BISHOP

TERESA GABELMAN

The Protectors Series

Bishop

Copyright 2020 Teresa Gabelman

Gabelman, Teresa (2020-2-26). Bishop (The Protectors Series) Book #15

Kindle Edition.

Editor: Hot Tree Editing

❋ Created with Vellum

CHAPTER 1

*B*ishop Valentino lay on his back, staring up at the ceiling. His heavily muscled arms positioned under his head as his body and mind relaxed before starting the day. This was his new place, his own. No sharing with his newly mated brother or other Warriors. It was empty of everything except a bed that he never slept on. He didn't sleep, but lying down, he could relax and think. Some called it meditating. He, on the other hand, called it preparing his mind and body for the shit show that was his way of life. Killing, capturing, saving… so on and so forth.

His eyes remained transfixed. He hadn't blinked, and he expected some would wonder if he was dead. That was how still he'd remained for hours. In doing so, he was in control of his mind and body. And the one thing Bishop had was control. He very rarely lost it and when he did, he could easily and quickly call it back and regain control over any situation.

The cell phone buzzed next to his leg on the bed, but he ignored it. He had exactly two minutes before he had to leave his place, and he wasn't leaving a second sooner. The phone quieted as he knew it would. He hated technology, missed the days when there weren't cell phones. It had been peaceful then, but now, everyone knew where you were because they could track you down within seconds because of the damn things. While that was good for many, for him, he felt trapped by it. Other than his brother, he was a loner. Viktor was the only person he could spend more than an hour with before wanting to kill them.

The only movement on his face was a slight tip of his lip. His brother had found his mate, Lacey. He was so damn happy for his brother. Bishop knew Viktor had been ready, even before Viktor himself had known it. Seeing his brother suffer for years after losing Emilia had been hard on Bishop, but he'd remained steadfast beside his brother knowing that someone out there would bring the brother he once knew back to the man he was today.

Knocking on the door downstairs finally had Bishop blinking. Sitting, he moved off the bed with ease and headed downstairs. He opened the door and stepped back, letting Viktor inside.

"You stop answering your phone?" Viktor grumbled as he walked inside.

"I had two more minutes before my day started." Bishop shut the door, brushing past his brother. "Call me now and I'll pick up."

"Smartass." Viktor scowled as he looked around the place. "A little empty in here."

Bishop grabbed his jacket off the kitchen counter where he'd tossed it, then loaded up on his weapons, all while rolling his eyes at his brother. "Haven't had a lot of time to shop, brother."

"Get yourself a mate." Viktor grinned, glancing at him. "Lacey already has our place decked out, looking sweet. As if we've lived there for years."

"Yeah, I'll pass on that." Bishop slipped on his leather jacket. "So when is lovely Lacey going to be inviting me to dinner?"

"Never." Viktor hissed, his eyes narrowing. "At least not until you stop flirting with my mate."

"Afraid she'll realize she picked the wrong brother?" Bishop grinned as he headed for the door, dodging Viktor's punch.

"I can't wait to bust your balls," Viktor grumbled, following him out.

"You do that every damn day," Bishop shot back. "Don't know what would change that."

"Oh, there's someone out there, and I can't wait for you to find her." Viktor climbed on his bike and put his gloves on. "Or for her to find you."

Bishop didn't respond as he got on his own bike. After sharing a kiss with Bonnie under the fucking mistletoe and his mixed feelings for her, Bishop had realized that maybe it wasn't in the cards for him to find a mate. He was okay with that. He didn't have time to devote to a female right now. His main focus was to find Orjyll, kill the bastard, and anyone who got in his way.

"Where we headed?" Bishop ignored his brother's "mate" bullshit.

"Meeting up with Steve at the warehouse." Viktor glanced at the darkening sky. Snow fell lightly. "Sloan finally released him to work missions. He wants him with one of us until we're sure his mind is right."

Bishop nodded, glad Steve was released, but he hoped it wasn't too early. Witches were on the menu, so to speak, and it was time to start putting the pressure on. His bike roaring to life, Bishop took off. His back tire slid on the icy surface of the road as he pulled out of his driveway, but Bishop expertly kept it up with ease.

The warehouse wasn't far from his place. He had given a realtor a detailed description of what he wanted and where. The guy had done a good job finding him a place quicker than Bishop expected and in the price range. It didn't feel like home yet, but soon it would. He'd always thought of building his own place, something he still would do, but now wasn't the time. They never stayed in one place long, and he wasn't ready to put down roots just yet. While Viktor wasn't since meeting Lacey, Bishop was still a free agent.

The snow came down harder the closer they got to the warehouse, making visibility near impossible. Fucking snow. He couldn't wait for sunny weather; he hated this shit. Pulling into the warehouse, he parked and got off the bike, following Viktor inside.

Bishop's eyes adjusted quickly to see Kira, Bonnie, and Mira, along with Ronan on the mats.

"You have to stop pulling your magic, Kira," Bonnie was saying with an edge of irritation. "Believe me when I tell you those around my asshole father will not be pulling theirs. From what I've heard, he's rounding up some of the most powerful witches and warlocks from every-where. I'm surprised I'm the only one with a hit on her head."

"Actually, you're not," Mira said, then frowned when Kira glared at her. "It's time they knew, Kira. I'm sick of keeping this secret."

"What secret?" Ronan snapped to full attention.

"Damn," Bonnie cursed with a hiss. "I bet old saggy ass wants her alive, though. I can't believe I didn't hear about this. Then again, I've been staying away from most witches since my price is mighty tempting, even to a goodie-two-shoes witch."

"You knew about this?" Ronan's voice rose as he took a step toward Kira. Anger radiated off his body and tone of voice.

"It's just rumors." Kira tried to lighten the implication of what was just exposed by Mira.

"Bullshit," Mira whispered, but they all heard her.

"Mira," Kira warned, but Mira ignored her, looking straight at Ronan.

"She was supposed to tell you. Promised me she was going to tell you, but"—Mira disregarded Kira's warning glare—"she hasn't so I'm telling you."

Bishop listened, knowing exactly how Ronan was feeling. Well, maybe not exactly, but having a price on a loved one's head sucked. He and Viktor had many prices on their heads over the years. It was something witches liked to do; both witches and warlocks had a reputation for being greedy. Made no damn sense to him since they could easily get anything they wanted without money by using their craft. Guess it was like a notch on their broomstick or something.

"This is nothing new, Mira," Kira said, but her eyes were on Ronan, who was glaring hard at his mate. "We've had a bounty on our heads since the day we were born."

"Actually, this is new," Bonnie added, her eyes briefly meeting Bishop's before going back to Kira, then Ronan. "Now whoever takes you can boast they bested the most powerful witch, bringing her to her knees."

Curses filled the air, Ronan's the loudest. Bishop remained silent, knowing Bonnie was right. He glanced at Viktor, who gave him a knowing look. It was now known that Emilia had gifted her powers to Kira, which made the hunt and takedown that much sweeter. Even a white witch would be hard-pressed to turn down such an accolade.

"She's right," Bishop said before Kira could dispute Bonnie's claims. "It is different now. Not only are witches on the lookout for you, but non-witches who want the money and don't care about the accolades of taking down the most powerful witch."

"I swear I'll kill the bastard." Ronan's cowboy twang

intensified with his rage. "I forbid you to put yourself out there like this."

"Oh shit." Bonnie shook her head. "He went there."

When Kira put her hands on her hips, Bishop realized Bonnie was right. Ronan did go there.

"Listen, cowboy," Bonnie tried to explain, no doubt trying to stop the shitstorm brewing, "forbidding a witch is like, ah... standing behind a horse and sticking a needle in his ass."

"What?" Ronan finally looked away from Kira to glare at her now.

"Yeah, what?" Bishop frowned, cocking his eyebrow at her.

"Hey, I'm trying to talk 'cowboy' here." Bonnie shushed Bishop. "And you heard me, Ronan. Forbidding a witch is like standing behind a horse and sticking a needle in his ass. You're for sure gonna get kicked."

"Okay, that made no fucking sense at all." Bishop snorted and shook his head.

"And you are no cowboy." Bonnie gave him a "duh" look before rolling her eyes.

Before Bonnie could continue, Kira held up her hand. "Listen, and listen well." Her voice was strong and sure. "No one is going to forbid me to do what I need to do to save my sister and niece. Not even you, Ronan. If you cannot stand beside me in this, then leave."

Bishop noticed Bonnie cringe as they all waited for Ronan's response. He stared at his mate, and Bishop felt for him. Damn, what a fucking decision. Stand back while your woman saved the fucking day, putting herself in danger every second or turn and walk away. Yeah, he didn't know what he would do in that situation, so he kept his damn mouth shut. Then again, he did know what he wouldn't do. He would never walk away from the woman he loved. Definitely not happening.

"I'm going nowhere," Ronan growled the words, leaning toward Kira. "But neither are you, alone."

"What's new? I've got an overprotective cowboy who won't let me out of his sight." Kira shrugged, then reached up and touched Ronan's cheek before dropping her hand. "I have to do this, Ronan."

"She really does. So back up, cowboy, and let her do her thang," Bonnie added, breaking their moment. This time Bishop cringed. Lord, that witch really didn't care what she said, when she said it, or who she said it to. She glanced over at Bishop with a grin. "How do you like my cowboy slangin' twangin' talk?"

"Can use a little work, witch," Bishop teased, then laughed when she flipped him off. He glanced over at Mira. "Where's Steve?"

"I'm here." Steve's voice sounded right beside him, making him jump.

"Son of a bitch." Bishop threw an elbow, hoping to hit Steve. "Haven't you been warned about being invisible and sneaking up on people, especially me?"

Steve became visible. "Sorry, just making sure I'm ready

to go. Haven't been invisible for a while and wanted to make sure I still had it," Steve replied, then grinned. "You had no clue, did you?"

Bishop glanced at Viktor, who was grinning like an idiot. "What clued you in?" Viktor answered before Bishop could. "The way he jumped like a little girl or his squeal of terror?"

"Fuck you, Viktor," Bishop spat before looking back at Steve. "Don't make me have to explain to Sloan why I had to kill you."

"Well, since Sloan knows me so well, I don't think you'll have to explain much," Steve replied, then headed toward Mira. "Make sure I have a nice burial, babe."

Bishop heard Bonnie snicker, but when he looked that way, she was straight-faced. "What?" she said at his look.

"Make sure she's ready." Bishop nodded toward Kira.

"Oh, okay, Sloan Jr." Bonnie saluted him. "What in the hell do you think I'm trying to do? Now, get out of here so we can work."

Bishop sent a glare her way, but when he turned to leave the warehouse, a grin broke out on his face. One thing about Bonnie was he loved giving her shit because she gave it right back to him. That was refreshing and something he wasn't used to with women. He liked it, a lot.

"You sure you guys aren't... you know?" Viktor said as soon as they walked outside.

"I'm sure," Bishop replied, wondering suddenly why he replied at all.

"Well, I think there's a spark there," Steve said as he passed them. "I know this shit. Bonnie just likes to play the tough girl, but I've seen her staring at you with googly eyes."

"Googly eyes?" Viktor laughed, staring at Steve.

"Yeah, you know," Steve said, then looked toward Bishop with his eyes all wanting and shit as he stared at Bishop. "Googly-eyed. Does no one know what that is? I swear I've even had to show the Warriors the googly eye," Steve said seriously as his eyes went back to normal.

"I swear to God, if you ever look at me like that again, no one, and I mean no one, will be able to identify your body," Bishop growled, his fangs bared and gleaming.

"Damn, this is going to be an awesome day." Viktor laughed before taking off on his bike, with Steve quickly following.

Bishop hung back, thinking of what Steve said, then glanced back at the warehouse before taking off after them. No, Steve was wrong. It was clear Bonnie had no real feelings for him nor he for her. They'd already got that shit out of the way, and he knew that's why they got along so well. Easy. Friendship. Done.

CHAPTER 2

*B*onnie watched Bishop leave then chuckled to herself. He sure as hell didn't know what to think about her, and that's the way she wanted it. She'd heard of Viktor and Bishop Valentino long before she'd met them, very well in fact, and no matter what her feelings for the man may or may not be, she knew his past. He had killed more witches than she was comfortable with. Bonnie had a code she lived by, somewhat, and well, she honestly didn't know how she felt about Bishop's past. If they had met up when he and his brother were on their killing spree of witches, would she have been one of their many kills? Probably, and that bothered her more than she wanted to admit.

"So, what next?" Kira said, breaking her out of her thoughts.

"Start out slow," Bonnie said, walking over toward a pile of mats and sitting down as she looked around. "Make me believe I'm not inside this building, but outside."

"Ah, and that's slow?" Kira snorted, putting her hand on her hip, staring at her. When Bonnie didn't respond but kept staring back, Kira sighed. "Okay."

Bonnie waited and waited. Nothing was happening. "Focus, Kira. You can do this. It's easy."

"Then you do it," Kira hissed, her eyes closed slightly.

Shrugging, Bonnie called on her powers, and suddenly the building around them disappeared. "Done."

She watched as Kira opened her eyes and gasped, "Seriously!" Kira spun in circles before glancing her way, her eyes wide. "Me thinks you have been holding out on us, Bonnie."

"Well, you *thinks* wrong." Bonnie stood, growing aggravated. "Kira, you haven't been using your powers, being afraid Orjyll will find you. You're out of practice. You should have been able to do this without even thinking hard about it. Focus, dammit. This is Witch Shit 101."

"Easy for you to say," Kira grumbled.

"And easy for you to do if you'd get the broomstick out of your ass," Bonnie replied, then smirked. "Bet if your honey over there was in danger, you'd call on those powers real quick."

Just as Bonnie's words were apparently registering in Kira's brain from her wide eyes, Bonnie formed a long, pointy icicle in midair that headed toward Ronan. She had to give the cowboy credit. He just stood there ready to take the ice missile to the chest, but before it hit its mark, Kira's hand shot out, and the icicle exploded into a million pieces, falling harmlessly to the ground.

"There you go." Bonnie smiled in triumph.

"Are you crazy?" Kira's eyes darkened in rage as she glared at Bonnie.

Shrugging, Bonnie thought for a minute. "Unfortunately, I'm batshit crazy, and many know it." Standing, Bonnie took a few steps toward Kira. "Looks like you need a nudge. It would be a shame if something happened to Drew." Bonnie let that settle in the air between them and knew she'd figured out a way to get Kira moving on her powers.

"You even think about it, I will tear you apart." Kira's eyes began to flow and swirl as an invisible vortex swirled around her.

Bonnie dropped her magic, and the building around them appeared again, but the same vortex continued. "How can you do that when you can't even do basic magic? You can't even touch me before I harm Drew."

The vortex swirled faster and stronger—even Ronan took notice. Mira backed up to hold on to something as Bonnie stood facing Kira. "Touch Drew and die," Kira sneered.

Knowing she was pushing it, Bonnie thought hard on what to do next. Should she push her further to see how strong Kira really was?

"Bonnie," Mira whispered in warning. "That's enough for now, I think."

It was actually an amazing sight seeing Kira standing there, a wind she produced from magic swirling around, her hair looking electrified as her eyes glowed unnaturally. Sparks were even zapping around Kira as she stood, her eyes deadpanned on Bonnie. Maybe Mira was right, that was enough, but then again....

"Bonnie." This time the warning came from Ronan, who was easing his way toward Kira.

Tilting her head, she gave Kira a smirk, then began moving her mouth as if casting a spell. She really wasn't, but Kira was so far into protecting Drew it didn't matter. Kira's arms shot out, and Bonnie was suddenly lifted off her feet, dangling in the air. She quickly used her own magic to protect her from what she knew was coming and damn, it was going to be painful.

Their eyes were locked on each other. Their will of magic was strong as it fought against each other. It felt as if Bonnie's body was being pulled apart as she hung in the air, but thankfully, she had been quick to use her own protective magic so she wouldn't be pulled apart limb by limb.

Bonnie was amazed by Kira's power, and deep down felt a sense of jealousy that Kira was the one Bonnie's mother had gifted her magic to. A sense of loss overwhelmed Bonnie, making her magic slip. She screamed out in pain just as Ronan tackled Kira. Bonnie fell to the ground hard, her body throbbing in excruciating pain.

"Oh God." Kira's voice sounded so far away. "Bonnie, dammit. I'm sorry."

"My fault," Bonnie managed to croak as a smile slipped across her face. "Now that's what I'm talking about."

"Get Slade," Kira ordered Mira. "Hurry."

"I'm fine," Bonnie lied. She wasn't fine at all. Ribs were broken, that she was sure of. "Now, all we have to do is get you to control all that power." Bonnie's voice was coming in gasps, but she needed to get it out.

"Stop talking," Ronan ordered, his hand on her shoulder. "Slade is on his way. Can't you use your magic?"

Kira shook her head as tears filled her eyes. "We aren't supposed to hurt each other. When we do, magic won't fix us. It protects witches against witches, or at least that was the purpose. Dammit, Bonnie, what were you thinking?"

"Of killing my father, and you are the only one who may be able to do that." Bonnie coughed and thought she tasted a hint of metallic… blood. Shit, this wasn't good. Maybe she fucked up pushing Kira too far before she was able to control it. "And for the record, I would never hurt that precious baby."

"I know that," Kira whispered, fear in her voice. "But you're right. I have to control this. I never realized just how…." Kira swallowed hard, looking away from Bonnie.

"Powerful my mother was?" Bonnie finished, then reached out for Kira, stopping when pain streaked through her body. "If I could take it from you, I would."

"Is that possible?" Mira, who was crouched at Bonnie's feet, asked.

Bonnie thought on that for a long minute, her breathing becoming more shallow. Damn, broken ribs hurt like a bitch. "I don't know," she finally said, then looked back at Kira. "But if I can, I will. It should have been me. My mother should have given me her magic."

Kira nodded, looking defeated. "I'm so sorry." She sighed, then stood quickly when Slade rushed inside with the new Warrior Ryker following close behind.

"Don't be," Bonnie said, then tried to smile. "I'm the idiot in this scenario."

"What happened?" Slade knelt down to look at Bonnie, who tried to talk, but it was becoming harder and harder to do so.

"I lost control," Kira said, her voice shaking. Ronan had stood and was holding Kira. "I hurt her. I think it's her ribs."

Slade carefully lifted her shirt, his eyes assessing before looking at her. "Are you having a hard time breathing?"

Bonnie nodded, her eyes shifting to Kira. Ronan had walked her back, giving Slade room to work. "I coughed, and I think I tasted blood," she whispered so Kira couldn't hear.

"Dammit." Slade's eyes narrowed as he took out his phone. "This is Dr. Buchanan. I need an X-ray room ready as soon as I get there. Ten minutes at the most."

Glancing at the new guy who stood staring down at her, she felt her eyelids drifting closed. He was really cute, she thought and wondered why in the hell her thought process went there when she was possibly dying. Nah, Slade would save her. Her eyes opened quickly, afraid of the darkness. They focused on Slade. He was pretty damn cute himself.

"Bonnie, we are going to have to move you." Slade's voice washed over her, sounding all doctor like. It was crazy how this man could shift from Warrior to doctor in a blink of an eye. "Ryker, help me, but be careful. I don't know what's going on until I see X-rays, and I don't want to cause more damage or shift her ribs."

Ryker stepped forward, putting one knee on the ground. "You're going to be okay, Bonnie." He smiled at her with a wink. "I've done this a hundred times and only made one Warrior scream."

"Ehhh," Bonnie managed to get out. "Got a pretty high pain tolerance, I think."

"Wait," Mira said before Slade and Ryker could lift her. She looked over at Kira. "We can move her more carefully and safely without jostling her."

Kira pulled away from Ronan, rushing up to Bonnie's side. "Yes, we can." Kira knelt in front of Bonnie. "We're going to put her in Mira's car. Go on out and be ready."

"Yeah… I don't know." Slade frowned, not liking the idea.

"Please, I did this to her." Worry etched on Kira's face. "We can do this. Trust me."

"Do it," Bonnie whispered, then licked her lips. "I trust you, but hurry the hell up. This hurts like a bitch."

Bonnie had transported herself hundreds of times over the years. She wasn't fond of it. Always made her sick to her stomach and gave her one hell of a headache, but she had done it. Never had she let another witch transport her, but she was too weak to do it herself. But Mira

17

was right. This was the easiest, less painful way to do it.

Closing her eyes, she waited for the weird feeling of weightlessness to hit her when she transported. Along with the pain, her body tingled, and she knew it was working. There was always that fear she would transport herself somewhere that she couldn't get back from. It had only happened once and it hadn't been pleasant. She really was putting all her trust in Mira and Kira, but what choice did she have? None. She was helpless at the moment, which was totally her fault. She shouldn't have pushed Kira to the point of no return, but dammit, she was anxious and ready to see her father suffer for everything he had done.

Feeling something hard under her head, she slowly slid one eye open. She was in a car, her head on someone's lap.

"Well, that's a first for me," Ryker's husky male voice said from above her. "Never had a beautiful woman appear out of thin air with her head on my lap."

"Yeah, well, there may be another first." Bonnie wheezed, nausea swirling in her gut. "I tend to throw up after transporting."

"Nah, actually that wouldn't be a first." Ryker chuckled, his large hand resting on her arm.

"Now that's a story I want to hear... later." Bonnie moaned when the car jerked, causing her to shift.

"Hold on, Bonnie." Ryker's voice soothed her. "You'll be as good as new soon."

She hoped like hell he was right. Bonnie felt herself relax, which was odd because of the pain she was in, but Ryker's voice, as he continued to talk softly to her, eased her in a weird way.

"Don't let me die," she whispered, not really knowing why. "I have some killing to do."

His silence, then sudden chuckle, almost made her smile. She was damn good at shocking people.

"I have a feeling you're too ornery to die," Ryker whispered, and she knew he was grinning.

"You have no idea," Bonnie whispered back, and then the darkness that was edging closer took over, and everything went black.

CHAPTER 3

*B*ishop walked around the old house. The smell was overwhelmingly disgusting. The odor of death, rotten food, and old blood filled his senses. Steve walked by with his shirt up over his nose, his golden eyes searching.

"Doesn't look like anyone has been here for a while," Steve muttered, kicking some boxes out of his way. "Are you sure this is the address? And why in the fuck does it smell like feet in here?"

Viktor checked his phone with a frown. "This is the address the informant gave me. Said a lot of activity in this area, especially this address."

"If it's witches, they could be glamming the place," Steve said, looking around. "Mira told me witches do it all the time. Though this place doesn't look glammed; it's a shithole. And maybe that's what they want us to see. But seriously, didn't they wear fucking shoes. Damn, it's gagging the shit out of me."

Bishop glanced at Viktor with a cocked eyebrow. Steve was right. A witch could hide in plain sight. Glamming, some called it, was when a witch used her magic to trick the eye. A person could be standing in a palace and not know it. Though this part of town, he doubted that. Witchcraft may not work on full-bloods, but magical elements could still fool them. Damn, he was obviously out of practice since he hadn't thought of that.

Walking toward the hallway, he searched for a door. "Did you notice if there were window wells?"

"No, but I'll go look." Steve rushed out, then came right back in. "Yep, there are."

"Then we have a basement." Bishop felt around on the wall in the hallway until his hand landed on a knob that by the eye, you couldn't see. Twisting the knob, it turned with ease and the door appeared and opened. "Found it," he called out, then headed downstairs.

The steps were old, rotting, and unstable. It was pitch black, but Bishop could see perfectly. Once at the bottom, he checked around and it looked empty, but he had a feeling that wasn't the case. The cluttered mess upstairs betrayed the cleanliness of downstairs. As he walked to the middle of the room, he frowned.

"It's clean. And has the bonus of no feet smell." Steve stomped around with his hands on his hips. "What the hell?"

Bishop looked around, his eyes narrowing. The walls

were too white. He glanced at Viktor and knew he noticed it too. It looked freshly painted.

"Go ahead." Viktor gave Bishop a nod. "See if you still got it."

Bishop smirked, then put his hands together and bowed his head. He cleared his mind as he focused. He hadn't done this in years, and it felt foreign as well as familiar all at the same time. Very strange emotions hit him at once, but he forced them back.

"Ah, don't think prayer is gonna help on this one, man," Steve grumbled, but Bishop ignored him. "Didn't think you were the praying type, though. Good to know in a pinch."

Still ignoring Steve, Bishop thought of the words Emilia had taught them years ago and hoped he was repeating them correctly. "Help me," Bishop hissed, feeling his body tingle and warm. He knew something was happening, but the magic here was strong.

He heard Viktor's low mumblings in his thoughts and continued keeping pace with his brother.

"Okay, freaking me out a little." Steve's voice sounded far away as Bishop focused. "You two priests in a past life or something? I mean, sorry, but you sure as shit don't look the part. Then again, I heard the Dark Guardians were once men of God, and they sure as fuck don't look—"

"Shut up," Viktor hissed, then all went silent other than their low mumbles of words they hadn't spoken in years.

"Sorry," Steve muttered. "Should I start praying? I'm sure I can throw some words together.... Whoa, what the actual fuck?"

Bishop slowly opened his eyes but continued with the words. Sure enough, it was working. The magic faded, showing the true vision of the basement, and what he saw turned him cold as ice. The walls were covered in a mixture of occult drawings. Bishop dropped his hands, walking toward one. He reached up to touch the red lettering, then looked at his fingers covered in red.

"Is that blood?" Steve walked up, looking closer.

"Yes." Viktor stood back, his eyes dark as night when Bishop glanced his way. "It's a summoning spell."

"Summoning what?" Steve asked, not sounding like he really wanted to know.

"Some of these symbols I've never seen." Bishop glanced around, ignoring Steve's question. "Some are fresh, very fresh."

"Damn," Viktor cursed, reaching down to the floor and picking something up. He handed it to Bishop.

"Son of a bitch," Bishop growled, staring at a picture of Bonnie. The symbol painted across the picture was dry. Rage slammed into him, threatening to consume him.

"What's that on the picture?" Steve took the photo and tentatively touched it.

"The symbol of death," Viktor answered as he continued to look around. "Which isn't shocking since she has a bounty on her head, but this... *this* isn't good."

Bishop turned to see Viktor holding another picture. Walking that way, he swore if it was another picture of Bonnie, he was going to lose his shit, but it wasn't. It was Kira, and the symbol painted in red blood was still damp.

"Call Sloan," Viktor ordered Steve. "Tell him we need a witch here now, preferably Bonnie."

"Ah, you think that's the smartest idea since her picture is here with a death symbol painted in blood on it?" Steve looked up from his phone with a frown.

Bishop agreed with Steve but knew Bonnie had the most experience with black magic. Some of these symbols he'd never seen before, and that was saying something. "Just call," Bishop bit out, then continued to walk around. Whoever did this meant business.

Steve cursed. "I thought we were supposed to have cell service everywhere. I can't get a fucking signal down here."

"Then go upstairs." Viktor stared at the ground where a huge pentagram was painted on the floor. He pulled his phone out and took pictures. "Do you remember ever seeing anything like this?"

"No," Bishop replied, shaking his head, his eyes going to the picture of Bonnie and Kira that Steve had set down. "I have a feeling Orjyll is behind it."

"Yeah, that's pretty much a given." Viktor frowned as he turned to head upstairs. "I'm going to check out more of the upstairs."

"Watch your back," Bishop warned, grabbing the

pictures of Kira and Bonnie. He stood there staring not at Kira's picture, but at Bonnie's. She didn't deserve this. From what he understood, she had spent her life plotting against her father to avenge her mother's death. Alone. She was one of the strongest people he had ever met, and yet, his feelings toward her confused the hell out of him.

"Hey!" Viktor yelled from upstairs. Bishop folded the pictures and stuck them in the inside pocket of his jacket. Hurrying up the steps, he stopped at the look on Steve's and Viktor's faces. "It's Bonnie."

"What?" Bishop growled with narrowed eyes. He swore if anyone hurt her, he would hunt them down and rip them apart. His instant rage took him back somewhat, but he ignored it.

"She's in the hospital. University," Steve added, looking a little nervous. "It seems training went bad. She pushed Kira into a rage by threatening Drew. Kira couldn't control it, and Mira said she hurt Bonnie pretty bad."

"Go on," Viktor ordered him. "We've got this and will wait until Sloan and the rest of them get here. Mira is heading this way with Damon to see if she can decipher some of the symbols. I'll call Raven also."

Bishop didn't have to be told twice. He was out the door and jumping on his bike. "Fuck!" he cursed as he pulled onto the street. Bonnie never thought twice about putting herself in danger, and it pissed him off. What in the hell had she been thinking? He knew how powerful Emilia was, and for Kira to not only have her own power but Emilia's too, made her a dangerous foe, especially as she had little control.

Running lights and Stop signs, Bishop fought with his thoughts. Would he be rushing to her if she didn't mean anything to him? What in the fuck was he doing? He should be back with Viktor trying to figure this shit out, not risking his ass or others by riding like a maniac to get to her.

Pulling into the hospital, he parked quickly, then jogged toward the emergency room. Heading toward the waiting room, he saw Kira and Ronan. His gaze then fell on Ryker, the new Warrior. His eyes narrowed, but Kira rushed toward him, gaining his attention.

"Slade was just out here," she said quickly, her eyes red and swollen. "She's going to be okay. A few broken ribs. I'm so sorry. I didn't mean—"

"Of course you didn't mean to do it." Bishop pulled her into a hug. "And she knows that."

Kira pulled away and nodded, wiping her eyes. "I just feel terrible. She's right. I don't know what I'm doing. I cannot control this. It's too much."

"You will." Ronan pulled her into him, his eyes meeting Bishop's.

Jill and Katrina ran into the waiting room, and Kira headed their way. Bishop nodded for Ronan to follow him. Once they were away from the women, he pulled out the pictures. "We were at a house in Newport that an informant told Viktor about. We found these."

Bishop glanced at Ryker, who walked up and gave

Bishop a nod before looking at the pictures when Ronan cursed.

"What is that?" Ronan growled, staring at the picture of Kira.

"Death symbol," Ryker hissed, his eyes narrowed as he stared at the picture.

"Who exactly are you?" Bishop glanced over at him.

"Ryker," he said with a small half-grin. "Think we already met."

Before Bishop could say anything to that, he heard her voice. Turning, he frowned when he saw Bonnie holding her ribs as she made her way down the hall and into the waiting room.

"What in the hell are you doing up?" both Bishop and Ryker said at the same time.

"Seriously, who in the fuck are you?" Bishop growled, glaring at Ryker.

"Ryker. Bishop," Bonnie introduced as she slowly made her way toward them. "Bishop. Ryker. Now that we got that taken care of, who is going to take me to the house?"

"Did Slade release you?" Bishop frowned down at her.

"No, he did not." Slade's voice boomed behind Bonnie, making her jump then cringe in pain.

"I'm fine. I'm wrapped, took some drugs, and ready to go," Bonnie said, then looked at Ronan's hand. Slowly, she walked that way and snatched the pictures.

Bishop watched her reaction as she stared first at Kira's photo, then hers. Anger and something else crossed her features as she looked up at Bishop. "Damn, they could have taken a picture of my good side." She handed the pictures back to Ronan. "Let's go. I heard Slade talking about a house and symbols. Is it black magic? And don't lie, because, by the symbol on our pictures, I can pretty much say it is."

"Some of them I've never seen before," Bishop said, then frowned, realizing he just answered her. "But you aren't going anywhere until Slade releases you."

"I've released myself." Bonnie turned slowly. "I can do that, you know. Come on, Kira. Let's see if we can help these Warriors figure this out so I can lay down and cry in peace. Kidding. I'm kidding. I'm going to live. I'm tougher than a piece of rawhide," Bonnie said before anyone could say anything.

Bishop cursed, shaking his head. "Dammit, Bonnie."

"Dammit, Bishop." Bonnie mocked him back as she waddled her way toward Kira. "Mira shouldn't be doing it alone."

"You heard everything?" Slade glared at her.

"Every single syllable. I have expert eavesdropping skills." Bonnie patted him on the arm as she slowly walked past. "Thanks for wrapping me up, Doc. I'm as good as new."

"Guess you aren't going to stop her," he asked Slade as he frowned when Ryker rushed toward Bonnie to walk beside her.

"Would it matter if I did?" Slade threw his arms out in defeat. "Women."

"Witches," Bishop growled, then walked up to the other side of Bonnie, glaring down at her as she painfully walked toward the exit. "Pain in my ass."

"Honestly, I'd rather have a pain in *my* ass," Bonnie hissed as she snapped at Bishop. "Broken ribs suck. And if you say sorry one more time, Kira, I'm going to zap you. This is on me."

"You're damn right it is," Bishop answered for Kira. "What in the hell were you thinking?"

"Why do people keep asking me that?" Bonnie grumbled. "For the last time, I was thinking of killing dipshit, aka, saggy ass, aka, my evil father."

Bishop glared when Ryker chuckled, then looked at Bishop with a smirk. "I'm Ryker."

"Fuck you," Bishop growled, really not liking the smartass at all.

CHAPTER 4

*B*onnie thankfully didn't have to ride on the back of a motorcycle. Though riding on the back of Bishop's bike had a certain thrilling ring to it. Okay, dammit, she found the witch-killing Warrior handsome as sin, but nothing and she meant *nothing* could come of it. The kiss they shared rocked her world, but never would he or anyone else know that. It was her secret. She had lied to him, herself, and anyone else who may have raised the question of a relationship between her and Bishop. Not happening. Actually, relationships for her were off the table. Period. A fling, definitely, but not with Bishop Valentino. A fling would never be enough for her with that man. She had already put herself through hell most of her life, and taking a taste of Bishop was a hell she just couldn't afford.

"You good?" Ryker said from the seat next to her. Ronan drove with Kira in the passenger seat. Bonnie and Ryker occupied the back. Bishop followed behind them on his bike. She could actually feel his glare on the back of her head through the rear windshield.

When Bishop had said it had been like kissing a cousin after their kiss under the mistletoe, his words had almost done her in, but that had been her plan all along. She shouldn't have taken it personally, but she did, and it sucked. Shaking the thoughts away, she sighed.

"Yeah, think the pain meds are kicking in, which is good and bad." Bonnie grinned, feeling a little flighty. Pain meds along with her magic didn't mix very well. Ryker sent a questioning gaze in her direction. "Good because the pain has eased. Bad because so has my brain. Feeling a little loopy, so forgive me if I say some stupid shit."

"Forgiven." Ryker's deep voice filled the back of the car. Bonnie continued to stare openly at him. He was a big man, barely fitting in the back of the car. Her head had fit nicely in his lap. That thought made her chuckle internally. She was also a sucker for a handsome smile, which was what he always seemed to be doing. He was a fine-looking man with his wind-blown sandy brown hair, golden skin, and matching eyes. But he wasn't the brooding, fickle-ass man with his dark, tattooed looks riding behind them.

"So, what's your story?" Bonnie laid her suddenly very heavy head back against the seat and continued to stare at him. "You mysteriously appear Christmas Eve, we don't even know your last name, and you spend hours at the hospital with a person you just met."

An uncomfortable silence followed her question. His

eyes shadowed briefly, but Bonnie didn't miss it. This guy had secrets. Huh, welcome to the club, buddy.

"I like long walks on the beach, puppies, and seafood with a nice tall glass of blood," Ryker said, his tone impressively serious. Bonnie rolled her eyes.

"This isn't an interview for *Playgirl*." Bonnie snorted, then lifted her head with a smirk. "Though I'm sure they'd love to have you for their spread."

"Thank you." Ryker nodded without blinking an eye.

"You're... welcome," Bonnie said slowly, then shook her head. "Okay, remain the mysterious Christmas Eve Warrior. Maybe Santa sent you."

The car stopped, and Bonnie looked out the window to see a house and knew instantly it had been glammed, and not in a good way.

"I'm no elf, Bonnie." Ryker chuckled, getting out of the car, then bent down to stare at her. "But I do like the mysterious Warrior. I think I'll go with that."

Bonnie smirked as he shut the door, then jumped when her door was jerked open. "Dammit, stop scaring me and making me jump."

"Sorry," Bishop said, but he didn't really sound sorry. No, he sounded pissed off. "You sure you're up for this?"

Actually, she wasn't sure at all. In the car, she'd felt relaxed, but now, standing slowly, she felt jittery as hell. It had to be the pain meds messing with her. She never did well on them and usually could fix her issues with magic. Nope, not this time. Suffering for her stupidity was what she had to look forward to until she healed.

"Nope," Bonnie answered honestly, letting Bishop help her out of the car. She stood and stared at the house, getting her bearings. "It's glammed."

"I know," Bishop replied, but continued to stare at her and not the house.

"The basement's not," Steve said as he passed and then stopped, looking at Bishop. "And by the way, how in the hell did you do what you did?"

Most times Bonnie had a hard time following what Steve was saying because he said so much off-the-wall shit, but this time she got it right away. "You unglammed the basement?" Her eyes widened.

"Yeah, he and Viktor did. At first, I thought he was praying with the hands and mumbling, which was weird." Steve didn't pay any attention to the glare Bishop threw his way. "Damn, man. Didn't know you were a witch."

"Warlock," Bonnie corrected with a grin when Bishop's eyes narrowed to slits.

"Oh, yeah. He's a dude." Steve nodded seriously. "Warlock. Does Sloan know about this?"

"I'm not a Warlock," Bishop growled through clenched teeth.

"But—" Steve said, then stopped, no doubt realizing he was treading on thin ice with Bishop. But Steve being Steve couldn't help himself. "What you did was magic, man. Hey, that has a certain ring to it. Bishop, the Praying Magic Man/Warrior."

Bonnie couldn't help it. She laughed, and it hurt, but she took great satisfaction seeing Bishop sneering and growling at Steve. "It really does have a ring to it," she added with a huge grin.

"What in the hell happened to you?" Raven walked up with a frown, saving Steve's ass from certain pain and probably death. "I'm not around you for an hour, and you end up in the hospital?"

"You're fired," Bonnie said, then chuckled. "Kidding. I was perfectly safe except from myself. Did something stupid and paid the price. Story of my life."

"Are you going to stand outside all day shooting the fucking breeze?" Sloan's booming voice rolled around them. "Or are we going to figure this shit out sometime this century. And you…"

Bonnie looked behind her, then back at Sloan as she pointed to herself.

"Yeah, you, smartass," Sloan growled. "You okay?"

"Tired, loopy from pain meds, and a little short of breath from broken ribs, but other than that, I'm golden," Bonnie said as if Sloan really gave a shit. Maybe a little part of her wished the boss man did care, but the look on his face told a different story.

"Good, because if you ever pull a stunt like you pulled today, putting yourself and anyone else in danger, you're gone." Sloan didn't mince words, ever.

The best thing would be for Bonnie to nod in submission of his order, but yeah, Bonnie never did what was best, obviously. "Then you might as well tell me to get my witchy ass out of here because training you know who, for you know what is going to be dangerous to all involved."

Sloan looked around as if noticing they were out in the open and frowned even more than he had been, which was amazing. "We'll talk about this later. Get in here and help Mira," he ordered, then disappeared back inside.

"Pain meds make you grumpy too?" Ryker asked as he passed, giving her a half-grin.

"No, that's just my loveable personality. Grumpy and honest to a fault," Bonnie shot back as she started toward the house and the dreaded stairs leading to the front door. Taking the steps slowly, she frowned. "You know we're being watched."

"Yeah, figured that," Bishop replied, taking her elbow and helping her up the steps. "Guess you don't know where they are?"

"Nope, but you'd be the first to know if I did," Bonnie said, stopping at the top to take a small rest. "Do me a favor, though. If they try to take me out, just let them. Broken ribs ain't no joke."

"Not funny," Bishop growled, but his eyes searched for possible threats to her, and didn't that make her feel all warm and fuzzy, dammit. "You should still be in the hospital."

"Sick people belong in the hospital. I'm not sick," Bonnie

replied, on the move again as she went for the door. "Believe me, you think I'm bitchy now. Give Bonnie a runny nose and all hell will break loose."

Bishop opened the door and ushered her through the house toward the basement. She knew it was glammed, could feel the magic all around her. Without even wondering why Mira or Kira hadn't unglammed the place, she used her magic to do just that. She turned to look and wasn't surprised at what she saw. The place was immaculate. Nothing out of place, clean, and with the best furniture money or witchcraft could buy.

"Dealing with some high rollers." Bonnie clucked her tongue. "Daddy must be paying well these days."

"You think this is connected?" Bishop asked, also looking around what was now a whole different perspective.

"I'm sure it is, especially with that god-awful photo of me you found with the death symbol. If I was a betting woman—and I usually am—I'd say it's definitely connected." Bonnie frowned, glancing at the steps leading down to the basement. "Seriously? Steps suck." She moaned, then started her descent.

Once downstairs, she looked around at all the symbols painted on the walls. It was a smorgasbord of the occult. Black magic, white magic, and a little satanic crap thrown in for the hell of it.

"Ever see anything like this?" Raven asked as her eyes took in everything.

"Looks like they were either confused as hell or they

want anyone who finds it to be confused as hell." Bonnie walked over to a symbol, studied it then threw in, "Or...."

Bishop followed her, also staring at the symbol. "Or?"

"They really want me dead and in a bad way." Bonnie continued to study the symbols as she moved around the room. "Do you notice one similarity?"

Raven walked over along with Mira and Kira. The four women's gazes raked around the room, but no one answered.

Pointing to a symbol that was a circle with a large A in the center, she pointed again and again. "Every single one has that symbol embedded into it somehow."

Ronan, Bishop, Viktor, Steve, and Sloan began walking around the room. "Son of a bitch," Bishop said as he walked up to Bonnie. "Why?"

"What does it mean?" Steve asked while he even stared up at the ceiling.

"It's the symbol for anarchy," Bonnie whispered with a frown, then pointed. "And that is the Star of Chaos, which also seems to be included in each one." The eight-pointed arrow was crudely incorporated along with the symbol for anarchy into each symbol.

Bonnie had actually never seen such a mess of symbols. Didn't really know what it meant. Then again, she was afraid she did. Glancing at Kira and Mira, she frowned, not liking where her thoughts were going, and by the looks on their faces, they were thinking the same thing.

She turned toward Bishop, then looked at Sloan. "I've never seen so many symbols representing different things. It's a mixture of the occult. Meaning this doesn't happen every day. You stick with your beliefs. You don't mix and match. This is mixed and matched in the worst possible way."

"This isn't good," Kira whispered as she continued to look around.

"No." Charger's voice filled the basement as he came down the steps. "It's not good at all."

Bonnie watched as Charger looked over at Raven but glanced away quickly as he began studying the basement.

"New one for you?" Bonnie asked, knowing what his answer would be. She was sure the Dark Guardians had seen some shit in their lives and dealings with the darkness that walked the earth.

"Actually no, it's not," Charger said, his voice low as he glanced up at the ceiling. "But it's been a very long time since the occults came together like this, and I seriously doubt this is an isolated incident."

"What happened then?" Steve asked, his eyes wide as he looked from Bonnie to Charger.

"Son, you don't want to know," Charger said, but Bonnie knew, and by the looks on everyone else's faces, they figured it out.

"Hell on earth," Sloan growled, then turned and stomped up the steps, phone to his ear. "Duncan, get me the owner of the house ASAP. I want them brought here."

Sloan's voice faded, leaving everyone in the basement silent as they realized what was to come. Bonnie glanced at Bishop, who turned to look at her. Her father wasn't waiting for the death of all Grail women to regain his powers. He was using the powers of all the occult to carry out his deranged plan. For the first time in a long time, Bonnie felt insufficient and unprepared in the face of her father's evil takeover, and that honestly scared the shit out of her. For so long, there were three, now four Grail females standing in his way. To the detriment of humankind, it seemed they were now only a bonus in the grand scheme of things, and anyone not in the occult was on the front lines.

A shitstorm was brewing, and if they couldn't put a stop to it, life on earth would never be the same again.

CHAPTER 5

*B*ishop left the house and walked around the neighborhood. Raven had followed him out, and he figured that was because of Charger's arrival. The tension was thick between the two, especially since Raven had transferred from the Dark Guardians to the VC Warriors.

"So are you official?" Bishop asked as his eyes scanned the houses and alleyways they passed.

"Yeah, signed this morning," Raven replied, her voice low. "Start training tonight if we finish here in time. Got any advice for me?"

Bishop slowed and glanced at Raven. "Don't show any weakness. Once the recruits realize you're a transfer, they will most definitely try to put you in your place and send you back to the Guardians."

Raven nodded, not seeming concerned about that fact.

"Point taken," she replied with a nod. "They still giving Katrina a hard time?"

"Women will always have a hard time in the program." Bishop watched as a car slowly came down the road, passed them, and then pulled into the house. Must be the owner. He turned to head back that way.

"Which is bullshit," Raven added, following him back.

"Bullshit, but fact," Bishop agreed. "But I seriously doubt you have anything to worry about. I've heard about you. Just go in, do your thing, and don't worry about anyone else."

"That's the plan." Raven smirked, then nodded toward the house. "Must be the landlord."

Bishop watched a beautiful blonde woman step out of the car, then head toward the steps, looking cautiously around. His eyes also scanned the area, then went back to her and noticed she had stopped and was watching him and Raven.

"Are you Sloan Murphy?" Her shaky voice carried toward them.

"No." Bishop walked to her. She was short, her straight blonde hair ruffling in the breeze. Definitely a looker, and her body was perfectly proportioned in a short skirt, blouse, and nicely fit blazer. "You own this house?"

"Yes," she replied, then glanced up at it before looking back at him and then Raven. "It's one of the properties I own. What seems to be the problem?"

Sloan walked out at that moment and headed toward

them. "I'm Sloan Murphy, VC Warrior." He nodded in greeting. "You must be Savannah Livingston."

"I am," she replied, sounding as confused as she looked. "Have the tenants done something wrong?"

Bishop and Sloan shared a look. "How much do you know about the tenants?"

"Just the normal information any landlord would know." She opened the file in her hand. "I don't know a lot of personal information, but their names are Cynthia and Tiffany Simmons. Sisters. Been here for six months. Cynthia works at a florist in Cincinnati, and Tiffany goes to school. Never late with their rent. Credit check was excellent. References all checked out."

"Were they the only ones living here?" Bishop asked, holding his hand out for the file.

The woman hesitated for a minute before letting the file go. "As far as I know. They are the only ones on the lease. If anyone else was to live here, they would have to be added." She frowned when Bishop looked up from the file. "I'm sorry, but what exactly is this about?"

"Follow me," Sloan said, leading the woman up the steps and into the house.

Bishop and Raven followed. His eyes going directly to the woman's legs in appreciation. Raven snorted, then nudged him out of the way as she blocked his view and went in front of him. Bishop chuckled, shaking his head. "What?"

Rolling her eyes, she reached back and grabbed the file, smacking him with it. "Pig," she hissed in a whisper.

Before Raven could follow Sloan and the woman in, Bishop used his hand to keep the door shut. "What is your problem?"

"Men." Raven turned to face him. "That's every woman's problem."

"What in the hell has gotten into you?" Bishop cocked his eyebrow. "I was just admiring a beautiful woman's—"

"Ass." Raven finished for him with a growl.

"—legs," Bishop corrected, then frowned. "You're not my keeper, Raven. Never will be, so you need to check yourself before even thinking of checking me. Got it?"

Raven tilted her head and stared at him. "Are you really that fucking stupid?"

"You are definitely pissing me off." Bishop sneered, his eyes narrowing. What the fuck was her problem?

"Guess that answers my question. Fucking idiot." She pushed his arm out of her way and slammed open the door but stopped. She didn't even look over her shoulder at him. "Have you even offered Bonnie your blood to help her heal?"

"What?" Bishop stopped, stumped.

"Never mind." She shook her head and continued. "I know many strong vampires who'd be happy to heal her as well as... you know."

Bishop actually reached out this time, stopping her, and he wasn't too gentle. "No, I don't fucking know." Bishop's anger soared, and he had no clue why. But the thought of any man giving his blood to heal Bonnie sent a killing rage through him. Why in the hell should that bother him so much? He looked at Bonnie as a… sister. Okay, that thought kind of made him sick to his stomach.

Raven watched him closely. "I'll be damned," she whispered as a smirk formed on her face. "You don't know if you're coming or going with her, do you? That sly little witch."

"Who?" Bishop was confused as fuck and it pissed him the hell off. "What are you talking about?"

Before Raven could answer, there was a commotion coming up the basement steps. Bishop looked to see the woman, Savannah, rushing toward them, her face pale and body shaking. Sloan was coming up behind her.

"Whoa." Bishop reached out to steady the woman before she fell. She sank into his arms. "Slow down."

"I didn't know." Her beautiful blue eyes stared up into his.

Bishop could understand the woman's fear. This definitely wasn't normal. Well, for them it was somewhat normal, but humans were definitely a different breed, especially a woman such as this. He continued to hold the woman, but his eyes rose to see Bonnie staring at him with a look in her eyes he had never seen before. Hurt, betrayal, and something else he couldn't quite put his finger on. But what he didn't understand was why. He wasn't fucking stupid as Raven had called him, but he sure as hell was stumped.

"Bishop, make sure Ms. Livingston gets home okay," Sloan ordered.

Any other time Bishop would be all over taking a beautiful woman home and even comfort her fears, but as his eyes once again met Bonnie, that wasn't something he wanted to do, and that shocked the shit out of him.

"I'll take her," Raven said, stepping forward, but Sloan stopped her.

"You have training," Sloan said, then nodded toward Bishop. "Go on. We're finished here for now. I'll fill you in when you get back."

His mind warred with him to refuse, but his sense of duty to the VC Warriors and Sloan had him turning the woman toward the door, but not before he once again noticed the confusing emotions on Bonnie's face as well as Raven's glare directed at him.

"Stay with her," he said to Raven, ignoring her glare. Jesus, women were going to fucking drive him insane if he wasn't already there, and in an odd way, he wondered if he was actually losing his mind.

She just gave him a snort, clearly pissed off.

"Did you hear me?" Bishop gave her a narrowed look.

"Oh, yeah. I heard you." Raven's sarcasm was thick. "I heard you real well. Loud and fucking clear."

"Steve, make sure my bike gets back to the warehouse," Bishop said after dismissing Raven's weird mood. "I'll get myself back."

"No problem." Steve gave him a wink that made Bishop want to punch him in the face. "Have fun."

Once away from the craziness going on inside with Raven bitching, Steve winking, and the hurt look on Bonnie's face, he helped Savannah into her car. Walking around, he got into the driver seat, moving it back to fit his much larger frame.

"Where am I taking you?" Bishop asked as he took the keys and started the car. When she didn't answer, he glanced her way. She was staring at the house. "Ma'am?"

"I'm sorry," she whispered, then rattled off the address. "I've just never seen anything like that before. And then when they explained to me exactly what it was, well, I just can't believe those two girls are responsible."

Bishop knew exactly where he was going. It was a very nice gated community. "I'm sure they know we've been there by now and won't be back, so I don't think you'll have any problems with them," Bishop replied, making a left-hand turn. "But you have Sloan's information if you need us for anything."

"Thank you," the woman said, and Bishop could tell she was staring at him.

She finally looked away, and the rest of the ride was quiet. Pulling up to the gate, the security guard looked into the car to see Savannah.

"Ms. Livingston, everything okay?" the man asked, looking at Bishop briefly.

"Yes, Fred. Thank you," she replied, and the guard

opened the gate. "Just follow the road. It's the first condo on the right."

Bishop pulled in and parked. Getting out, he went around and opened her door for her. "I'll make sure you get inside."

Once at the door, she keyed in a code and opened the door. She turned to look up at him. "You can come inside."

The invitation was clear in her voice as well as her eyes. Damn, he actually had to think, and it didn't take long for him to realize that it just felt wrong. Not many times in his life had he turned down an invitation from a beautiful woman like Savannah Livingston. Today was a first for him. The more he thought, the more he realized how long it had been since he'd had a woman, any woman. And didn't that make his mood foul as fuck.

"I need to be getting back," Bishop replied, not really knowing how to turn down a fucking invitation for sex. And he knew if he went through that door, that's exactly what was going to happen. Jesus, he was losing his fucking mind. Viktor would laugh his ass off if he ever found out.

"Oh, okay." She seemed taken aback by being refused, and by the looks of it, that didn't often happen if at all. No, he was the fucking dumbass who was her first, he was sure. "Well, ah, thank you again."

"Ma'am." He gave her a nod, then turned and walked away toward the gate. Four times he thought about going back, but each time he stopped himself and wondered if he needed to see Slade. Something was definitely wrong with him.

Not even waiting for the gate to open, Bishop jumped it and took off in a jog heading toward the warehouse where his bike better be. His mind kept going to the woman with a body that would bring any man to his knees, and he wasn't even getting hard. Holy fuck, his dick was broken. Okay, that made him chuckle, realizing how stupid of a thought that was... or was it? He frowned as he kicked his speed up a little bit.

Thinking of Raven's attitude, he had a feeling she knew something, but what? What in the hell was going on? Not really wanting to jog with a hard-on, he kept the woman from his mind, thinking of anything else, but fear for his dick made him continue with thoughts of her legs, ass, and large tits in that button-down white shirt showing a healthy amount of cleavage. Glancing down, he cursed. Nothing. Suddenly, Bonnie's image came to mind, confusing him even more. His cock jerked, making him trip to a stop. His eyes widened as he stared down at himself while cars passed by. A car horn blared, and he glanced up at his surroundings. Cursing, he took off, determined to get to the bottom of what in the hell was going on. Raven knew exactly what his and his dick's problem was. He was sure of it.

"Jesus!" he growled, his eyes glowing black. If Raven didn't have answers, Slade better because no fucking way in hell would he live life with a broken fucking dick.

CHAPTER 6

"Y ou should be resting," Raven said as she and Bonnie walked into the warehouse.

"No way am I missing your first night of training." Bonnie held her ribs, secretly wishing she was still in bed, but she didn't want to miss this. Not on her life. She had a feeling some asses were going to get kicked, and she wanted to be there to support the ass-kicker.

"I asked Bishop to give you some of his blood so you can heal," Raven said absently as she set down her bag.

Bonnie gasped. Her stomach swirled with panic as she reached out, stopping Raven in a bruising grip. "You did what?" she hissed, then bent slightly. "Ouch, that fucking hurt."

"You heard me." Raven grabbed a chair and walked her over toward the mats. "Sit down before you do more damage."

"Raven, you can't ask Bishop things like that about me," Bonnie said as she sat down. She continued to stare at Raven, her eyes wide in panic.

"Why is that, Bonnie?" Raven put her hand on her hip, glaring down at her. "Afraid your little spell is weakening because you're hurt. Well, you're probably right."

"I don't know what you're talking about." Bonnie looked away from Raven quickly. "Spells don't work on full-bloods. And why would I do a spell on Bishop? I have no reason to do a spell on Bishop. Plus spells wouldn't work on Bishop anyway, like I said."

"You ramble when you lie." Raven smirked, then narrowed her eyes at Bonnie as she knelt down. "I've been around enough demons, witches, and magic to know when someone is under a spell."

"I didn't put a spell on Bishop," Bonnie whispered as a few trainees jogged by staring at them. "And I don't ramble or lie. Magic doesn't work on—" Bonnie shut her mouth since she began to ramble again about something she had already said multiple times. She'd also said Bishop's name fifty times, or at least it seemed like that many.

Raven snorted. "But you put a spell on yourself, didn't you?"

Bonnie shook her head, clamping her mouth shut.

"Afraid you're going to ramble?" Raven chuckled as she knelt down on Bonnie's level. "Don't know why you did it, but I know you put a spell on yourself so Bishop doesn't find you attractive or something to that effect. I know you're in love with him. I've seen it. I also know he has feelings for you, or at least I saw it before you did the spell. Why, Bonnie?"

Bonnie remained silent. Her heart was beating a million miles a minute. She was sweating like crazy, and she honestly felt like throwing up. Dammit, this wasn't good. No one was supposed to find out ever, or at least until she killed her father or he killed her.

"You're wrong," Bonnie said, then clamped her mouth shut again.

"No, I'm not, and I'm not letting up on it until I learn the truth." Raven stood slowly. "And I can be a real pain in the ass, witch."

"You going to chat all night, or do you think you can find time to join us?" Jax said from the mats.

Raven continued to stare at Bonnie, who glanced at Jax, then pointed his way before looking at Raven. "He isn't talking to me."

"No, but I am." Raven gave her a warning look. "Tell me or I tell him. I'll give you till the end of training to decide. It's wrong, Bonnie, and you know it."

"And to think I came here to support you," Bonnie called out after her as Raven started jogging to warm up. She gave Bonnie a backward wave as if dismissing her.

As it turned out, she wasn't the only one who wanted to watch Raven's first training session as a VC Warrior. Everyone other than Sloan and Bishop was there. Charger had just walked in and leaned against the wall, watching from the shadows.

After warm-ups, they began drills. Raven did them with ease, no problems at all. Bonnie could tell some of the trainees were talking about her, a few making remarks that Bonnie could hear. She knew Raven heard because her golden eyes had become black, but that was the only indication. Other than her black eyes, Raven was cool, calm, and collected. That was until the sparring began.

Bonnie actually stood up and moved closer so she could watch. She'd heard Raven was badass, but now she was going to see firsthand. The first round Raven sat out watching. Bonnie looked on. It was easy to spot the assholes in the trainee program. Katrina was going with a guy and doing really well until she got a good sweep, taking him to the ground. When she stood to let him up, he swung out, hitting her hard in the jaw, sending her crashing into the wall.

Glancing at Blaze, she saw the anger on his face, but he remained where he was, not saying a word. Damn, that had to be hard for the Warrior. Katrina shook it off and went back in and continued for a few more minutes. When it was time to switch partners, Raven walked over and stood directly in front of the guy who'd hit Katrina.

"Oh shit," Bonnie said when she saw the smile on the guy's face. She glanced at Raven to see her smile was bigger. Nervous energy made Bonnie jittery. She looked over at Charger, whose expression was deadpan as he stared at Raven.

Jax gave the command to begin, and Bonnie realized the guy never had a chance. Raven was all over him with punches, kicks, sweeps, and hell, Bonnie didn't know what else. It was a total massacre and a sight to see as everyone stopped to watch. Jax commanded them to stop and Raven did. She went to find another partner, but the guy punched out, not expecting Raven to catch and stop the punch. There were gasps and excited curses from the other trainees. Raven shook her head at him, grabbed him by the shirt and head-butted the asshole, knocking him out cold. She stepped over his body, searching for her next partner, but no one would even look her in the eye except Katrina, who walked up to her giving her a high five.

Glancing at Charger, she watched as he turned and walked out of the warehouse with a proud grin on his face. Damn, bet he hated losing Raven, she thought, then continued to watch the rest of the training. Jared had to actually walk the guy off the mat after he woke up.

"Guess you learned a lesson," Jared was saying as the guy wobbled his way toward her. "Don't piss off a female who's more badass than you." Jared winked at her as he passed with a huge smile.

Bonnie grinned, seeing the large goose egg knot on the guy's forehead. Raven didn't even have a red bump that she could see. Soon the training was over, and Bonnie considered transporting her ass out of there before Raven could start on her again, but after what she saw tonight, she really didn't want to piss her off.

"You ready?" Raven said after coming out of the back, her hair wet and hanging down her back.

Bonnie nodded, noticing all the guys staring at Raven. "I think you've scared the shit out of all of them," Bonnie whispered as they walked out.

"Good." Raven nodded but then grinned. "Just the way I like it."

"Charger looked pleased," Bonnie added as they walked out to the parking lot. "He had a big old proud grin on his face when he left."

Raven shrugged, tossing her bag in the back of the car. It had started snowing again, and Bonnie was freezing. Raven didn't seem fazed, but vampires rarely were by the weather. Once they were inside the car, Raven started it and turned on the heat. "You need anything before I take you back? I have a meeting at the warehouse in about half an hour."

"No, I'm fine," Bonnie said, happy that Raven must have forgotten about their earlier conversation. "But thanks."

"Don't be thanking me yet." Raven backed out of the parking spot. "You have until we get to the compound to tell me what in the hell you think you're doing messing with Bishop."

"Shit," Bonnie mumbled, her hopes of Raven forgetting dashed. "I'm not messing with Bishop. It's for his own good. I'm no good. He needs someone like that woman, Savannah, or whatever her name is."

Raven pulled to the side of the road and stopped, then glared over at Bonnie. "Bullshit."

"No, actually it's not bullshit." Bonnie glared back. "I have a bounty on my head, Raven. A lunatic father who will stop at nothing to see me dead. He will go after anyone and everyone associated with me. As a matter of fact, I should have left a long time ago, but I've stuck around trying to help Kira get ready. This is not anyone's fight but mine. If feelings develop between me and Bishop, his life won't be worth anything."

"You love him." Raven's glare softened.

Bonnie opened her mouth, but no words came out. She cleared her voice and looked away. "Love has nothing to do with anything. Just trust me. It's best this way."

"Oh, I trust you with my life," Raven said, her tone stating clearly she meant it. "But I don't trust you to make the right decision on this. What you are doing is wrong, Bonnie. You cannot play with people like this and expect everything to be okay. Let Bishop make his own decisions. He is a Warrior. A man who, by the way, is going to be all kinds of pissed off when he finds out, and he will find out either by you or me."

"Please don't, Raven," Bonnie begged, her eyes round with fear.

"If he asks me, I'm not lying. It's against everything I believe," Raven stated firmly. "But…."

"But?" Bonnie asked hopefully.

"I will not seek him out to tell him." Raven sighed, then frowned at her. "But think about what I've said. The way you are going about this is going to lead to heartbreak, and I'm afraid that heartbreak is going to be yours."

"You can't break something that's already broken, Raven." Bonnie glanced away to stare at the snow hitting the windshield. "And you speak to me about Bishop. What about you and Charger?"

"Oh, you are so wrong about that. Believe me when I tell you a heart can break a hundred times in a hundred different ways," Raven replied, then turned the lights on the car back on. "And me and Charger are different. He knows exactly how I feel, and I know exactly how he feels. Nothing similar at all with our situations. Give Bishop the same benefit. He's a good man and deserves that much."

"But I'm trying to save him." Bonnie tried to justify her actions.

"No, you're controlling him," Raven shot back. "There is no justification in that, Bonnie. And save him from who? Your father? He's been against worse in his lifetime, I'm sure."

"From me," Bonnie whispered, then shook her head and looked toward Raven. "From *me*," she repeated louder.

"What if he doesn't choose to be saved from you?" Raven asked, her head tilted as if trying to understand. "Oh, that's right. You've taken his choice away."

"Why does this matter so much to you?" Bonnie sighed, not understanding why Raven just wouldn't let it go. Let her do what she needed to do, what she felt was best.

Raven was silent for a long minute, just staring out the windshield. "I've had few friends in my life. I consider you one of those few."

"But you barely know me," Bonnie said, confused, never having had a friend. A true friend. It was foreign to her.

Raven smiled as she finally looked her way. "Pretty cool, huh."

Bonnie laughed, then nodded. "Yeah, it is." She had actually felt that connection with Raven too. "Never really had a friend before, so I'm sure I'll fuck up a lot."

"Don't worry. I'll beat you back into shape." Raven grinned as she pulled back onto the road.

"Ah, is that what friends do?" Bonnie gave her a sideways look.

"It's what I do," Raven said, then laughed at Bonnie's frown. "Don't worry, I won't head-butt you."

"Can you show me that move?" Bonnie asked with a grin. "I sure could use that knowledge."

"I'll show you anything you want to know." Raven pulled into the compound. "You'll be one badass witch. Now, go get some rest, and I'll see you in the morning."

"Thanks," Bonnie said, opening the door, but stopped. "And, Raven, I've never had love in my life. I don't even know what love is. Bishop deserves much more than I could ever give him."

She got out quickly, then slammed the door before she could hear anything else from Raven. Her mind was already on overload, and she didn't know what to do with all the emotions rambling around in her head and heart.

Bonnie was ready for a shower and bed. This day had sucked, and tomorrow looked like it was going to suck even more. She made it to the door, hit the code, and as the door opened, she turned to look at Raven. With a wave, she ducked inside, hurried to her small room Sloan had given her, and closed herself in. The tears fell, hard and fast. Shit was getting too real for her. Maybe it was time she pulled a Bonnie and disappeared. It was her definite go-to when things got hard. The security she felt at disappearing wasn't there this time. No, her heart hurt, and that's when she knew she had overstayed her welcome. Bonnie Grail didn't deserve peace, not yet. Not until her mother rested in peace and her father was dead by her hand.

CHAPTER 7

*B*ishop slammed his way into the warehouse seeing that training was over. He looked around for Raven but didn't see her anywhere.

"Bike's out there," Steve said, walking up to him. "Not a scratch."

"Good thing." Bishop frowned, not in the mood to talk to anyone other than Raven. "Where's Raven?"

"She took Bonnie back to the compound. She should be back here any minute," Viktor said, then frowned. "Why, what's up?"

Bishop shook his head. Viktor was the last person he wanted to talk to about this shit. "How'd she do tonight?"

Viktor smiled. "She kicked everyone's ass. It was pretty fucking amazing."

"Damn! Was hoping to see that." Bishop felt his mood

lighten slightly. Even though she called him a fucking idiot, he still wanted to see what she was capable of. "Charger show up?"

"Long enough to see how she did," Viktor replied, then glanced toward the door. "Then he left without a word to anyone."

Bishop nodded, then angled to see Raven walk in with Jared, Duncan, and Sloan. He headed toward her. "Need to talk to you."

"Where's Damon and Sid? Ronan is on rounds, so he won't be here." Sloan glanced around as he asked Bishop before he could take Raven outside.

"No clue. Just got here myself." Bishop took Raven's arm and headed outside.

"What?" Raven said, her tone of voice calmer than it was earlier when she was calling him an idiot and a pig. Yeah, he'd forgotten about that until now.

"Why don't you tell me what the fuck happened back at that house?" Bishop crossed his arms and watched her closely.

Raven shrugged. "A bunch of occult shit was found. Trying to figure it out." Raven glanced away from him. "You know, you were there."

His mood took a turn for the worse. "You are seriously going to act like you didn't call me a fucking idiot or a pig?"

. . .

"*O*h, that," Raven said, finally looking at him. "Yeah, sorry. Just had a moment. Girl time."

"You're a fucking vampire." Bishop sneered. "You don't have girl time. Cut the shit, Raven. What in the hell is going on?"

"Are you going to help Bonnie heal, because if not, I'm going tonight to make her take my blood, or find someone to give her blood. I could probably call one of the Guardians—" Bonnie eyed him closely.

"The fuck you will," Bishop roared, then frowned, confused.

"Shit." Raven shuffled from foot to foot, looking nervous. "I can't do this. It's not fair."

"What's not fair?" Bishop questioned, not liking being in the dark.

"You've been confused about your feelings for Bonnie." It wasn't a question Raven was asking; it was a statement. "You kissed her, felt nothing, yet lately, the thought of another vampire giving her his blood is driving you into a rage. Why do you think that is?"

"The fuck if I know," Bishop said, not really comfortable talking about this with Raven, but fuck, he didn't feel like he had a choice.

"Think about it, Bishop," Raven urged him, looking conflicted. "I really don't want to be the one to tell you this, but I don't think Bonnie will. She will probably take off before she would do it, and if she leaves, she's as good as dead."

The thought of something happening to Bonnie made his head spin, making any other thoughts impossible. He just stared at Raven.

"She's a witch." Raven's eyes opened as if trying to force the answer into is head.

"I know that," he replied with agitation. "Tell me something I don't know. I'm getting damn tired of this guessing game."

Raven remained quiet as she stared at him, looking as if she was going to call him a fucking idiot again. *She's a witch.* He knew that, dammit. He frowned with a curse.

"She can't use magic on me," he said, his eyes narrowing.

"But she can on herself," Raven added, then clamped her mouth shut. When Bishop remained silent, she sighed. "Come on, man. For a witch hunter, you sure as hell don't know much about witches. She put a spell on herself."

Bishop was trying to get his head around everything he'd heard when Jared came outside.

"Is there a problem out here?" Jared asked, walking next to Raven.

"No," Raven replied. "No problem. Just going over a few things."

Bishop didn't say anything, his mind still trying to put shit together. Why in the hell would Bonnie put a spell on herself? And what did that have to do with him?

"Good," Jared said, then clapped Bishop on the shoulder. "Come on, Sloan's ready to get the show on the road. Damon and Sid are pulling in now."

"We're coming," Raven said, then waited until Jared returned inside before turning back to Bishop. "I've said all I'm going to say. I've actually said too much. You need to figure this out before it's too late, Bishop. Her life depends on it."

Raven walked away, but Bishop stopped her. "She put an aversion spell on herself?"

Looking over her shoulder, she nodded.

"But why?" Bishop frowned, feeling more confused than he had before, but his mixed-up feelings were starting to make sense.

"That's not my story to tell," Raven said, her voice low with a tinge of sadness. "But I will tell you this. You break her heart, I *will* break you."

Bishop watched as Raven disappeared inside. Anger mixed with disbelief hit him hard. None of this made any sense to him. Damon and Sid walked up.

"Meeting over?" Damon asked, glancing toward the warehouse.

"What?" Bishop shook his head, trying to focus. "Ah, no. Hasn't started."

"Shit, hoping we'd at least be late," Sid said as he passed. "Need to see my mate. She's probably left me by now."

"You good, man?" Damon asked, watching Bishop closely.

Bishop looked at him blankly for a minute. "No, I'm not." Bishop headed toward his bike. "Tell Sloan I'll get filled in later. I have to go. Something's come up."

"You need help?" Damon called out.

"No." Bishop hopped on his bike, started it, and took off. It was time to get answers, and the person who had the answers wasn't there. So he would go to her. He really tried his best to keep his anger at bay until he heard her out, but it was hard. Why in the hell would she do something like that? He felt played and it pissed him off. Magic wasn't something he took lightly, especially when it was used against him, and he had a bad feeling that's exactly what was going on.

Pulling into the compound, he parked then jogged to the door. Keying in the code, he burst through the door, slamming it behind him. Taking the steps two at a time, he headed toward her room. Once there, he knocked on the door, but she didn't answer. Tuning in, he listened closely and could hear a heartbeat and knew she was inside. He knocked again. Still nothing.

He tried the knob and the door opened. He looked inside and saw her curled up on her bed under the covers. Bishop closed the door behind him. Walking to the end of the bed, he stood there watching her sleep. A sudden strong urge to protect her overwhelmed him. She looked so small and defenseless lying there. This small woman had lived a life of pure hell with no end in sight.

His gaze left her to look around the sparse room. There wasn't much in the space other than her clothes she had worn earlier folded neatly on the only chair in the room. Walking backward, he moved the clothes and sat down, leaning his head against the wall, his eyes staying on her. He would wait, not having the heart to wake her yet.

Yeah, he would wait, at least for a little while. Crossing his arms, he continued his vigil. Some would call what he was doing creepy, but suddenly it didn't feel that way to him. This felt right, like he belonged here… with her. Feelings he thought he had for her when he first met her came rushing back to him in waves.

With a curse, things started to become clear to him. She was hurt, which weakened her magic. And now she was sleeping, weakening it more. For a fact, he knew Bonnie had put an aversion spell on herself. Bishop wouldn't leave until he knew why.

She stirred, her legs moving in jerky movements. A small whimper filled the room before she quieted. He sat up, ready to go to her if needed, but she seemed to calm. He relaxed, but only for a minute. She again started to struggle, this time in earnest. He stood and went to the bed, afraid she was going to hurt herself.

Leaning over, he cringed at the fear on her sleeping face. "Bonnie," he whispered, putting his hand gently on her shoulder. "Wake up."

Once his hand made contact with her, all hell broke loose. She began to fight demons he couldn't see. It broke him to see her fear while still asleep caught in a nightmare he wasn't in to protect her.

"Bonnie!" he said louder, this time with more force. "Wake up."

"No, please," she whimpered, her arms fighting to get out from under the covers. "Take me, not him. Me! Bishop! No! Please!"

Bishop whipped the covers off her and picked her up, holding her tightly to him. "Bonnie! Stop! Wake up!"

She smacked at him, and he knew she was fighting something, trying to come out of her nightmare. He kept calling her name until finally, her eyes popped open, wide in fright, but then relief flashed across their beautiful green color.

"Bishop?" she whispered as big wet tears slipped from her eyes. "You're okay?"

"Yes, of course I am." He wiped a tear away from her cheek with his thumb. "And so are you. You're safe. I've got you. It was just a nightmare."

She slowly shook her head, staring up at him. "What are you doing here?"

"To heal you," he replied after a moment of silence. "And to find out why you've put an aversion spell on yourself. It's time for truths, Bonnie, and I'm not leaving until I have it. All of it."

"She shouldn't have told you." Bonnie's head dropped, but he lifted it so she could see his face.

"Raven didn't tell me," Bishop said, then frowned. "I guessed. You're damn lucky I'm an understanding man. At least for the moment."

Bishop looked down at her body. She only wore a tank top that barely covered her. His cock stirred, and he sighed in relief. His dick wasn't broken. At least with her it wasn't. He had a feeling for any other woman it was.

"Time to come clean, witch." Bishop's eyes rose to meet hers. "And it better be good. I don't take magic being used against me lightly."

"I did it for you, not against you," Bonnie whispered, then bit her lip.

"That's a very fine line, Bonnie." Bishop stared at her lips, then bent his head. Their lips met, and within a second, he knew for a fact what he'd felt under the mistletoe had not been real. This right here was as real as it came, and deep down, it scared the fuck out of him.

CHAPTER 8

*H*er nightmares were real. They came every single time she closed her eyes, making her hate sleep, but unfortunately, her body needed it. Bonnie had gone days without closing her eyes, but the toll was always a high price for her. It made her magic unpredictable and right now, that was dangerous.

Hearing her name repeated over and over again had Bonnie fighting from the darkness. She hated the darkness and never slept without a light of some sort. In her nightmare, she reached for Bishop, but he was being pulled away from her. Nothing worked. Not her magic, nothing. He was mouthing something to her, but she couldn't make out what he was trying to say. The blackness was swallowing him, and she begged whatever it was to take her, not him. And then she heard her name, felt herself being pulled away.

The voice became harsher, but still felt safe. Opening her eyes against the heavy force was no easy feat, but she did it. Bishop's image focused at her wide-eyed gaze. She was sure he'd said something to her and she'd responded, but her brain was still in the nightmare so she had no clue what was exchanged.

"That's a very fine line, Bonnie." Bishop's voice was low and held a hint of anger.

"Huh?" She frowned, wishing her mind would clear.

His eyes narrowed. "Why did you use an aversion spell?"

Even though she felt safe in his arms, she needed to move away from him. It was too easy to give in, and the kiss they just shared proved her magic was weak. She gasped in pain when she tried to push away from him.

"Dammit." Bishop held her still. "Be careful."

She watched as he put his wrist to his mouth, his fangs gleaming. "Stop." She grabbed his arm before his fangs could make contact with his skin. "I'm fine."

"No, you're not," Bishop replied, gently pulling his arm away. "I know most humans don't like the taste of blood, but only a few drops should do, and your pain will be gone."

In all honesty, Bonnie wondered what the big deal was about the blood of a vampire. She had never herself tasted any but knew others who had. With a nod of agreement, she watched as he used his fangs to puncture his skin, then held his wrist out to her. The two beads of blood appeared, and she slowly lowered her mouth to his wrist.

His blood hit her tongue as a tingling sensation strummed through her body, consuming her with feelings. Her senses were in overdrive. The taste of him, the smell of him, and the feel of him caused a moan to catch in the back of her throat. His blood was warm, which surprised her. She thought it would be cold with a metallic taste, but she was oh so wrong. His taste was something she couldn't describe in words and the way it made her feel was hypnotizing, as if she couldn't get enough. The pulls of her mouth on his wrist became a little frantic, shocking her, but she couldn't stop.

It was actually Bishop who stopped her. "That's enough. Too much isn't a good thing."

Bonnie's eyes were wide as she pulled her mouth away, touching her lips with her fingertips. "Now I know why you're so addictive," she said, then cleared her throat. What the hell was she saying? "I mean your blood. Your blood is addictive."

A half-grin formed on his lips as he stared down at her. "How do you feel?"

"Great." Bonnie sighed, wanting nothing more than to jump in his arms and…. Wait a minute. This so wasn't her. She moved away from him, surprised and relieved the movement didn't hurt. "I mean yeah, it feels much better. As if it didn't happen."

"Good." His grin slipped as he stood. He grabbed the single chair in her room, then placed it next to the bed and straddled it. "Now, about that aversion spell."

Bonnie needed to get her ass in gear and stop being a slobbering mess. It was just blood. He was just a man and she needed to steer clear. Not only for her own sanity, but his as well. Digging deep for the smartass she knew she was, she pulled the covers over her bare legs.

"What about it?" She shrugged and felt her nipples harden as his eyes dropped to her white tank top. Yeah, no bra, white, and well… shit, she couldn't blame him for looking. It was like they were screaming, "Hey, look at these ta-tas, big boy." Fighting the urge to tell him where her eyes were like she had done to countless men in the past, she sat still, secretly loving the lust in his gaze. Yeah, she wasn't going to say a damn word for more reasons than one.

Finally, his gaze rose. Their eyes met and what came out of his mouth made her smile… dammit.

"Huh?" His voice was deep, rough, and her body ached at the sound.

"What about it?" she repeated slowly, a tinge of smartass rearing its ugly head.

Bishop's eyes narrowed slightly as if realizing what had just happened. "Bonnie, stop playing games."

"Games?" That snapped her out of smartass right into anger. "I don't play games, Bishop. I don't have time for games. None of us do. The reason for my aversion spell is my business. Mine alone."

"Not if it involves me," Bishop growled, leaning forward slightly.

Okay, this was getting way too personal. Bonnie didn't do personal, just like she didn't play games. Her life was too fucked up to get personal with anyone, let alone someone who could steal her heart and then die because of her. Not happening. Not on her watch, and not while she drew breath.

"Don't flatter yourself, Warrior." Bonnie cocked her eyebrow at him. "This aversion spell has everything to do with anyone who comes into contact with me."

Bishop stood fast, knocking the chair out of his way as he leaned over the bed and was right smack in her face. "Drop the fucking aversion spell, Bonnie."

Whipping the covers off, she got up on her knees and leaned toward him. The only thing was he didn't move, and they were now nose to nose. "Don't even think you can order me to do anything. Good luck with that." She snorted, but her eyes narrowed; she wasn't backing down. "Many have tried and failed."

Healed from his blood, she felt stronger, much stronger. She doubled her power on the spell as a "fuck you" to his order. His expression clued her into the fact he felt her magic. His phone began to ring, but he ignored it. Finally, it stopped only to start up again.

"You going to answer that?" Bonnie said; they were still nose to nose, and honestly, her eyes were starting to cross.

Backing up slightly, he answered. "What?" he all but shouted into the phone. "Dammit. I'll be there."

Bonnie couldn't help it. She was fucking turned on by his intensity. Yeah, the aversion spell didn't affect her, so her attraction to this man was off the charts. Maybe it was time for her to walk. Move on and away from everyone she was beginning to care about. It never ended well for those people. Her eyes rose from the bed to his where he continued to stare at her.

"What?" she whispered, tired of the fight, yet fighting was what she was best at, thanks to her piece-of-shit father.

"Drop the aversion spell," Bishop demanded, his golden eyes narrowed.

"No." Bonnie's voice wavered slightly. With her whole being she wanted to do as he demanded and wasn't that right there a mindfuck?

"Now that I know I will never give you peace." Bishop reached out and touched her cheek. "Drop it, Bonnie."

"My magic is strong. I could even make you hate me." Bonnie countered, but sat back on her heels and stared up at him as if in defeat. The thought of him hating her, gutted Bonnie. Goddess, she was exhausted.

"Your magic *is* strong, but I could never hate you." Bishop pulled his hand away as a frown formed across his lips. "You can't push everyone away."

"I've done a damn good job so far." She shrugged as if the thought of the loneliness she had suffered over the years didn't faze her.

"Actually, you haven't," Bishop replied, with such confidence Bonnie seriously wanted to slap him.

"Excuse me?" Bonnie put her hand on her hip, not realizing she was pressing her boobs out until his eyes shot downward briefly before lifting back to hers.

"I'm here, aren't I?" He answered, his eyebrow cocked making him look sexy as hell.

"Kissing you was like kissing my cousin. Now, who did I hear that from recently? Christmas Eve I believe it was." She cocked her eyebrow right back at him.

"That would be me, but I think I just proved to you that was a mistake." Bishop followed with an honest to God growl, but he did keep his gaze on hers and not her boobs.

"No, that was magic." Damn, she kinda liked sparring with this man. It was invigorating to the point she wanted to jump him. Ugh, she needed to get her shit together, and fast. All her mind went to was jumping this Warrior. Before she knew what was happening, he moved so fast she was in his arms, pressed against the hardness of his body.

"Now that I know, I will fight it and I will win. Amp up that magic, witch," Bishop hissed, staring down at her before his lips slammed against hers.

As far as kisses went, Bonnie had never been kissed like this before in her life. It was all-consuming, touching her mind, body, and soul. It was rough yet tender, and she couldn't get enough. It felt right… too right, and by the feel of his lower body, she knew he definitely was not thinking of her as his cousin.

As abruptly as the kiss started, it stopped, and she felt empty. How odd. Opening her eyes slowly, they met his.

"That's the best you can do?"

At first, she thought he meant the kiss and wanted to

slap him for the insult, but then her mind started to function, and she knew exactly what he meant. Her magic.

"You took me by surprise," she shot back. She tried not to wince at the rasp in her voice from the passion of the kiss. It didn't even sound like her own voice at all.

"Bullshit." He pressed his hardness against her with purpose, as if proving to her that her magic spell had no effect on him. "Never, and I mean never, try to trick me again with spells. And if you run…"

She knew he caught her guilty expression before she could hide it.

"…I will find you," Bishop finished after giving her a warning look. "You do not control me or my feelings, Bonnie. At least not with witchcraft."

"Why? Why do you even care?" She pulled slightly away from him. "I'm a witch. You're a witch killer."

"Was," he corrected. "And I only kill those who deserve to die. Witches included."

"I will only bring you pain, Bishop. That's all I ever bring anyone." She tried to not only reason with him, but herself as well. Her mind screamed for her to do what he warned her against and that was to run, but her heart had other plans. "A happily ever after is not in the cards drawn for me. Never has been."

Bishop cupped her face and kissed her quickly, stealing her breath and her heart a little bit more. "I've never dealt those cards now, have I?" He backed away from her, then headed to the door. "Get dressed. Sloan needs to see us. I'll wait out in the hallway."

"You're making a mistake," she whispered as the door closed behind Bishop.

"Makes life interesting," he said from the other side of the doorway, actually making her smile just as a tear slipped from the corner of her eye.

CHAPTER 9

"*N*othing yet?" Wyrick stood in front of a computer screen staring over it at Orjyll, who just walked into the room. "But I know they got the message. It shouldn't be long now."

Cursing, Orjyll's hands fisted in anger. He hated to wait for anything. Waiting to regain his powers had made him that way. Fucking Grail females. Every single one of them were going to pay, and pay dearly. At first, he'd just sought them to kill them, but that was before. Now he had other plans. They would suffer in the most violent, deranged ways he could come up with, and damn his mind was morbid.

"It better not be," Orjyll said, then headed toward the window and looked out. He hated Wyrick. He was a snobby bastard who thought he was better than anyone, but time and time again, Orjyll proved him wrong. No one in his presence was better than him. He was once the most powerful warlock, and he would be again. The only reason he allowed Wyrick to live was because he needed him… for the moment. As soon as that moment was over, he'd kill the asshole himself.

"This stuff takes time," Wyrick said in his usual condescending tone. "You need to be more patient."

Orjyll's face became a vision of rage. He stared through the reflection of the window. Patient? Waiting for years and years to regain his powers had run his patience very thin. For now, he knew Wyrick didn't fear him, but he knew what the bastard's true fear was. Sloan Murphy. A sick grin formed at the corner of Orjyll's cruel mouth. He wondered briefly if Sloan Murphy would like to make a trade. His traitor of a daughter for the man who tried to kill him. Even with a man he hated as much as he did Sloan Murphy, he would definitely make that trade.

He continued to stare at his reflection, seeing the lines creasing his skin. He needed youth. Losing his power and not able to perform that spell of youth on himself drove him mad, but what drove him to the edge was having to ask someone like Wyrick to do the deed. His hair was thinning and turning an ugly gray.

"Call Roberta for me," Orjyll demanded without turning around. He was once a very handsome man who could have any woman he wanted. Now, only a spell returned those looks.

"Why?" Wyrick asked, and Orjyll knew he now gained his full attention. One thing about Wyrick was he always needed to be number one. The other warlocks and witches he surrounded himself with were below him, or so Wyrick thought. "What do you need?"

"My dick sucked," Orjyll said with a flippant edge. "Unless of course you want that honor."

This time, Orjyll did turn only his head to look at Wyrick. That was one secret Wyrick would die to keep. Orjyll had walked in to find a young warlock on his knees pleasuring a very wicked Wyrick. Orjyll had actually stood and watched just to make sure Wyrick knew he was there.

"I don't know what you think you saw, but...," Wyrick sputtered, only stopping when he saw Orjyll's expression.

"Your perversion to the young warlock is what I saw, but who am I to judge? Hmm? You want cock? That's your business." Orjyll turned fully toward him. "Just make sure the warlocks are agreeable because I don't need that drama upon my house."

The hate on Wyrick's face flashed very quickly, but Orjyll spotted it right away and knew he needed to watch his back. "Now, I need to freshen up," Orjyll said, which was his way to tell Wyrick to use his magic to bring his appearance back up to par. Seeing the hesitation, he knew Wyrick was wondering if this was a good time to take Orjyll out. "Careful, my... friend. Those around me have been given strict orders that if something happens to me, to take you out first."

"You wound me, Orjyll." Wyrick's fake shock pissed Orjyll off even more. "I would never."

"And that's the smartest words you've spoken today. Believable is another matter," Orjyll said, feeling the magic working. He felt stronger, more vibrant, and horny as fuck. Anytime this spell was used on him, everything outside and inside his body came alive with an almost violent vibrancy. His cock throbbed, which was why Roberta had been summoned. She was a beautiful brunette, who didn't remind him of anyone. That's the way he liked it. No memories as he released his lust upon whoever lay underneath him.

"Roberta is on her way." Wyrick's eyes went to Orjyll's dick then quickly away. He knew without a doubt, given the chance, Wyrick would be more than happy to kneel in front of him, but Orjyll didn't roll that way. He didn't frown on it, not at all. It just wasn't his choice. During his younger days as a warlock, he had been involved in hundreds of orgies. Many opportunities had presented themselves, and he'd had a few males service his cock, but a female's lips and tongue were his preference.

What really pissed him off about Wyrick was his complete denial of his sexuality. If Orjyll did enjoy the same sex, he sure as hell wouldn't give two fucks what anyone else thought. Wyrick's complete refusal to admit —even when caught with his cock in a man's mouth— that he enjoyed men said a lot about Wyrick. At least in Orjyll's way of thinking, and in his house that was all that mattered.

"Make sure you notify me as soon as she's on," Orjyll ordered, glancing once again at the computer. With the help of magic, his office was what he was accustomed to. High tech and the most expensive equipment witchcraft could buy. That was one good thing about Wyrick; he had good taste.

"Have you thought about possibly making a deal with

your daughter?" Wyrick asked, sitting down in the computer chair and turning it to look at Orjyll. "You would make an amazing team."

Eyes narrowing, Orjyll glared at him. "She is a Grail, or have you forgotten the curse?" Stupidity was something Orjyll could barely tolerate. "She dies in order to have my powers restored. Unless you have something useful, don't suggest anything at all."

"No, I haven't forgotten." The anger in Wyrick's voice was there, but he tamed it. "But once she helped you kill the other Grail females, we could take her out."

"Sure, Wyrick. As soon as she contacts us, I'll bring that up to her," Orjyll said with so much sarcasm, it dripped from each word. "You fucking idiot. I don't pay you or keep you around for idiotic suggestions. Don't even open your mouth unless you have something useful to say."

There was a knock on the door before it opened. "Did you need me?" Roberta asked, her eyes going from Wyrick then to Orjyll.

"Come in," Orjyll demanded, his gaze roaming her body, though he felt nothing. Wyrick's stupidity totally did away with his hard-on. "Let me ask you a question, Roberta."

"Sure," the witch said as she came further into the room. She was young, but very smart and ambitious. Her venture into the black arts was an asset to him. Especially as she was beautiful, intelligent, and had an evil side that he enjoyed very much.

"Do you think I should bring my bitch of a daughter in as a partner?" Orjyll felt Wyrick's unease.

At first, she hesitated, as if not really knowing how to answer. Her eyes shot nervously between Wyrick and Orjyll. She was definitely smart because both of them were powerful in their own rights. "Ah, no," Roberta finally stated. "I think that would be a horrible mistake. She has already proven where her loyalty lies, and it's not with you. Plus she's a Grail, and...."

Orjyll frowned. "And?" he asked after she trailed off.

"I haven't collected the bounty on her yet," Roberta replied, then a wicked smile spread across her beautiful face.

Orjyll's head fell back as he laughed, but then cut it off abruptly. His eyes zeroed in on Wyrick. "I think maybe you need to take lessons from her, Wyrick. She seems to be the smarter of the two."

Taking Roberta's hand, Orjyll led Roberta into the bedroom, his sexual need returning with a fury. "Knock if she comes on," Orjyll ordered before slamming the door shut, but not before missing the glare full of hate shooting toward him from Wyrick. Soon his need for the bastard would be at an end, very soon.

∾

*R*aven walked out the warehouse, her mood dark and grim. She needed to go back to the Guardian house and get her belongings. She really didn't know where she was going to go. They just had a meeting with the Warriors and Sloan, stating they were going to build housing for the recruits because some had long commutes and others were out of state with no real place to go. Unfortunately, that didn't help her now, but she knew her time with the Guardians was over. It was time to move on. She had some cash, but not enough to rent anywhere. Maybe a week in a motel at the most.

Heading for her bike, she frowned. She knew her dad—damn that was weird to think—would help her, but she needed to do this on her own. Strapping her bag on the seat, she felt someone coming up to her. Being aware had kept her safe and she was ready for anything, but one whiff of the air, she knew only one person with that scent.

"What do you want, Kane?" Raven said before turning around.

Kane chuckled with a grin. "Never could sneak up on you."

"Yeah, well, you kind of make it a priority not to get sneaked up on with demons wanting a piece of your ass." Raven shrugged. She really needed to get her stuff and find a place to stay before it got much later. "Listen, I really need to take off."

"Val left," Kane said with a frown. "He quit, packed his shit and took off."

Dammit. Raven really hated to hear that, but what she had with Val was an understanding between them both. Nothing serious. "Okay." Her single word reply sounded uncaring even to her own ears. She wondered briefly when she had become so cold to everyone and everything around her.

Kane's eyes narrowed. "That's it? That's all you have to say?"

"What do you want me to say?" Raven frowned, not liking his attitude, which made no sense at all since she was thinking herself as being cold. Damn, she was moody as fuck. "We weren't serious, Kane. He barely noticed I was gone."

"Obviously he noticed. Now we're two down." Kane sighed, running his hand through his hair. "We can't afford to lose any more when there weren't many of us to begin with."

"Listen, I—" Raven started, but Kane stopped her.

"I know why you left, Raven. Charger is a dumbass." Kane's gaze turned sympathetic. "He couldn't see what was in front of his face or he ignored it—when in fact we all saw it. I think Val began to have feelings for you. He and Charger had a beat down the night you signed on with the Warriors."

"Val had no right," Raven hissed. "Charger had nothing to do with my decision."

"It wasn't Val who started the fight. It was Charger." Kane corrected her. "And you never could lie worth a shit. He's hurting, Raven."

Confused, Raven shook her head. "Then he shouldn't have let Val go."

"What in the hell are you talking about?" Kane was the

one who now looked confused. "Charger doesn't give a shit about Val. I mean, sure, he hated losing a man, but Val's ass kicking was a long time coming."

"Listen, I'm sorry, but this is where I need to be. I can't continue with the Guardians." Raven was done with this conversation that was going nowhere, plus it was totally confusing the hell out of her. "I'm going now to get my stuff."

Kane stared at her as if he wanted to say more, but just nodded.

"I'm sorry, Kane," Raven said, feeling as if she was letting him down. "I didn't come to this decision lightly. It's something I have to do."

Kane reached out and pulled her into a hug. "I always looked at you as a little sister, Raven. Just be happy and watch your ass."

Raven nodded, tears clouding her eyes. Kane and she always had a good relationship. "Watch yours too, Kane. And slow down on the whores. You can do much better. You need to find your mate and settle down."

"Settle?" Kane pulled away with a grin, lightly fake punching her in the chin. "Honey, that word isn't even in my vocabulary."

"She's out there and is going to find you," Raven warned with a knowing stare.

"I'm very hard to find." Kane tossed her a wink, but then his expression turned serious as he moved to leave. "Things are not what they seem with Charger."

Raven opened her mouth to ask him what he meant by that as she watched him walk away, but he stopped without turning around before she could respond.

"I'm here if you ever need anything, Raven. You may be a VC Warrior now, but to me, you will always be a Dark Guardian." With that, Kane disappeared.

Watching Kane ride away hit Raven hard. She'd never felt more alone than she did at that moment. Her life was spiraling out of control and she had no clue on how to stop it. She thought leaving the Guardians and getting away from Charger was what she needed, but she wasn't sure even that was going to stop her spiral. She needed to get a fucking grip and get over it. Her life was complicated, had always been complicated. So why in the hell did she think a switch was going to change that fact? If she'd learned one thing in her long life, people came and went. Nothing and no one were forever.

CHAPTER 10

*B*ishop walked out the door, closed it behind him, and then wondered what in the fuck just happened. Leaning against the wall, he softly banged his head against it. Damn! Her words had torn at him. Was she saying she was a mistake?

Closing his eyes, he thought of the kiss. Their kiss was nothing compared to Christmas Eve under the mistletoe. No comparison at all.

Without a doubt, he knew if he had stayed inside while she dressed, they wouldn't be leaving that room anytime soon. Viktor had called him, informing him that Orjyll had made contact, and to bring Bonnie to Sloan's office.

Not telling Bonnie was a conscious decision on his part because honestly, he didn't know if he wanted her to go. It felt like he was putting her in harm's way, but Bishop knew that wasn't fair. This was something Bonnie had to do, and it wasn't for him to deny the closure she needed where her bastard of a father was concerned. And he fucking hated it.

Every protective instinct inside his soul burned for him to take her and go. Leave and let everyone else deal with the evil Bonnie had endured all her life. But he also knew that until this was finished and Orjyll was dead, Bonnie would never have a life. She would always be looking over her shoulder and even with him at her side, that was not living. And it definitely wasn't a life she deserved to have. He was afraid she was the only one who could defeat her father, and that knowledge terrified him.

Opening his eyes, he stared at the closed door, knowing that his mate—yes, mate—was behind it. Bishop had never been more certain of anything in his life now he could push past her aversion spell. She was human; he was not. He had no clue how she felt other than her thinking they were a mistake, but he was willing to prove her wrong.

Thoughts of the past pushed their way into his present and he stared into the distance. His stomach twisted in knots, knowing one day soon he would have to confide in her how many witches he had killed. She was a witch; he had been a witch killer and damn good at his job. Swallowing hard, he realized he was afraid of losing something he wasn't even sure he had. Bonnie was complicated, no doubt about it, and at that moment, he knew he would die for her.

As the door opened and she looked up at him, Bishop knew that the first time he ever saw this beautiful woman, he would have died for her. Pushing himself off the wall, he scanned her from head to toe. She was beautiful. Her rounded face, rose-kissed cheeks, and large, expressive brown eyes called to him like no other. He was done denying it.

She was his.

"This—" Bishop waved his hand toward her room. "—is not over."

"It should be," Bonnie whispered, barely able to look at him. "I'm bad news, Bishop. Didn't you learn that with my mother? Nothing good ever comes with a Grail woman."

"Bullshit." He really tried to keep the anger from his voice, but with Bonnie, his emotions were hard to control.

"You'll see," Bonnie warned, once again looking at him. "So will Steve and Ronan. I don't want to say it or think it, but our track record is piss poor."

"Honestly, to this point, it's the people you've surrounded yourselves with that's been piss poor," Bishop said, truly believing that. "You've been let down... I'm sure by those you've trusted. Seen people turn their backs on you because of fear or greed, but never will I do that. Neither will Steve or Ronan. We are in this to the very end."

Bonnie looked as if she was ready to say something, but instead, she closed her mouth and sighed.

"What?" Bishop urged her to continue. He wanted to know what was in her thoughts.

"I'm a witch. You've hated witches for most of your life." Bonnie cocked her eyebrow at him. "And I've hated your kind most of mine. You really think that's the best foundation for a relationship."

He wasn't surprised by her words, because he had actually thought them himself. Spent many long nights thinking them. "A weak foundation can be reinforced with the right equipment and materials."

She frowned at him, and he noticed she fought a smile. The smile won. "Have you ever even built anything before?"

Bishop chuckled. Even with what he knew they were getting ready to walk into in a few minutes, she made him laugh. "I'll have you know I'm an excellent builder, with many structures under my belt."

Bonnie shook her head with a smirk. "You've been warned."

"I have, but you have to promise me something," Bishop replied, growing serious. All joking put aside for now.

"I don't make promises until I know what they are." Bonnie's voice shook, indicating she didn't like where this was going.

"You don't run," Bishop said point-blank, staring directly into her eyes. He could always see a lie in the eyes, and Bonnie's were no different.

"That's a promise I will never make," Bonnie answered with no hesitation whatsoever. "If anyone's life depends on me running, I will run."

"And what about your life?" Bishop didn't like her answer but wasn't really surprised. This was who Bonnie was and one of the reasons he was so drawn to her. She was loyal to those she cared for.

"I have no life as long as my father breathes." Her reply sent his emotions into overdrive. He grabbed her, pulling her to him.

"I swear to you I will do everything in my power to keep you safe, Bonnie." Bishop held her against him tightly, daring anything or anyone to harm one hair on her head.

"Then you will have no life either."

He heard the tears in her voice, and it killed him. Before he could respond, his phone rang again. She pulled away instantly, turning from him, and headed down the hallway. He glanced at his phone to see his missed call was from Viktor.

With a growl, Bishop rushed forward and stopped her. "I haven't had a life until you walked into it," Bishop growled down at her. "Don't think you know what my life consisted of before you met me."

"Killing witches," she spat, and he knew instantly what she was trying to do.

"It's not going to work, Bonnie." Bishop warned her with a glare. "You're not going to push me away that easily."

"What do you want from me?" Bonnie's voice rose to a higher pitch. "I don't have anything to give anyone. I don't have anything left. I don't even know if I had anything to begin with. My whole life has been trying to take my father down. Do you have any idea what that does to a person, let alone a young girl so bent on revenge? It's all I think about, every single minute of every single day. I have nothing but hate in my blood and if I'm not careful, evil will join that hate. I wake up in the mornings praying to the Goddess that my soul hasn't turned against me and that I still have some good inside. It terrifies me to become what I had to pretend to be."

"I want all of you. Everything. From the good to the bad," Bishop said while wondering where in the hell that came from, but it was true. He wanted all she had to offer.

"You have no idea what you're saying." Bonnie tried to turn away from him, but he wouldn't allow it. "You have no idea what I've done for revenge. Things you and your brother would have hunted me down for, only to burn me for the witch I was, had to become."

"You did it for the good of others." Bishop tried to reason with her, but he had a feeling reasoning with her at this moment wasn't something that would easily be done.

Bonnie laughed, but no humor registered in the hollow sound. "Revenge is a personal vendetta and has nothing to do with the good of others. The truth about me is ugly, and the truth always comes out. You ask me why the aversion spell. That is why. Once the truth comes out, it saves me the heartache of watching people walk away in disgust and hatred. Betrayal is hard to see in another's eyes, and I've seen that look more than I ever care to admit. Selfish is what I am, Bishop. Nothing more, nothing less."

He knew without a doubt that anything he said at this point would be a waste of time. She wasn't ready to admit she was worth anyone seeing anything other than what she saw in herself. She needed to be shown, and once he'd saw past the aversion spell, he'd known she was worth that fight. Actually, the first time he laid eyes on her he'd known she was worth any fight that put itself between them.

Taking her hand, he remained silent as he led her downstairs. Soon she would see, and if it wasn't soon, he would spend the rest of their lives proving to her that she was good, no matter what her past dictated. For once in his life, he had purpose, *real* purpose and he'd be damned if anyone took that away from him.

CHAPTER 11

$\mathcal{B}$onnie walked downstairs to Sloan's office with Bishop. The room was overflowing, and she had a sudden feeling of unease. Seeing a man she had never seen before, she frowned. He was a tall, slim guy in a *Big Bang Theory* T-shirt, skinny jeans, and wearing black-rimmed glasses. He was actually handsome, in a nerdy type of way with his mop of unruly brown hair. He was bent over a computer that Lacey sat at.

He straightened and turned toward her, his smile widening. "Bonnie."

"Jinx." She smiled back, finally realizing who the guy was by his voice. "So I finally get to meet the master behind the screen."

"Hear that, Lacey? Master," Jinx said proudly with a puffed-out chest. "I've been telling her that for years, but finally, someone who knows perfection when she sees it."

Lacey turned, rolling her eyes. "Congratulations, Bonnie. You've created a monster."

Bonnie grinned, but it slowly faded when she noticed the look Lacey was giving her. She looked at Jinx. "He contacted you, didn't he? That's why you're here?" Bonnie's tone turned serious.

"Yeah, the Wicked Warlock of the West found a way past my VPN and ordered me to summon you," Jinx replied, none too happily. "How the hell he did it I don't know, but I'm helping Lacey make sure everything here is more secure."

"When?" Bonnie said, trying to ready herself for this meeting with her father.

"Not much longer." Lacey turned back to the computer.

"You don't have to do this," Bishop said from behind her.

"The hell I don't," Bonnie said as she looked around at the Warriors who were waiting for her answer. "I will never run from that bastard. We've been trying to get hold of him for weeks."

"Yeah, that's no easy feat on the dark web," Jinx said without looking away from the computer. "Anyone can get lost there and not be found."

"But he found you." Sloan's eyes narrowed.

"There is that and it shook my confidence, which only makes me more anal." Jinx pushed his glasses up. "But that won't happen again. I can only think this evil dude had a computer guru like me."

"So now you're calling yourself a guru?" Lacey glanced at him over her shoulder, making Bonnie smile.

She needed to be relaxed and on her game when she talked to her father. Their banter was easing her tension. Orjyll would be able to tell if she was nervous, scared, and not her normal "fuck you" self. He would prey on that, and she couldn't afford to give him that satisfaction.

"Babe—" Jinx said, then cringed after taking a quick glance at Viktor, who stood frowning at him. "Sorry, habit."

"That habit is bad for your health," Viktor replied, his voice deep without a hint of joking.

"Yeah, tell me about it." Jinx whistled low, then turned back to what he was doing.

"You get used to the threats," Steve reassured with a grin. "I get at least four, maybe more a day. So, are you a gaming guru too?"

Jinx snorted. "Shit. Try guru master. There isn't a game on the market I can't beat."

"Please." Lacey shook her head with a loud sigh.

"Listen, baaaa—Lacey," Jinx said correcting his slip, then looked at Steve. "How in the hell have you survived here?"

"It ain't easy, bro." Steve shook his head. "Definitely not easy."

"You guys done shooting the shit?" Sloan growled,

eyeing both Steve and Jinx. After they shared a look, they both nodded. "Then hurry the hell up."

Jinx practically pushed Lacey out the chair. "What in the fuck have you gotten me into?" he whispered, but everyone in the room heard him, including Bonnie.

"Stop being a puss and help me." Lacey stood and went to another computer. "Okay, I think we got it."

"Yeah, no one is going to be able to break their way into this system." Jinx sounded confident.

"Good, 'cause your life depends on it," Jared tossed out as he glared at Jinx, his eyebrow cocked.

"Every single day, bro," Steve reminded Jinx, then shrugged and walked away. "Every single day."

Bonnie chuckled, but felt nervous tension overwhelming her. She used her magic to calm herself down. Hearing someone else come through the door, she saw Mira and Kira, followed by Charger and Kane. She honestly didn't know how they were going to fit anyone else in the room. She looked around for Raven, but she wasn't there.

"Where's Raven?" Bonnie asked, a frown dipping her brows. Her gaze met Charger's, but it was Kane who answered.

"She's probably getting her stuff and trying to find a place to stay," Kane said, nodding at Bishop as he passed.

Anger consumed her. "You kicked her out?" She directed her question to Charger.

He glanced her way but didn't answer. One thing Bonnie hated was being ignored or looked over as if she or her question didn't matter.

"I'm talking to you," Bonnie said, stepping in Charger's way when he tried to pass. Bishop grabbed her arm, but she pulled away. "Did you kick her out of a place to live just because she transferred?"

Charger stopped, then finally looked down at her. His eyes were dark as he leaned into her space. "Her decision, not mine." He growled the words, obviously not liking the confrontation.

"Watch yourself, Charger," Bishop warned but remained where he was.

"Charger," Sloan called out, and Bonnie stepped out of his way, but not before she saw regret flash briefly in Charger's eyes. "Heard you lost a man."

Surprise flittered through Bonnie to hear that and instinctively knew it was Val. She pulled her phone out and sent a quick text before putting it back into her pocket.

"Don't get involved, Bonnie," Bishop whispered, making her jump.

After rolling her eyes, she gave him a sideways glance. "I have no idea what you're talking about." Her lie sounded just that even to her own ears.

"Any luck finding Vanessa's son?" Sloan asked Charger, and Bonnie paid close attention.

"No," Charger said, irritation clear in his voice. "No clues. Nothing."

"What's his name?" Bonnie asked, and prayed silently to the Goddess that Orjyll didn't have him.

Charger glanced her way but remained silent. He opened his mouth but stopped as he glanced over her head. Turning, Bonnie saw Raven standing at the door staring at Charger.

"So much for staying out of it," Bishop growled at her, but she ignored him.

"His name?" Bonnie repeated, looking back at Charger. "If my father has him, I may be able to find out. And the quicker we get him back, the better. My father is not... kid friendly." And wasn't that an understatement. Orjyll despised children. The why of it she didn't know, but he was a cruel, unfeeling asshole the best of times, but throw a kid in there, and yeah, he was every child's monster hiding under their beds, or in their closets.

"My son's name is Kevin." Vanessa's voice rang out behind her. Vanessa had been used by Pike who was working with Orjyll, helping grow his army of half-breeds. The Warriors had also learned that Vanessa's son had been taken and used for her cooperation. With Pike dead she had told the Warriors everything she knew, and it was very useful information. The search for the little boy was high priority.

Bonnie cringed, realizing Vanessa had heard her. Dammit. Honestly, she didn't have anything against this woman, but she did have loyalty to Raven. Turning, she saw Vanessa and Katrina passing Raven in the doorway and walking inside. She went straight to Charger.

"Why?" Vanessa's wide blue eyes stared at her. "Do you know something that will help me find him?"

Dammit, Vanessa really shouldn't be here. No way was she bringing up her son if she was present. Who knew what the hell Orjyll would say, and she really was sorry to say that could ruin Bonnie's plan. Not that Kevin, Vanessa's son, wasn't important. He was, absolutely. If Orjyll had her son, there was no telling what he would say, and that could drive Vanessa right over the edge.

"Did Pike give you any hints where your son could be?" Bonnie knew time was of essence; it always was with children.

"No." Vanessa shook her head, and Bonnie could tell she was trying to keep the tears at bay.

"Are you ready?" Jinx asked Bonnie as he sat down at the computer.

"Not yet." Bonnie shook her head, still looking at Vanessa. "Listen, if my father knows anything about your son, I can get it out of him, but you need to leave."

"But—" Vanessa started to argue, but Bonnie stopped her.

"No. I refuse to do anything with you here." Bonnie stood firm. "Not only is finding your son of the utmost importance, but so is finding Orjyll. If you lose your shit, if *anyone* here loses their shit, then all could be lost, and I don't know when the next time contact with him will be made."

The room was silent for a second as they all stared at her, but at least no one was disagreeing. That was a plus with this group.

"Out of anyone in this room," she continued, "I know this bastard better than anyone. I know how he operates. I know the depth of his evilness. I know how to get under his skin. And honestly, I want Mira and Kira gone also, as well as Steve and Ronan," Bonnie said, then waited for the blowback from that bombshell.

"Wait a minute." Kira frowned, taking a step forward. "I should be the one here, especially if I'm the one who is going to defeat him."

"This is what he wants. Every Grail woman in this room to hear his words." Bonnie knew it was time to become the bitch she knew she was, deep inside. "If I don't get my way, then I walk and you'll be screwed. Take it or leave it."

Bonnie knew Kira was pissed, but so be it. If she had her way, it wasn't going to be Kira and Orjyll in the final showdown. It was going to be the person who deserved to take the bastard to his grave the most, and that was her. Sure, Mira and Kira's life had been a living hell, but nothing compared to what she had been through. This was her right, and she was going to do everything in her power to take that right back. They may hate her for it, but yeah, what was new? She was hated by many and could still hold her head up.

She waited as Steve and Ronan ushered Mira and Kira out the door. Both Steve and Ronan gave her a nod of

TERESA GABELMAN

understanding, which she didn't need but appreciated. Her eyes went to Vanessa.

"I will do everything I can to find out where your son is, Vanessa. You have my word on that, but with you here, that will not happen. I cannot take the chance." Bonnie waited for Vanessa's decision.

Glancing up at Charger, who gave her a nod, she let Katrina lead her out the room, but she stopped in front of Bonnie. "He is my life."

"As he should be," Bonnie replied immediately. "I promise to do what I can, but you have to trust me."

"That's not easy for me." Vanessa gave her a sad smile.

"Yeah, you're not alone in that," Bonnie mumbled her reply, then waited until Vanessa and Katrina were out the door and it shut behind them. Her eyes then went to Charger, then everyone else. "If you don't think you can remain cool and calm keeping your mouth shut, then leave."

She glanced at Sloan, who had a small grin on his lips as he stared at her before he looked around at everyone present. "You heard her. If you're going to have a problem, then get the fuck out." When no one moved or said a word, his attention went to Charger. "Don't make me regret you staying."

Charger glanced from Sloan to Raven and then down at Bonnie. "Do it."

Bonnie nodded, then glanced at Jinx. "You heard him." She nodded to the computer. "Do it."

"Jesus, this shit is intense," Jinx said, his eyes round as saucers under his glasses. "Okay, one evil Warlock coming right up."

Bonnie swallowed hard as she sensed Bishop step closer to her. It comforted her in a way, but it also made her more nervous as the conversation after this showdown was going to get ugly, very ugly.

CHAPTER 12

*R*aven kept her place near the door, feeling as if she didn't belong. Yet when she received the text from Bonnie to come, she didn't hesitate. She had just gotten off her bike at the Guardians' and was ready for the hard task of getting her belongings as well as shutting the door to that part of her life when Bonnie's text arrived. It couldn't have come at a better time.

As she watched Vanessa, along with Katrina, pass her and head straight toward Charger, the action nearly tore her dead heart out of her chest. She sucked it up and doggedly appeared emotionless. That's what Guardians did. Wait... she wasn't a Guardian anymore. No, she was a VC Warrior now. Looking around the room at the emotionless stares of her new comrades, she realized yeah, she was definitely in the right state of mind.

Even though she wanted to tear every hair out of Vanessa's head, as well as tear her from limb to limb, she felt for the young woman as she talked about her son.

Anyone, especially a woman, could see the pain radiating from her. No matter who the mother was, or father for that matter, a child was a child—an innocent thrust into a cruel world, especially the one she lived in. At that moment, she pushed her feelings aside for the woman and made a vow to do everything in her power to find the kid. Yeah, she wasn't as heartless as she let others believe.

Her eyes met Charger's more than once, and it was a fight to keep every single emotion locked away and hidden from his gaze. No way in hell would she ever show him weakness again. Never. She was here for Bonnie. That was it. She hadn't even known Charger would be here.

Her mind wandered as she leaned against the wall. She heard Bonnie kicking Mira and Kira out, along with Steve and Ronan. She had to grin at that. Bonnie was definitely a force to be reckoned with. She loved it. Next, it was Vanessa who was being led out of the room. Their eyes met briefly as Vanessa passed, but no words were spoken. As she looked toward Charger, surprise flittered through her—he wasn't staring at the beautiful woman who'd just left the room, but at her. She held his gaze until she heard Bonnie say, "Do it."

The room was silent as a guy named Jinx, along with Lacey, worked on a computer. A moment later, they stopped and stared at the monitor before looking at each other. Raven's eyes roamed the Warriors, stopping on her father, Jared, who glanced her way. He gave her a cocked eyebrow, but that was it.

Jinx turned and motioned for Bonnie to say something.

Raven watched as Bonnie physically prepared herself by straightening her shoulders and taking a long, deep breath.

"Hey, saggy ass," Bonnie called out to the room. "You wanted me. Here I am."

Everyone remained silent, only a slight buzzing came over the computer. The screen black.

This time it was Lacey motioning her.

"Father, wherefore art thou, asshole," Bonnie continued, her tone a mix of boredom and sarcasm. "Come on, you summoned me. You scared, you piece of shit? It's just me, your loving daughter."

A crackle came over the intercom, but then went silent.

Raven watched Jinx and Lacey work frantically on the computer as Jinx mouthed, "Fuck," then pulled at his hair and flipped the monitor off twice with such vigor she couldn't help but grin. Then she felt bad until she saw Bonnie chuckling behind her hand.

"Okay, Daddy-o, stop wasting my time. Got things to do, people to see, and a father to kill. Oops, let the cat out of the bag. Oh well, fuck you," Bonnie said flippantly. "Catch ya later, dickhead." She then gave Jinx and Lacey the cut signal.

"Damn, if he was listening, I'd say he's pretty pissed about now." Jinx eyed Bonnie with raised eyebrows.

"Good." Bonnie grinned with a nod. "The bastard hates any type of disrespect and gets sloppy when his rage takes over his thought process. The angrier I make him, the better."

"Do you think he was listening?" Raven said, and felt Charger's eyes slam into her, but she ignored it. "And if so, could he be listening now?"

"He could have been," Lacey replied, glancing over her shoulder at Raven. "And no, we've cut the audio from our side."

"Do you want to try again?" Jinx asked, standing up and stretching. "I'm free all night."

"Let him stew for a while if he actually was listening," Bonnie answered before anyone else. "And yeah, I want to try one more time. I'm serious when I say if he has that little boy, the quicker we can get him away, the better. That is now my main concern."

Raven glanced at Charger who was talking to Kane, but then turned and walked her way. Raven acted like she was busy by looking around at everyone but him. Dammit, she wished someone would start talking to her. She started to go to Bonnie, but he was there before she could take a step.

"How's it going?" Charger's voice seemed to cocoon her, and she hated it.

"Fine," she replied, making herself stare right at him.

"You did good with training." Charger appeared visibly relaxed, but she felt some tension coming from him.

"It wasn't too bad." Raven realized how damn stupid

and awkward this conversation was. "Listen, I'm fine. You don't have to worry or feel guilty."

"Who says I'm worried or feel guilty?" he shot back, his eyes narrowed, then shifted toward something behind her. She turned to see Kane walking back in with Vanessa.

"Oh, yeah, my mistake." Raven laughed bitterly. "I forgot who I was talking to for a second."

"What in the hell is that supposed to mean?" Charger growled, not looking too relaxed now.

Raven ignored him as she stepped to the side. "I'll get my shit out tonight and be out of your way for good." She turned to walk away, but he snatched hold of her arm, turning her back around.

"This was your choice, not mine," Charger whispered harshly.

Once again, she glanced at Vanessa who was watching them closely. She jerked her arm away from him with a sneer on her face. "Was it?"

Raven left him with only those words. Spotting Bonnie standing alone, she headed toward her.

"You okay?" Bonnie asked as if knowing her turmoil, and maybe she did.

"Never better," she replied, and they both knew she was lying out her ass.

"Yeah, okay." Bonnie gave her a sideways glance before looking around. Quickly, she pulled Raven toward the back of the room away from everyone. "I need a favor."

"That depends on what the favor is," Raven replied, giving her a stern look.

"I want you to have my back," Bonnie whispered, then pulled Raven closer. "Please."

"What am I having your back for, Bonnie?" Raven frowned, not promising anything until she knew exactly what she was being asked.

"Dammit, why are you guys so untrustworthy?" Bonnie cursed, making Raven grin. "Just freaking promise me. I don't even know if it's going to happen, but if it does, I need someone on my side."

"Okay, but why can't you tell me?" Raven questioned, not feeling good about this for a second.

Bonnie bit her lip as she looked up at the much taller Raven. "Because I'm afraid you'll say no and I'll be alone."

"Well, fuck!" Raven finally said, then squeezed her eyes shut. "You're lucky I like you. I don't like many people, especially smart-ass witches. Shit, this is going to get me in trouble, isn't it? Yes, Bonnie, I've got your fucking back. Shit."

Bonnie beamed, then hugged her, surprising Raven. She couldn't remember the last time someone hugged her like that. "Thank you!" Bonnie said, then pulled away. "I'll try not to let you regret it."

"Great! Just fucking great!" Raven threw up her hands, knowing that she would never go back on her word. "So when do you think I'm going to know about this thing you need me to have your back for? I swear, if it puts you in danger, I'm going to be pissed."

"Ah, no comment," Bonnie said, then quickly slipped away.

"Bonnie!" Raven called out after her, but she managed to get away. Raven headed in the direction Bonnie had gone.

"What happened?" Steve asked as he walked in with Mira.

"He was a no-show," Jinx said in disappointment.

"Actually, I'm not really surprised." Bonnie shrugged, then looked at her phone. "I say give him half an hour and we'll try again."

"Maybe he was dropping a stink pickle," Steve said, gaining the silence of the room. All eyes went to him, and Raven couldn't help but laugh.

"A stink pickle?" Jinx frowned, then a grin split his face. "You mean a shit?"

"Yeah, man." Steve nodded. "Warlocks shit too."

Jinx laughed so hard he gagged, then gave Steve a high five. "Dude that's the funniest shit, pun intended, I've ever heard. Stink pickle has been uploaded to my vocabulary."

"Holy fuck, I think we've met another Steve." Jared shook his head, looking a little afraid. He then looked at Raven. "What in the hell are you laughing at?"

"He's funny." Raven grinned when Steve turned to give her a high five.

"Thanks, Rave," Steve said with a huge grin. "Just stick around. There's more to come."

"Yeah, stick around and you'll want to kick his ass daily." Jared cocked his eyebrow at her.

"Dude, why do you always have to ruin my mojo?" Steve frowned at Jared. "Let me have a moment."

"Your mojo is going to get you killed," Sid warned Steve, then high-fived Jared.

"So it's not safe to hang with him?" Jinx jabbed his thumb toward Steve.

"No," the whole room erupted, which caused Steve to flip everyone off.

"Nice knowing ya, dude." Jinx snorted, then sat down at the computer.

Raven shook her head and caught a glimpse of Charger leaning against the wall staring at her, ignoring everyone else and what was going on. Her body tingled, but she shut that down real quick. He was bad news for her— her heart and mind. She needed to mold herself into a VC Warrior, and quick.

"Hey!" Lacey said loudly over the talking. "It's showtime!"

Raven glanced at Bonnie, who paled slightly, but appeared to quickly pull herself together. "You got this," she told Bonnie, who nodded at her.

"Fuck yeah, I do," Bonnie said, then walked closer to the computer, her head held high. "Everyone who needs to get out, get out now. Playtime is over."

"Damn, Sloan," Jared said in all seriousness. "Looks like Bonnie may be taking over your job soon."

"Nah, I wouldn't work with you assholes if ya paid me," Bonnie said, then laughed when Jared looked at her shocked.

"Well, you'd definitely fit right in." Sid chuckled. The room then became silent as the door shut behind Steve.

Seeing the vulnerable side of Bonnie, even if it was only for a split second, and now seeing her as the hardass she portrayed herself to everyone, told Raven she would most definitely have this woman's back, no matter what. She glanced at Bishop, who stood behind Bonnie with a proud look on his face. What Bonnie didn't know was that there would be others standing with her also, and Raven felt a ping of jealousy over that.

Keeping her eyes off Charger, Raven focused on what was about to happen. She needed to keep her mind clear and be ready for anything. That was her life as a Guardian once upon a time, and it was her life now as a VC Warrior.

CHAPTER 13

*B*onnie rolled her head around on her neck as if getting ready for the fight of her life. It was ridiculous, but she felt like she needed to be relaxed again. Man, dealing with her asshole of a father was exhausting. She watched as Lacey looked away from the computer, then around the room. Viktor remained vigilant beside her, as if to protect her.

"I'm turning on the audio," she warned everyone, then looked at Bonnie. "You ready?"

"No," Bonnie said, then grinned. "But go for it."

The sound of the audio thumping to life sent Bonnie's heart racing. She had a feeling this was it, and steeled herself.

"Yo!" Bonnie said loudly, just as she took a step closer to the computer.

"I still have doubts you are from my sperm." Orjyll's

voice came over the speakers. "Your vocabulary is barbaric."

Bonnie rolled her eyes. "Whatevs," she responded, making damn sure her vocab was not to his liking. "So finally worked up the nerve to talk to me, huh? Where ya been hiding? Or maybe you thought your bounty on me worked and you've been hiding, not wanting to pay."

"We had some technical difficulties," Orjyll admitted, surprising Bonnie. He never admitted to anything closely resembling failure unless... "Wyrick can't seem to do anything right." ...he blamed someone else.

Bonnie's gaze shot to Sloan's, whose eyes narrowed dangerously. She leaned over in his line of vision and shook her head. "Oh, so you haven't killed him yet? Still finding him useful? Hey, Wyrick. Enjoying the evil side of things? Ya know, when the man, excuse me, the bastard you work with puts a hit on his own daughter, *your* life isn't worth shit."

"You're a real smartass, aren't you?" Wyrick's voice filled the room, making Sloan stand up slowly. Bonnie waved her arms in warning. So yeah, the warlock shot Sloan, but there wasn't a damn thing—other than threatening him—that Sloan could do in this moment.

"You have no idea, traitor," Bonnie replied, getting a nod from Sloan. "You'll get yours, Wyrick. If not from saggy ass, then Sloan, so don't get too comfortable. I'm really surprised you're still around. Good old Dad don't usually keep those more powerful close for long, so you must really be a pussy."

Okay, Bonnie had to admit she kinda got off on being a bitch. She was damn good at it. But only to those who deserved it. She actually gained a thumbs-up from most of the Warriors in the room. She gave them a proud bow.

"Are you finished?" Orjyll hissed, reminding her of a snake.

"I'm not even close to being finished, *Dad*." Every time she called him that, the sarcasm was thick and evident. "You contacted me, so what in the hell do you want this time?"

"Who is there with you, Bonnie?" Orjyll asked, his tone softening, as if asking for a favor.

Okay, this was a good time to find out how much Intel Orjyll was getting about them. Taking a deep breath, she really put her acting cap on and went for it.

"Sorry, guys, but I'm going to name drop," Bonnie warned everyone, then shook her head when Jinx looked at her as if she had lost her mind. "We got a few Warriors here working the system, Jace and Chase," she lied.

She wiggled her eyebrows at Jinx, who looked relieved.

"Then we have VC Warriors Deke and Zeke, they're twins, who really hate you by the way," Bonnie said, then glanced at Sid and Jared. "You boys want to say something to dipshit?"

"Yeah, fuck you," Jared said, then glanced at Sid. "What about you, Zeke?"

"You're a dead motherfucker," Sid added, gaining a thumbs-up, this time from Bonnie.

"Told you they hated you. Not a shocker there." Bonnie smiled. "And then we have Pike, Vanessa, and little Kevin, but I don't think they want to talk."

The silence in the room was deafening as Bonnie held her breath and waited for Orjyll's response. She decided to speed it up a notch.

"What? Demon got your tongue?" Bonnie added, and knew his response was going to come quick and filled with evilness directed right at her.

"You think you're clever don't you, bitch," Orjyll growled, the threat in his voice clear, making Bishop come even closer to her.

"Where's the kid, Orjyll?" Bonnie demanded, now done with the games.

"Ask Pike." He chuckled as if he just pulled one over on them, but boy oh boy, was he wrong. Her gaze met Bishop's briefly. Orjyll just gave his hand away. Pike was definitely a plant, and obviously the only plant. He also didn't know Pike was dead.

"I'd have to go to hell to do that since the asshole is dead as in worm food, compliments of a VC Warrior," Bonnie happily informed him. "Now, where's the kid?"

"I'll tell you what, daughter," Orjyll said after a moment of silence. Well, not complete silence. They all heard a woman's voice in the background whispering something, but it was garbled. "You for the boy. Easy trade."

Bonnie felt the tension in the room explode, the man beside her ready to say something, but Bonnie stopped Bishop. "Name the time and place, asshole. It's time I put a stop to you, and I'm more than ready."

"Oh, but baby girl. Momma didn't will her powers to you," Orjyll said, then laughed. "That must really make you feel like nothing. Your own mother willed her powers to someone else and not her own daughter. You're pathetic, Bonnie, and so was your mother."

"Time and place." Bonnie kept all emotion out of her voice. "Or are you too afraid to face me?"

"I'll get back to you on that," Orjyll said, then chuckled again. "I'm sure the Warriors are trying to trace this, so I need to be going just in case the mighty Warriors have broken the dark web's deep secrets, but I will stay in touch."

"You do that, Orjyll," Ryker said as he walked into the room. "And how about asking for me next time instead of your daughter."

Bonnie looked up at Ryker in shock, but he was focused on the computer where Orjyll's voice echoed from. What in the hell was he doing? She grabbed his arm to shut him up, but he paid her no mind.

"Ryker!" Orjyll's voice said loudly, filling the room, and Bonnie actually heard a small shake in his tone. Holy shit.

"In the flesh," Ryker said, hatred dripping from every word. "Looks like I'll be seeing you real soon."

"Looking forward to it," Orjyll said quickly, sending

shock through Bonnie. Orjyll legit sounded a little frightened. Who the hell was this guy? "And, Bonnie, you should be careful who you hang out with. Bet you haven't told everyone your story now, have you, Ryker?"

Orjyll's laughter was evil and loud before it was cut off. Bonnie glanced over at Jinx and Lacey, who were once again frantically typing. It wasn't until Jinx stood up cursing that she knew they were off audio.

"What in the hell are you doing?" Bonnie slammed her hand on her hip, glaring up at Ryker. "I was trying to get him to tell me where the kid was, dammit."

"He wasn't going to tell you anything," Ryker growled at her, then cleared his voice. "But I will find him and kill him."

"Oh, is that so?" Bonnie snorted, pissed that this guy just ruined her plan.

"We didn't get a trace, but that's not surprising. I would have been shocked as shit if we had," Jinx announced, before taking stock of the tension in the room and quickly sitting down and shutting up.

"And how do you plan on doing that when I'm the one who will be killing saggy ass?" Bonnie asked, knowing she was going to have to announce her plan and soon.

This time a grin tugged at the corner of his mouth. "Why do you call him that?"

"Do you even know how old the asshole is?" Bonnie snorted. "Believe me, when he doesn't have anyone to do his magic-of-youth crap, he looks like the Crypt Keeper."

"So let me ask you the same question, Bonnie Grail." Ryker cocked his eyebrow at her. "How are you going to kill him when you don't have your mother's powers?"

Okay, here it was. It was time for her grand plan. Glancing at Bishop, she shrugged then looked back at Ryker. "I'm taking her powers back from Kira."

Ryker laughed, then shook his head. Bishop and the rest of the Warriors started talking at once.

"You got a death wish?" Ryker said above the noise.

"No, but I can control it and Kira is having a hard time, and we're running out of time. While we run around like fools trying to find him, he is growing his army. You can believe that. If we wait too long, it may be an army we can't beat." Bonnie didn't want to get into the details with everyone around. Bishop wasn't going to like it, neither would the other Warriors. It was dangerous as hell to transfer powers, but she'd do what she had to. And her top priority was to kill her bastard of a father before he won this war and ruled the fucking world. Damn, how fucked up was that?

"If you survive it," Ryker again warned her, and this time Bishop caught on to it.

"What in the fuck do you mean, if she survives it?" Bishop demanded, his voice harsh with concern.

"When a witch transfers her powers to another witch by force and not by the will of death, it usually doesn't end well for the witch receiving the powers," Ryker said, looking from Bishop to Bonnie. "Does it?"

"Only if the witch receiving the powers doesn't know what she's doing, which I do know what I'm doing and...," Bonnie replied, then stopped talking as she stared at Ryker. "Wait a minute. How in the hell do you know about this? Who are you really?"

Ryker smiled, then raised his arms. A breeze started in the room. As his wrist began to twirl, the wind picked up, causing a vortex. Bishop pulled her back, as Jinx jumped up from the chair to run away.

"What the fuck have you gotten me into, Lacey!" Jinx yelled above the roar.

Bonnie looked around to see furniture moving, the Warriors grabbing on to something to keep them on the ground, and Sloan's angry expression.

"Ryker!" Sloan bellowed. "That's enough."

Ryker dropped his arms, and everything stopped, suddenly falling to the ground. "She asked."

"You're a warlock," Bonnie whispered in shock. "A vampire warlock."

"Actually, I was a warlock first," Ryker said, his eyes growing black. "And then I met Orjyll. I remember you, Bonnie Grail."

Bonnie's mind whirled as she tried to place him, but couldn't. So many people have been in and out of her life, she just couldn't— Oh, Goddess, she did remember him. "I do remember," she whispered, her hand going to her mouth. "I watched you die."

"Yes, you did." Ryker leaned toward her, but Bishop pushed her behind him, putting himself between the threat. "Don't worry. I'm not here for her."

"That would be the biggest mistake of your life if you were." Bishop growled the warning, taking a threatening step forward.

Bonnie peeked around Bishop. "I tried to save you."

"And that's why you live," Ryker shot back, just before Bishop's fist caught him under the chin. "Whoa, I'm here to help. Not harm her. She's the reason I'm here. To pay back a debt." Ryker worked his jaw back and forth.

"Holy fuck, I think I just dropped a stink pickle," Jinx whispered, but it was loud enough for everyone to hear.

"Jesus." Sid slammed his hand on his forehead. "I can't handle another one like Steve."

CHAPTER 14

*B*ishop felt a rage he had never felt before. For this man to even think he had the power over whether Bonnie lived or died set his blood boiling. Viktor held him back, barely.

"If you think you have the power to touch her, you are mistaken," Bishop roared, his eyes narrowing with warning. "Never threaten her again."

"I didn't threaten her," Ryker said, rubbing his jaw. "Though if I wanted her dead, she'd be dead."

"Dammit, Ryker," Sloan bellowed. "Shut the fuck up before I have Viktor let him go."

"Calm down, brother," Viktor hissed, then forced Bishop to look at him. "Calm down!"

Bishop pushed Viktor away from him, regaining some control. He then pointed directly at Ryker. "Stay the fuck away from her."

"You know, 'her' is standing right here." Bonnie stepped between them, her voice shaking with anger. "And 'her' can speak for herself."

Bishop's gaze snapped toward her. "Bonnie."

"Bishop," she shot back, then gave him a narrowed glare before looking back at Ryker. "Who are you to Orjyll?"

Ryker removed his hand from his jaw and actually grinned at her. "You're smart."

"Genius, but that's beside the point," Bonnie said without missing a beat. "Now stop with the bullshit and answer the question."

"I was his apprentice before your mother put a binding spell on him," Ryker answered, his eyes never leaving hers. There were murmurs throughout the room, but Ryker didn't flinch. "He was the most powerful, and when he accepted me, I didn't waste time. I was one of many. Everything seemed normal. I was blind to what was going on around me because I was so eager to learn. It wasn't until other apprentices who weren't as… loyal, I guess you could say, started to disappear that I started to question what exactly was going on."

"Questioning anything to do with Orjyll was not a very wise thing to do," Bonnie replied with a shake of her head.

"Yeah, I realized that the hard way." Ryker seemed to relax, but Bishop was tense and ready to tear the man's fucking head off if he made a move toward Bonnie. Even though Bishop listened to every single word, his focus was honed to protect.

"Is that a thing with witches and warlocks?" Jared, who had been unusually quiet, asked. "Being an apprentice?"

"Mostly warlocks," Bishop answered the question, his eyes never leaving Ryker. "And they usually remain loyal. Isn't that right, Ryker?"

"Yeah, that's exactly right," Ryker responded without delay. "But my loyalty ended the day I learned exactly what that bastard was doing. Only the dark ones remained loyal to his evilness."

"Did you know my mother?" Bonnie asked, and Bishop noticed the stiffening of her body as she asked that question. It was odd how in tune he was to her and her body language.

"No. I never met her, and I'm sorry for your loss," Ryker said and sounded sincere. "That happened after I escaped."

"That's a lie." Bonnie frowned, taking a step back from him. "Even though I only saw you once, you were there when I was there."

"Adam," Sloan said, and Bishop noticed Sloan didn't sound concerned at all. Their eyes met. "I know his story. I trust him, or I would never have called him in. Adam's the only one in this room who can confirm his story."

"He's not lying," Adam responded, coming forward. "So far."

"Make sure to let me know exactly when he lies," Bishop ordered Adam.

"You know I will," Adam replied with a nod.

"You know, I'm about done with your badass attitude." Ryker's "nice guy" routine took a turn quickly. "I can easily walk out of here without a second thought."

Before Bishop could respond, Sloan was in his face. "I'm two seconds away from kicking you out," Sloan said in warning. "If you can't control yourself, leave."

Out of respect to Sloan, Bishop didn't respond the way he wanted to. Instead, he gave a curt nod to Sloan, who backed off. He'd give Ryker a few more minutes to explain before Bishop went off on him.

"Chill, Bishop," Viktor hissed quietly toward him. "Hear him out."

After a few minutes, Ryker glanced away from Bishop to look at Bonnie. "Someone told Orjyll I was asking questions, snooping around. As I said, I wasn't the only apprentice, and they seemed to be coming up missing. A few I became close with. It didn't make any sense. If they'd just left, they would have reached out to me, but one day they were there and the next, gone. Their things were left behind. Nothing was taken."

"Yeah, that happened a lot," Bonnie agreed with a nod. "I could only imagine where they went, but I was smart enough not to look for trouble, so I remained on course."

"At that time, my course was to learn my craft from the best. Our courses were much different," Ryker replied, then his eyes darkened. "That is until I found out exactly what was happening. Then, Bonnie Grail, our course was one and the same."

"What happened to you?" Bonnie asked. Her voice shook only slightly, and Bishop really wanted to shield her from any more pain but knew that wasn't possible. She was a strong woman, and if he even tried to intercept anything Ryker was about to say, she would raise all kinds of hell.

Bishop looked from Bonnie to Ryker and actually saw a haunted look followed by regret flash through his eyes before he shielded it. "My powers were stripped, and I was turned into a vampire. What I now know is that Orjyll was trying to use magic to change humans into vampires. That was a fail. At the beginning of his scheme, he had a few vampires he paid handsomely to turn us so he could start his army. He realized that wasn't working fast enough for him, so he started with the serum."

"The serum makes changing humans easier and faster," Bonnie said, more to herself, but everyone heard her. "But it was flawed. Changing humans into half-breeds instead. He used you to find the best way to create his army."

"Orjyll was not teaching the apprentices coming to him in droves," Ryker growled, his answer evident. "He was grooming us for his army. Once we were turned and starved of blood, we would do anything in order to feed. Even though the serum was flawed, it fit his purpose because half-breeds were unpredictable, stronger at the making, and quicker to become rogue. At that point, he didn't care about the serum as long as it produced his army."

"Goddess," Bonnie whispered, then shook her head.

"That's what he was doing. I knew it was odd when witches and warlocks would just disappear, and new ones showed up. It was a revolving door. Why didn't he do that with me?"

Bishop also wondered that exact thing, but quickly realized the truth. "Because you were an asset to him, and you did his bidding, or so he thought."

"He's right." Ryker nodded. "You asked no questions."

"Makes me sound heartless." Bonnie sounded defeated, something Bishop wasn't used to hearing in her voice. "But I didn't know. Or maybe I did in a way but refused to address it until I found a way to kill the bastard. My fear of being found out and losing that chance trumped everything else."

"No, not heartless. You were very smart, Bonnie," Ryker replied, his eyes narrowing. "He thought you were a dark witch. Well played, by the way. That isn't easy to pull off, especially with dark witches all around you. If you had asked questions or snooped around, I seriously doubt you'd be here today, and there would be one less Grail female. You did what you could in order to stop his madness."

"I didn't do enough." Bonnie's voice was very low. Bishop heard her whispered words. The regret in her voice ate at him. "How did you escape and why did you come back?"

"A witch who Orjyll trusted turned on him. She let some of us go. At least the ones of us who weren't totally gone." Ryker's tone turned grim. "Being turned, then starved, I was on the verge of bloodlust."

"And that's where I come in." Sid stood, moved toward Ryker, and stood by his side. "I found this asshole stalking a man. When I confronted him, he begged me to kill him. Said he would kill if I didn't. He didn't try to fight. He just knelt on the ground and begged for death so the bloodlust would stop."

Something shifted within Bishop as he stared at Ryker. Each of them in this room had been on the verge of bloodlust, and none of them forgot that feeling. Usually, it was from being newly changed, and that was nothing compared to being starved of blood. Newly changed vampires were given small amounts of blood, which increased over time. Being starved of it was a totally different situation. And for someone in the midst of bloodlust to stop themselves and ask to die said something about that individual.

"I knew without a doubt there was something different about Ryker, so I took him into my care. Soon after, I realized he would make a great Warrior and took him into the unit I was in at the time," Sid replied, his eyes finding Bishop and then Bonnie. "I would trust him with my life. If I didn't, he wouldn't be here."

"You went back for revenge," Bonnie said, and Bishop knew she answered her own question from earlier that Ryker hadn't.

"For over five years I honed my skills, set a course that only I knew about to take him down. I learned about your mother and knew it was the right time for me to strike." Ryker hissed in anger. "And he was ready for me. I underestimated him and the people he surrounds himself with. Even after my training as a Warrior, I underestimated him and almost paid the price. After using my magic to change my looks—"

"Wait a minute." Jared spoke up. "You said your powers were stripped."

"They were for many years, but once Emilia Grail put a binding spell on the bastard, I regained them." Ryker then looked down at Bonnie. "Your mother was a hero to many. She didn't die in vain, Bonnie."

"Yes, she was," Bonnie agreed, shifting from one foot to the other. Bishop knew she was trying her best to control her emotions, but he felt her turmoil and hated it for her.

"As I was saying, even after disguising myself, Orjyll knew my plans, had known my plans and was waiting for me. To even think this is an easy mission is a deadly mistake. In my mind, everything I had planned out was foolproof. I was wrong. And if it wasn't for Bonnie, I would have paid the price of believing I could take down Orjyll alone." Ryker's mood shifted as anger and rage rang through his voice. "I can never repay you for what you did for me that day."

"I couldn't just stand there and watch what happened to you, happen." Bonnie's voice was strong. "Orjyll didn't realize that I was much slyer than the idiots he sent to kill you. I thought I'd failed. I didn't realize you'd actually escaped."

"Barely escaped," Ryker hissed, then glanced at Bishop. "I was punished by fire. Everyone in this room understands fire to a witch is a death none wish ever to face."

"I couldn't just stand there and watch it happen. I tried

to transport him, but I thought I'd waited too long." Bonnie shook her head as if trying to shake the memory from it. "I watched you burn."

"Because of your magic, which I felt, I used mine—together with yours—and transported, leaving the impression I was still there." Ryker took a step toward her, and Bishop allowed it. "Without that moment of you trying to save me, I would have died. I owe you my life."

Clearly uncomfortable, Bonnie looked away from Ryker but nodded. "I've done a lot of shady stuff in my life, but watching someone burn to death is something I couldn't do, even if it meant being caught."

"Well, thank you for taking that chance. Because your fate would have been much worse than mine," Ryker said, then looked around the room. "Don't take my word for any of this, ask Bonnie. Orjyll is a force not many have seen. Without his powers, he is still a force, so if he ever regains those powers, there will be no stopping him. People are going to die. Innocent people."

This time it was Bonnie's turn to look around the room. "I have repeatedly said how dangerous my piece-of-shit father is. Even without full power, he is more dangerous than anything walking this earth." Bonnie's eyes stopped at Bishop. "There's a lot to think about because this needs to end before it's too late. No matter the price, it has to end. If that price is too high for you, then you need to walk away."

"Magic, even bound by a curse, is a fickle beast," Ryker added. "Pain and time can weaken magic. Even a binding spell cannot completely stand the test of time. How much has Emilia's spell weakened? No one knows other than Orjyll and that, my brothers, makes him dangerous and someone to fear."

"You afraid?" Jared asked Sid with a don't-give-a-shit attitude.

"Not even close," Sid announced, cracking his neck back and forth.

"You have a human mate." Ryker looked toward Sid. It wasn't a question. "Then you should be terrified."

Bishop saw Bonnie shiver before she tried to hide it. He shared a look with Viktor, and then his gaze went to Ryker. "It seems that you and Bonnie are the only ones in this room who has had a close relationship with the bastard," Bishop said, not liking the fact they needed this guy, but smart enough to know they did. "Whatever information you can supply is welcomed."

"Is that the only 'I'm sorry for being a dick' I'm going to get?" Ryker asked with a smug grin.

"If you think that's what that was, then you're mistaken." Bishop snorted with a shake of his head. "I still don't fully trust you, but so far, by Adam's account—who I do trust—you're telling the truth. And I never apologize."

"Ain't that the fucking truth." Viktor finally moved away with a snort. "Take my word for it when I say you'll be waiting for eternity if you think you'll be getting an apology from his stubborn ass."

Bishop and Ryker continued to stare at each other until

Ryker finally looked at Sloan, who began talking to him. His main concern was keeping Bonnie safe, and he didn't care who was pissed off in the process. If this guy thought Bishop was going to apologize for that, he was going to be very disappointed.

CHAPTER 15

*B*onnie had felt numb as she listened to Ryker's account of what he'd endured under her father's apprenticeship. Was she shocked? No, not one bit. Her eyes gazed around the room as everyone now talked in groups. A few looked her way. Her gaze met Mira's and then Kira's before she quickly looked away. Her piece-of-shit father was the reason these good people were being affected. Her mother even had a hand in it if she was being totally honest.

A feeling of sadness overwhelmed her. It wasn't fair. This was her cross to bear, but these people had been dragged into a war that was ready to explode into something this world had never seen unless someone stopped it. She had to be the one. There was no question about it. It had to be her. For most of her life, she feared becoming her father. She had a feeling the evilness was going to have to win in order for her to do what had to be done.

She wasn't naïve enough to think this was all about her.

It wasn't. Not at all. But as of right now, she, Bonnie Grail, was Orjyll's number one enemy. He knew it and she knew it. Seeing Ryker staring at her, she realized he knew it also.

"Don't blame yourself," Ryker said as if reading her mind. "You are just an obstacle in the grand scheme of things."

Bonnie snorted. "Story of my life," she said—her favorite saying. "And blame? I know where it goes."

"Do you?" Ryker cocked his eyebrow at her. "Do you really, Bonnie?"

"Don't patronize me, Ryker." Bonnie's attitude kicked in, and she didn't realize her voice had raised quite loudly. "I know more than anyone who is to blame. I also know how demented and ruthless one has to be even to understand the lengths Orjyll will go to get what he wants. I know the evilness it's going to take to bring him down. Kira doesn't. That's why it has to be me."

Realizing the room had become silent, she shrugged, even when Bishop growled his displeasure at her words. The sooner they understood she was doing this, the better for everyone involved.

"What do you mean?" Kira, who hadn't been in the room during her announcement earlier, looked confused.

"You're going to transfer my mother's power back to me," Bonnie informed her without hesitation.

"No." Kira shook her head. "I'm not."

Bonnie hadn't really wanted to approach Kira this way, but it seemed everything related to her father turned out to be a shitshow. No reason for this to be any different.

"Then I suggest you spend as much time with your loved ones, because we will lose," Bonnie said as bluntly as she could.

"That's not fair," Mira said, standing up for her sister. "Kira is powerful in her own right. She can do this."

Even with Mira saying those words of support for her sister, Bonnie, along with everyone else, saw the fear in her eyes. "You're right. She is very powerful, but power is not what it's going to take. Knowledge is the key."

"And that's what I've been working on." Kira replied in frustration.

"Knowledge of how Orjyll thinks, works, acts, eats, sleeps as well as what makes him tick, what buttons to push and when," Bonnie added without missing a beat. "Who to throw under the bus in order to get a step ahead... that is something you could never do, not believably anyway."

The room was silent as they all looked at her. Yeah, she hated the spotlight, despised it actually, but she knew it was where she needed to be. The sooner everyone in this room figured out she was right, the quicker this would be over, either way.

"I used Drew to get you to use not even a third of the power you possess." Bonnie knew she needed to make a point, so she went for it. "Half of me meant that threat, but the other half of me would go to my grave before ever harming a hair on that girl's head. I'm not all good like you and Mira. I never will be. It is a continuous fight to stay in the light when at the edges, darkness is always calling to me. You know what I say is true. I was formed in the womb of a white witch by the seed planted from a dark warlock. My fate was sealed that day. It's up to me and me alone to fight every single day on which fate will win—light or dark. My fight may be over sooner than I think because no white witch can ever defeat my father. And if you think otherwise, then we all need to bow down to him right now and concede. You know I speak the truth."

"But you could die," Mira said. Her eyes filled with tears. "No, you can't do this."

"Not only that." Kira stepped up until she was in front of Bonnie. "He's your father. Whatever you do unto him will come back at you threefold. If you survive the transfer to defeat him, you will die."

"And it will be worse than anything you do to him," Mira whispered loudly, her voice shaking with tears. "You can't do this, Bonnie. Kira is the only way."

Bonnie's gaze didn't leave Kira, and she saw the depth of understanding in the woman's eyes. Kira knew that Bonnie spoke the truth. Bonnie was the only one who could defeat Orjyll with her mother's powers.

"When?" Kira finally said as she straightened her shoulders.

"Kira!" Mira cried out. "No! She can't do this."

"No!" Bishop's voice broke over Bonnie, but she ignored him. This was not his decision.

"As soon as possible," Bonnie replied, then glanced at Ryker. "I don't want Orjyll to even get a hint of this, and I need time to prepare. Tomorrow isn't soon enough, but I'm not in the right frame of mind to do it now."

Kira nodded, then turned and walked out of Sloan's office with Ronan following. Mira rushed up to Bonnie and grabbed her in a hug while Steve held Drew.

"Please, Bonnie," Mira whispered in her hair. "Rethink this. There has to be another way."

"We both know there isn't," Bonnie whispered back and hugged her close. "It has to be me. I think it's always had to be me, but my mother being my mother, refused to see it, so she transferred her power to Kira, hoping it would be enough. It's not."

Mira pulled away, her eyes overflowing with tears. Putting her hand over her mouth, she rushed back to Steve, who pulled her close to his side.

Bonnie could sense Bishop pulsing with anger beside her, felt his stare, and yet she ignored him. She didn't have the energy to battle him. Her emotions were too raw and open. She needed to seal the cracks in her tough exterior before tomorrow, and dealing with Bishop was not in her best interest, nor was it in his.

"Not that I need your permission," Bonnie said toward Sloan, "but I'd like to have the support of the Warriors."

Sloan ran his hand down his face, not answering her. His

golden eyes looked behind her, and she knew he was looking at Bishop.

"This is my decision and mine alone. It will happen with or without you, but backup would be much appreciated." Bonnie hoped she sounded stronger and more confident than she actually felt. In truth, she was scared to death—not that she feared death. She never had, but since discovering her connection with Bishop, she realized she'd never experienced real life. Nothing but revenge had filled her soul, and then Bishop had shown up. Her soul now sought something more than revenge, and it made her fear more real. If she failed, she failed him and those around her who she had begun to care about.

"I want to know everything, every single step that is taken, and I demand Bishop and Viktor to be involved." Sloan looked back at her. "The Warriors are and have been in this fight. We aren't going anywhere and will assist in any way you need us to."

Bonnie nodded, then gave Sloan a half-grin. "Those words were hard for you to spit out, weren't they?"

"You have no fucking idea," Sloan hissed, not looking happy at all for having to follow her lead.

"You do vampires," Bonnie said, digging deep for the smartass in her. "I do evil, piece-of-shit, saggy-ass, dipshit warlocks. Stay in your lane and I'll stay in mine."

She was surprised to see a grin start to tip his lips before it was gone. "Get the fuck out of my office," Sloan growled at her, but before he turned back to his desk, he stopped and looked straight at her. "And don't die tomorrow."

"Gonna miss me?" Bonnie did grin up at him.

"No. The paperwork is a bitch." Sloan actually gave her a wink, making her chuckle. She turned and almost ran straight into Bishop, who was glowering first at Sloan and then down at her.

"I don't find this funny." Bishop's sneer actually looked very sexy on him. "And I didn't agree to it."

"That's a shame on both counts because I was really hoping you'd have my back as I would have yours." Bonnie then patted him on his chest. "And actually, the paperwork remark was pretty funny coming from Sloan."

She moved past him, and he let her, which was for the best. She wasn't going to change her mind. It was a done deal. She glanced at Raven, who gave her a nod, then she walked out of the office. Heavy footsteps followed her, but she didn't stop until a large hand gripped her arm and turned her.

"I can't let you do this, Bonnie." Bishop shook his head. Turmoil swirled in his darkening eyes. "As a Warrior, I can't stand by and watch you put yourself in danger."

"And as a man, Bishop?" Bonnie cocked her head. "What does the man think?"

"They are one and the same," Bishop shot back, but he didn't sound so sure.

"No, they're not." She shook her head but gave him a

small smile. "But it's okay. Neither the Warrior or the man can change what fate has planned for me. Do you remember asking me a few short hours ago why the aversion spell? Well, this is why. Sloan would never have agreed so willingly to give me the go-ahead for what I'm about to do, no one in that room fought to stop me, not even you. So no, I will not release the spell I've put on myself. It's easier this way. Believe me, Bishop, I don't want to die, but if that is what the Goddess has decided for me, then there's nothing that's going to stop it from happening. I will defeat my father, but at least this way, no one will suffer for what I've decided to do."

"Bullshit." Bishop leaned close to her, so they were nose to nose.

"Is it?" Bonnie asked as she leaned away to really see into his eyes. "My life for the lives of millions? I don't think that is bullshit, Bishop, and if you dig deep into yourself, I think you'd agree. This is the Warrior talking, not the man. Forget me and find someone who is much better for you than I could ever be. I'm rotten to the core, and I really don't want you to see that side of me."

Bonnie knew he was fighting the aversion spell she'd doubled on herself, but he was failing. He didn't have much to say back to her, and that definitely wasn't Bishop. He was finding it hard to care. His mind and heart would be in a battle that wouldn't be won until she was out of the picture. This is the way it had to be.

Reaching up, she touched his cheek with a sad smile. "You're a good man, Bishop." Removing her hand, she continued to stare into his confused state. "Once this is over, you'll agree this was for the best."

Waving her arm, she disappeared, knowing exactly where she needed to go. She hated transporting with a passion, but it was convenient. It always felt she was out of control, tumbling toward something as she passed through colored fog. It was beautiful, but always scrambled her brain and zapped her energy. Closing her eyes, she focused on where she wanted to be, and soon the disoriented feeling stopped, and she opened her eyes. The field was exactly the way she remembered. The full moon sent light across the snow-covered ground. Everything looked crystallized, giving it a fairy-tale feel. This was where she found her peace. It grounded her for what was to come.

With a snap of her fingers, a book, candles, and a blanket appeared. She sat and picked up the book. It was her mother's words to Bonnie and in her writing. This would be the third time she'd read the letter, and maybe the last. Tonight was devoted to reading between the lines of her mother's story in hopes of finding a small glimpse of hope for her own future. She wasn't afraid to face what needed to be taken care of, but as a vision of Bishop flittered through her mind, she was afraid never to know the love of a man.

With a shake of her head and a snort, she opened the book. Damn, her thoughts were so jumbled. She needed to suck it up and do what needed to be done. She didn't have time for thoughts of love and a future that wasn't written for her. It was time she faced that and stopped this nonsense. The words on the page blurred as a tear slipped from her eye, smearing the ink of the word *love*.

"Story of my life," Bonnie whispered to the empty field.

CHAPTER 16

*B*ishop stood staring at the empty spot. He knew he would never get used to seeing someone disappear in front of his very eyes, and he had seen some weird fucking shit. Only powerful witches could transport.

"She needs you."

Frowning, Bishop turned to see Daniel sitting on the steps and looking down at his iPad or whatever in the hell he always had with him. "What?"

"Bonnie," Daniel said without looking up. "She needs you now more than ever, but she's pushing everyone away."

"And how do you know this?" Bishop headed toward Daniel, who continued to stare at the screen. Once Bishop made it over to him, and leaned against the railing, he was surprised to see the screen blank.

Daniel remained quiet until he looked up at Bishop, the color of his eyes clear and swirling. Everyone knew something special was going on with Daniel, but no answers had been forthcoming. Pam and Duncan had been trying to find someone like Daniel out there to get answers, but so far, nothing. He was growing quickly in body and mind. He looked to be a teenager, but his speech and knowledge said he was much older than that.

"I just know." Daniel shrugged, then smiled. "You like her."

Bishop nodded but felt unsure again. "Guess you wouldn't by chance know where she disappeared to?"

"Nope," Daniel replied, and Bishop felt a deep sense of disappointment. "But Ryker does."

"Thanks," Bishop said, then looked at the blank screen again. "What are you playing?"

Daniel looked down at the screen, then back up at Bishop. "Nothing, man. It's off." Daniel laughed, shaking his head as he stood. "You grown-ups sure do make stuff hard."

"Tell me about it." Bishop chuckled. "Maybe we should learn from you."

"You'd all be better off," Daniel said seriously, and then he grabbed Bishop's arm, his hand tightening as he squeezed. "Then again, this stuff comes and goes. Don't understand it yet, but sometimes I just need to let it out to the person who is meant to hear it."

Bishop stuck out his hand to Daniel, who took it in a manly handshake. "I appreciate it, Daniel."

"She doubled up on the aversion spell." Daniel let go of his hand, then turned to head up the steps. "Don't let her get away with it. She's a sly one who thinks of everyone else other than herself. She shouldn't be alone. Not tonight."

"Daniel," Bishop called out just before the kid disappeared upstairs. Daniel stopped and looked at him, shaking his head.

"I can't answer that." Daniel's voice sounded distant. "All I can tell you is what I've already said. Death will happen; it always does. But whose death, I don't know. Hey, tell my dad I'm going up, would ya?"

"Sure." Bishop gave him a nod as Daniel turned and continued on his way. This kid was one of a kind. Once Daniel and the Warriors learned what he was capable of, he would be an asset to the team. His knowledge was undeniable, and he was in awe of the kid. That was definitely saying something because not much awed Bishop Valentino.

Heading back into Sloan's office, he saw Ryker talking with Sid and Jared, but headed toward Duncan.

"Hey," Duncan said, then looked behind him. "She okay?"

"No," Bishop replied, then sighed. "But Daniel told me to tell you he was heading upstairs."

"Thanks." Duncan nodded, then frowned. "I promised

to take him somewhere. He probably got tired of wait-ing. I better get going."

Bishop stopped him. "Have you found out anything more about his abilities?"

"No, not really, other than they are getting stronger." Duncan frowned. "Why, did he freak you out? He doesn't mean to."

"No, he didn't," Bishop said, then laughed. "Well, maybe a little bit. But damn, he makes you think and knows things he shouldn't know."

"Tell me about it." Duncan frowned, then clapped Bishop on the shoulder. "Listen, you need anything, let me know."

"Thanks." Bishop nodded, then considered Daniel's words. It wasn't Bishop who actually needed anything. It was Bonnie. Anger hit him, instantly thinking of the aversion spell. With a curse, he headed toward Ryker.

"What's up?" Jared said as soon as Bishop walked up. "You doing okay, man?"

"I'm good. It's Bonnie who isn't," Bishop said, then looked at the blank faces of Jared and Sid before looking at Ryker, who wore a frown. "Is the aversion spell working on you?"

"So that's what she's done. I was wondering why there wasn't more of an uproar about her single-handedly putting her life on the line. Sneaky." Ryker replied, without answering the question.

"What do you mean? Spells don't work on us." Sid frowned, looking between Ryker and Bishop.

"It does if she puts the spell on herself," Ryker said, then chuckled. "I can now see how she tricked that bastard for so long. Smart. Damn smart."

"Yeah, you've said that," Bishop growled, then realized he needed to keep his cool since he needed the guys' help. "Listen, she disappeared and—"

"What do you mean she disappeared?" Jared gave him a sideways look. "You mean, poof and she's gone, or she walked out the front door? You know this witch and spell shit is making my ass uncomfortable."

"So you're telling me she put a spell on herself?" Sid asked, and rolled his eyes when Ryker only nodded, not explaining anything. "Can you tell me why, or is it some fucking big witch-secret thing?"

"She's put an aversion spell on herself," Ryker said, then frowned. "Witch-secret thing? What in the hell is that?"

"I don't know." Sid threw his hands up. "You tell me. And what the hell is an aversion spell?"

"Bonnie put an aversion spell on herself so no one cares what she does, or when she does it because they have no feelings for her one way or another," Ryker said, his eyes going back to Bishop. "But it hasn't worked fully on you, has it?"

"No. At least not completely." Bishop frowned, then sighed. "But I'm confused as fuck. She's doubled the spell. Whatever in the hell that means. Can you get me to her?"

Ryker stared at him for a long minute before he closed his eyes and began mumbling something under his breath. His eyes slid open, showing only white, which was creepy as fuck, and his hands began jerking.

"Dude, give me a rogue vampire any fucking day. This shit is just weird," Jared whispered, then cursed. "And why in the fuck am I whispering?"

"You ever transported before?" Ryker said as his eyes opened and looked normal.

"On wheels, yes." Bishop had a feeling he was not going to like this.

"Don't think that's what he means," Sid informed Bishop, as if he didn't know that.

"No shit." Bishop shot him the stink eye. "Guess she's not somewhere I can GPS to on my bike."

"Afraid not." Ryker chuckled, as his smile grew. "I'm going to really enjoy this."

"What in the fuck is that supposed to mean?" Bishop was second-guessing asking for this favor from a guy he didn't know if he could fully trust.

"It means hold onto your nuts, man." Ryker grinned, then lifted his hand grabbing onto to Bishop's. "'Cause you arc in for onc hcll of a ridc."

"Wait. What?" Bishop frowned, then everything went black. It felt as if his legs gave way, and he was spiraling out of control. Never in his life had he felt anything like this before, and was on the verge of losing it, but regained his control. Taking slower breaths, he let the feelings of disorientation flow through him as colors swirled around him. Almost as fast as it happened, it all stopped at once, and he stood in a field. It took him only a second to get his bearings, but he was aware of his surroundings immediately.

His eyes quickly scanned for danger before landing on Bonnie, who sat in the middle of the field on a blanket surrounded by candles. Her head was bent as the moon shined down on her, making her glow in a beautiful light. His footsteps were heavy on the snow-covered ground, and he knew the minute she realized she was no longer alone. Her shoulders stiffened slightly.

Slowly, her head turned toward the side. "How?"

"Ryker," he answered as he walked around and stood before her. "I wasn't finished talking to you."

She looked up at him, the moonlight reflecting in her eyes, making them sparkle. "You transported here?"

"I would have walked through hell, Bonnie," Bishop answered honestly. "Transporting was easy."

She continued to stare up at him, her face emotionless until finally, a small smile tipped one corner of her full lips. "You hated transporting," she stated, her words filled with truth.

"I said it was easy," Bishop replied, a smile also forming across his lips. "I didn't say I liked it."

Closing the book on her lap, she slowly stood. "Why are you here?" She tilted her head, looking as confused as he had been feeling. "You shouldn't be here."

"You can triple your aversion spell, but it's not going to work." Bishop reached out and touched her cheek. "At least on me."

"You're not going to stop me from what I need to do," she whispered, and pressed her face into his hand as if seeking his touch.

"Maybe not, but I refuse to let you face it alone." Bishop opened himself up so she could see the truth in his eyes. He shielded nothing. "I will be honest with you. I have fought my feelings for you from the beginning. You say you're rotten to the core, but you're wrong. I see deeper than what you portray on the surface. I've seen the goodness in you. Maybe you're right. You will have to bring out the evilness we all possess inside ourselves in order to do what it takes to win against your father. But I will be there once it's over to help you find the good, which is all I see when I look at you."

"Are you for real?" Bonnie whispered, then she reached out to touch him. "I have done everything to turn you away from me, but you keep coming back. I don't know if I have the strength to resist you anymore. I don't know if I even want to, and that scares me more than anything that I'm sure to face in the next few weeks."

"Do you trust me, Bonnie?" Bishop cupped her face with both hands as he stared down at her. When she nodded, he leaned in and kissed her softly. "Drop the spell."

He knew the exact moment the aversion spell was dropped. The intense feelings he had for this woman were far more powerful than anything he had ever felt in his life. His statement about walking through hell for her didn't even come close to what he would do for this woman.

"Never again," he whispered as he picked her up and held her close to him. "Because now I know my true feelings, and nothing you can do or say will change that."

CHAPTER 17

*B*onnie had known the moment Bishop entered her sanctuary. How she knew she wasn't sure, but before he spoke, the identity of the intruder formed crystal clear in her mind. What did shock her was that he'd let Ryker transport him just so he could be with her.

When he'd asked her to completely drop the aversion spell, she did it because, honestly, she wanted to know for herself. Tomorrow she could die. It was as black and white as that. Tonight could be her last night. It was her reality. As she had sat alone in her private, beloved spot, reading her mother's words, she'd felt lonelier than she had ever felt.

His appearance and approach were like a calling to her heart. For once, she was going to follow her heart instead of her instinct. It was time she finally thought of herself; it may be the last time she ever got the chance.

In his arms, she felt safe, something she had never in her

life felt before. It was foreign and yet felt so very right. As they kissed—and this man could kiss—she let herself go and enjoyed whatever Bishop had to offer.

He broke off the kiss and set her back on her feet. Taking his jacket off, he wrapped it around her. "You're shivering."

"It's not from the cold," she said shyly, glancing up at him under lowered lashes. "So, what do you think of my field?"

Bishop didn't even look around. He just stared at her. "Beautiful." His deep voice sent more shivers down her body.

"You didn't even look," she scolded as she pulled him down on her blanket to sit with her. "This is where I come when I need to get myself together. I've spent a lot of time here alone. You're the first person who's ever been here with me."

This time Bishop did look, but a frown formed on his lips. "How safe is it here?"

Bonnie rolled her eyes, then chuckled. "Perfectly safe." Then she frowned. "Then again, I guess I need to block when I come here since Ryker found me so easily. Not sure how he did it. It's rare, but I don't know how powerful of a warlock he is."

"Where exactly are we?" Bishop did another look around before eyeing her. "And am I going to have to be transported back?"

Laughing, Bonnie nodded. "Yes, but I promise to make your transport back more pleasurable."

Bishop cocked his eyebrow. "Is that so?"

She nodded, feeling a blush color her cheeks. This was so unlike her, but she was enjoying the flirtation. Something about possible death changed one's perception, that was for sure. She started to say something, but his frown stopped her.

"About tomorrow," Bishop said, and her heart dropped.

"I don't want to talk about tomorrow," Bonnie said quickly, the walls she let down, flying back up at his words. "If you only came here to talk me out of it, then you've wasted your time."

She held her breath, waiting for him to speak, but he remained quiet as he stared at her. She started to scoot back from him, but he quickly stopped her. "That is not the only reason I'm here, but if you think I'm okay with you putting yourself in danger, you definitely don't know me very well. And that is the Warrior and man talking."

Bonnie's eyes opened in surprise at him, throwing that last part back at her. "I understand that, but it's happening, and I don't really want to spend what's possibly my last night talking or arguing about it."

"Are you afraid?"

Bishop surprised her by his question. "I am, but not for why you think," Bonnie replied, deciding to be honest with him. She was tired of the game—not that it was ever a game to her—but she didn't want to be vague anymore. Her whole damn life had been vague. It was time to speak her mind and be damned the consequences. "I'm afraid tomorrow… if things don't go as planned and I do die, I will die without ever knowing the touch of a man."

The look on Bishop's face was priceless, so much so she wished she'd kept her damn mouth shut. She was queen of too much information, dammit.

"You've never—"

She shook her head and started to look away, but he stopped her by cupping her cheek. "I've been kind of busy trying to stay alive, revenge, and stuff. Little hard to find time for Tinder."

"Tinder?" Bishop frowned, his eyes narrowing.

"Never mind, not important." Bonnie waved that away because obviously someone like Bishop would never ever have to use a dating app to find a willing woman. "Sorry, ignore what I just said. This place always makes me wish for things not within my reach."

"First of all, never apologize to me for speaking your truth." Bishop's tone was low and serious. "And second… anything you wish for, I will see to it that it comes true if it is within my abilities."

"Why couldn't I have met you a long time ago? Why does my father have to be the spawn of the devil?" Bonnie whispered, her heart shattering, knowing this moment was fleeting. For as much as she wanted to live in the moment, she knew tomorrow or a few weeks from now could be the end for her. "And why would your refusal to make love to me shatter me to my very soul?"

"Because a long time ago, I hunted your kind. You aren't

responsible for picking your parents," Bishop said as his eyes roamed from her face and down her body, then back again. "And I would be a fool to refuse you anything, especially something as special as what you are offering me. And I'm no fool."

Bonnie stood slowly, removing his coat as she did so. He took it from her and tossed it behind him. His eyes never left hers as she undressed. She could use magic, but this seemed so much more personal. Plus, she was a nervous wreck and would probably accidentally transport herself out of here instead of undressing.

As she stood before him bare, he continued to stare into her eyes, which made her weirdly self-conscious. In a fluid motion, he was on his feet before her. Without touching Bonnie, he leaned over and kissed her softly. Their tongues teased each other before he pulled away. His eyes finally left hers and slowly roamed her body. She held her breath, afraid to breathe, and prayed to the Goddess she didn't see disappointment in his eyes.

"I have never seen anything more perfect." Bishop's voice rumbled throughout the field, over her body, and into her heart. "You honor me, Bonnie Grail. This is a gift I will cherish."

A tear leaked from her eye, and she wanted to wipe it away but was afraid to move just in case this was a dream, and it would wake her up. With ease, he pulled his shirt over his head, throwing it on his jacket. Their eyes met again as he pulled her against him.

"If at any time you change your mind, one word is all it

will take for me to stop," Bishop whispered against her forehead.

"Then I will remain silent," Bonnie said softly, but she knew he heard her when he made a masculine groan in the back of his throat. "I want this, Bishop. And I want it to be with you. I have never felt this before for anyone, only you."

"Tell me that this place is safe because I have a feeling my Warrior instincts are going to hell for the next few hours." He groaned as his hands touched her, his lips against her neck.

"No one will ever see us," she promised, then realized everything he said and pulled back to stare up at him with wide eyes. "A few hours?"

"At least," he said after his eyes did another once-over of her body. "Believe me when I say I am going to take my time and enjoy every single second of you and your body, but I have to ask."

"Ask what?" She ran her hand down his hard chest to the flat washboard abs, loving the feel of him.

"Are you sure?" His question had her eyes leaving his chest to look up at him. She tiptoed and kissed him with as much passion as she could work up over her nervousness.

"For the first time, I've never been surer of anything in my life." Bonnie smiled, feeling confidence she hoped he saw. "Not only will you be my first, but possibly my last."

"Oh, I will be your last, but not for the reason you

think." Bishop's eyes narrowed dangerously. "No other man will ever touch you in this way while I live. Do you understand me?"

She nodded and was surprised she agreed one hundred percent with his alpha declaration. She didn't want any other man, never would. "I'm yours," she said without hesitation.

"You are mine." He sealed it with a hard kiss, as if even talk of another man set him on edge.

She pulled away a little, breaking their connection. "I don't share either, Bishop." She felt it was only fair he agreed to her terms also.

"No other woman could even compare to you in my eyes." Bishop took her face in both hands, gently forcing her to look up at him. "And you will live. There will be many more nights and days like this in our future."

Bonnie nodded, knowing if she opened her mouth, she would scream at the unfairness of the moment. She knew her chances of surviving any of what was coming her way was dismal, but for tonight, she was going to enjoy every second. She just prayed this wouldn't ruin his life. That was what the aversion spell had been all about—not to let this happen at all, yet selfishly, she was letting it happen.

Pushing all that aside, she focused on what was happening now and not in the future. That was hard for her to do, but as he stepped out of his jeans, she sighed as all thought left her brain. He was a big man in more ways than one. Curious, she reached out and gently touched him, letting her fingers feel the silky hardness of him. His swift intake of breath made her bolder. She wrapped her fingers around him as she explored his body. It wasn't long before he was stopping her.

"Did I hurt you?" she asked him, worried she had done something wrong. Seriously, could she do it wrong? Was that even possible? She should have really done some research before attempting this so as not to make a fool of herself. "I'm sorry."

"No, you absolutely didn't hurt me," Bishop assured her quickly. "And stop apologizing. I just needed to stop you for a minute so I could gain control. I want this to go slow for the first time, and you, beautiful, are making that very hard to do."

A large grin broke over her face. "You really liked that?" Bonnie couldn't help but ask. She didn't care if she sounded like an idiot. She was happy she did something right to give him pleasure.

"More than you know." Bishop chuckled. "Soon, you will learn, as I will learn, what pleases you."

"Good, I'm a very fast learner." Bonnie grinned, then kissed her way down his chest, stopping just above where the waist of his jeans had been. "Very fast."

"Jesus." Bishop groaned, making her smile spread across her face.

CHAPTER 18

*B*ishop carefully laid her on the blanket, but he worried she was too cold. Not that he wasn't planning on warming her up, but still, it was cold and she was human. "Are you too cold?" Damn, he couldn't believe he had her naked and spread out beneath him, and he was worried she was cold, but he was.

She reached up and touched his chin, running her fingers along his jawbone. "You really are a gentleman, aren't you?"

"Hell no. Never once have I been called a gentleman." Bishop growled down at her, then smiled. "But I want you totally focused."

Bonnie chuckled, then waved her hand toward the side of them. A large fire appeared, and the warmth quickly spread over them. "Better?"

"Much," he replied. Surprise flickered through him when she pulled him down for a kiss, her certainty unexpected. Not that he'd been with many inexperienced women. Hell, he couldn't seem to think of one in his long life, but Bonnie seemed very comfortable and at ease. It was he who was a little nervous if he was being honest. Pulling his lips away from her, he had to ask, "Aren't you nervous?"

Frowning, she shook her head. "No."

"You're not?" Jesus, he couldn't shut the fuck up. What in the hell was wrong with him?

"Should I be?" Bonnie pushed away from him and sat up, facing him.

"No," he replied, then shook his head. "I mean, I don't know. Maybe."

"Are you nervous?" She cocked her eyebrow at him, then laughed at the face he made.

"Fuck no." He bristled. "I know exactly what I'm doing, what's going to happen, and—"

"Bishop, I was just kidding." Bonnie soothed him; at least, she tried to. She sighed, looking away from him. "If it was anyone else here with me, I would be very nervous."

"Who in the hell would be here with you other than me?" Bishop's body stiffened, making her head jerk back toward him.

"No one," Bonnie assured him, her cheeks turning red in a blush as she sighed. "I guess I am a little nervous, but not for the reason you probably think."

"Meaning?" Bishop knew he was making a fucking mess

of this, but dammit, he wanted to make certain she was sure and that she was comfortable. Seriously, what in the fuck was wrong with him? He wanted her more than he wanted anything in his life. She was naked, beautiful, and obviously wanted him. And here he was talking and asking stupid fucking questions.

"I'm not nervous because it's you, Bishop. I trust you and believe me, that's saying something because I trust no one. I've wanted this for a long time, to feel wanted by someone, and after meeting you, I wanted that someone to be you," Bonnie said, looking straight into his eyes, but then she shifted her gaze away. "What I am nervous about is being a disappointment. I can only imagine the women you've been with, and I know I could never come close to—"

"Stop." Bishop put his finger against her lips, then gently forced her to look at him. "You are the most self-assured woman I have ever met."

"I am very self-assured," Bonnie agreed, but wasn't cocky about it. "But I've never opened my soul to anyone. Ever. To give myself to anyone this way is not easy for me, but right now, in this moment, it's the easiest thing I have ever done in my life because it feels right. To disappoint you... yeah, that makes me nervous."

"I would never be careless with your soul, Bonnie." Bishop made sure his tone conveyed the seriousness of his statement. "And this is right. And as for disappointing me, not possible."

A tear leaked from her eye, and he caught it with his

finger as he pulled her to him. He knew her life had not been easy. He didn't know it all—he was sure of that—and for the first time in his life, he wanted to know everything about this woman. Never had he felt that way about anyone. Even with the aversion spell, he'd had an attraction to her, but since she had dropped the spell, his emotions were all over the place. Bishop was a man who kept his emotions closed off to everyone. Most Warriors were. They had to be with what they dealt with every day. It hardened them to the point emotions were foreign to them, or at least for him. But this woman had unleashed every single one of his feelings.

As he stared into her eyes, Bishop saw himself reflected in their depths, and he liked what he saw. A man who'd finally found what he had been searching for, but he'd never known it until this moment. He also saw the trust she was fully giving him, and he swore he would not betray the trust he knew wasn't easy for her to give.

Slowly, he lowered his lips to hers, capturing her mouth in a tame kiss, wanting to take it slow, but slow wasn't easy. Bishop wanted nothing more than to claim her. Instead, he controlled that instinct. He'd be damned if he ruined this first for her. Even if it killed him, he would make sure her trust in him was never questioned.

Focusing solely on Bonnie, he realized her kiss was becoming more impatient, and he internally smiled. And to think she was afraid of disappointing him. He could smell her passion, feel it in her body, and it pleased him more than anything ever had. Deepening the kiss, he roamed her body with needy fingers, and nothing felt sweeter than her curves. She moaned as his hand brushed against her breast, and she even arched as if asking for his touch. More than happy to oblige, his large hand cupped her breast, his fingers plucking at her sensitive nipple.

Bonnie squirmed against him. The sweet moans in her throat drove him crazy, crazy to the point he had to talk himself down so as not to move too fast. That plan almost failed in a major way when her small hand wrapped around his cock. He hissed, their lips parting.

"Did I hurt you?" she whispered, her voice husky and sexy as fuck.

"No," he assured her, his voice strained with the undeniable need to claim her. "Quite the opposite."

"Really?" Her womanly smile almost did him in. His reaction was like a teenage boy copping a feel for the first time. She moved her hand up and down, gripping with just enough tightness that he wanted to lie on his back and let her finish him off. It felt that fucking good. Damn!

Bishop let her explore his body until he was at the point of no return. Alert to danger, he glanced around before stopping her and quickly covering her body with his.

"My turn," he growled, then gave her a wicked smile as his mouth began to worship her body.

～

*B*onnie sucked in her breath, her eyes closing, and for once in her life, she lived in the moment. Instead of worrying about how to stop her madman of a father, what steps must be taken, and the absolute horror if he succeeded in his evil plan, Bonnie wiped her mind clean of all that to enjoy a moment for herself. Her eyes stared at the clear night sky above. With the stars winking down at her, she cherished the sensations that the man above her bestowed upon her. Never in her life had she felt wanted by another, but that was by her own doing. She had never trusted anyone enough to even think it was possible, but this man changed that.

The stars above blurred. She blinked as tears slid into her hair. She knew what a few short hours could bring and thanked the Goddess for leading Bishop to her tonight. Bonnie's fear—her true fear—was never feeling wanted by another before she died. Her eyes moved down and landed on Bishop who was kissing her stomach before he looked up at her. Her hope was she would have a little more time, but nothing in this world, *her world*, was promised, especially tomorrows.

Soon, her mind went blank of anything other than what this man was doing to her body. Strung tight, her body was alive like never before. As his hand moved to her very core, his fingers working their way inside her, she cried out at his touch.

"Relax." His deep voice soothed her, but was he serious? Relax when he was doing such amazingly wicked things to her body? "You are so tight, and I just want to make sure you're ready for me."

"Relax?" Bonnie chuckled, sighed, and hissed all at the same time. "Easier said than done. My body feels like it's going to explode."

His smile was full of male pride as he winked at her. "You haven't felt anything yet."

"Oh Goddess." Bonnie bit her lip. How was that even possible? As he continued to kiss and suck at her breast, his fingers ignited a fire inside her as they worked in and out slowly, then picked up speed, taking her to the edge of something she wanted to go over so badly. She cried out in frustration a few times until she couldn't take it anymore. "Please, Bishop."

Bonnie had never begged for anything in her life, ever, and it honestly shocked her a little that she did now. He moved up her body, their faces inches apart. He kissed her softly.

"Use your magic to dull the pain," he whispered against her lips. "I don't want to hurt you."

Slowly, she shook her head. "No." She looked into his eyes. "No magic. I want to feel everything."

"Bonnie—"

"I trust you," Bonnie whispered, touching his cheek as she opened her legs wider with a slow smile. "Are you going to make me beg, Bishop? Because if you are, I'm the queen of paybacks."

Bishop chuckled and growled at the same time. "You definitely are a witch, aren't you?"

"You have no idea," she shot back, then prepared herself for what was to come.

Her heart raced so fast she swore he could feel it. Her body trembled with need and anticipation. Bishop's handsome face blocked her view of the world around her, and she was fine with that. He was all she wanted to see at this moment. She groaned as the tip of his hardness touched her.

"I'm sorry," he whispered, just before he pushed inside her.

Words escaped her, as did all thought. Burning pain flushed through her body for only a second. She'd had worse pain in her life, but the fullness and the absolute feeling of being owned shocked her. Her eyes opened wide as they searched his.

"Bonnie?" He sounded worried as he started to pull his body out of hers. "Hey. Are you okay?"

"Shut up." She hissed, wrapping her arms around his neck as she also wrapped her leg around him, holding him to her. "If you pull away from me, I will turn you into something horrible."

"I'm a vampire." He chuckled, sounding relieved by her words. "Spells don't work on me."

"Are we going to talk or are we going to fuck?" Bonnie said bluntly, then smiled at his shocked expression. "This may be my first time, but I'm no prude. Make love to me, or I'll find someone who will, Warrior."

"Damn." He hissed, then his eyes narrowed as if her words finally sank in. "Anyone other than me touches your naked body, they will die the most gruesome death possible."

"I really like when you talk caveman," Bonnie teased, then gasped in pleasure when he moved.

"Look at me," he demanded, his tone serious.

She did, and she would never forget what she saw reflected in his eyes. The intensity staring down at her changed her instantly. She wanted to live. For all of her life, she had been prepared to die knowing what her future had in store for her. It had always been safer for her to prepare for her exit from the world, but now, with just one look from the man above her—the man inside her—that all changed.

"No man will ever touch you the way I have touched you tonight." Bishop's words were a vow, and his tone clearly stated he meant every single word. "You are mine, Bonnie Grail."

There was so much she wanted to say to him, but the words were taken from her as his body moved slowly at first, and then quicker, as if he were making his words true with the action of his body. The pain was gone, replaced with a feeling she couldn't even explain in words. She could only feel, and Goddess, it felt so right. She matched his movements with thrusts of her own, unable to get enough.

Their eyes held, each watching their passion in the reflection of each other's eyes. It was bliss. It was what she had been searching for during her darkest hours, and yet, never once did she think she would find it. But she had, and she found her true desire in the most unlikely of men. A witch hunter. Story of her life.

All thoughts left her as his fingers tortured her in such an arousing way she didn't even know if she could recite her name if asked. Their bodies worked together in unison, and she no longer knew where she ended, and he began. It was like they were one. Her body was building toward something amazing, and she wanted to experience it more than anything, and yet, she knew it would end this moment—her first, and she wasn't ready for that.

Bonnie realized that it didn't matter what her mind was ready for. Her body under Bishop's talented hands was making all the decisions.

The strength in Bishop's body built. The veins in his neck and arms bulged as his eyes turned black as night. Bonnie immediately gave in to what was to come. She opened herself up completely because no way in hell was she going to miss out on this moment.

As Bishop pumped into her, he threw his head back with his eyes slammed shut. She could see his fangs lengthen and wanted nothing more than for him to sink them into her skin. Okay, that shocked her a little, but she pushed it to the back of her mind as she watched his passion for her unleash. It was such a beautiful thing she took a mental snapshot. Never in her life did she want to forget this moment.

"You are mine." He roared as he thrust inside her one last time, his fingers working her into an ecstasy that blew her mind. Her body tightened like a bowstring, then released in such an explosion of pleasure she was sure she'd died. And if she was dead, what a way to fucking go.

Hearing her name, she slowly opened her eyes and realized she hadn't died but was staring up at Bishop, who seemed worried until a slow smile spread across his face.

"What are you smiling at, witch hunter?" Her voice was low and raspy.

"You, witch." Bishop carefully picked her up and held her to him. "I'm smiling at you."

CHAPTER 19

*N*ever in his life had Bishop felt so fulfilled then he did right now. Holding Bonnie in his arms while watching the fire burn set him at ease. Not that he wasn't alert for danger. That was embedded into him, but his mind was silent for the first time in such a long time. He knew he should get back to the compound, but he couldn't make himself move. He had barely managed to force himself to get his jeans on, but his training had him dressing just in case of trouble. Fighting naked was not ideal in any situation. They were out in the middle of nowhere. Actually, he had no clue where in the fuck they were, and that puzzled him. Bishop always knew where he was, what was around, but this woman had definitely bewitched him. Now wasn't the time for complacency, and he, better than anyone, knew that.

"What are you thinking?" Bonnie snuggled closer as she turned her head to look at him.

Bishop's eyes roamed the area. "Right this second?" he asked. She nodded. "Where we are."

"Oh." A look of disappointment crossed her face. "You're back to Warrior mode."

"Bonnie, I'm always in Warrior mode. It's who I am, and right now, especially because of your safety." Bishop tugged her closer.

She had put on his shirt, which looked more like a dress on her. Turning in his arms, she nodded. "I understand, but we're safe here," she said, still not saying exactly where they were. "Are you already regretting this?"

Her blunt question took him by surprise to the point he had to think of what she just asked him. His hesitation wasn't good, at least in her eyes. She went to push away from him, but he stayed her. "I will never regret what we have shared. Why would you even ask me that?"

"I don't know. You've just been so quiet. I figured—"

"You figured wrong." He didn't even let her finish. "I guess I could ask you the same thing. Regrets?"

"No, I don't regret it. Absolutely not. It was definitely the best thing that has ever happened to me." She didn't hesitate in her answer.

Male pride swarmed him as well as feeling honored that he was the best thing that ever happened to her. Damn, what man wouldn't want to hear that from a beautiful woman? He went to speak, but she continued.

"I guess you could say you were on my bucket list,"

Bonnie added, then went to snuggle back against him, but he stopped her.

"Wait, what?" Bishop frowned, hoping like hell he didn't hear her right. "Your... bucket list?"

"Uh, yeah." Bonnie gave him a cheeky grin. "I added you to it after I saw you the first time. It's a good thing, Bishop. I mean, I have a lot on my bucket list, and you moved right up to number one."

He seriously didn't know what to think about this. He continued to stare at her to see if she was messing with him, and sure enough, a huge grin broke out on her face. He grabbed her, then gently laid her on her back in a move so swift she gasped. "So what else is on this bucket list? Any other men, perhaps?"

"No." She shook her head, then bit her lip. "You moved him right off the list."

"Who?" Bishop growled, and his eyes narrowed.

"I'm kidding, Bishop." Bonnie kissed his frown away. "No man other than you has made my bucket list."

The rage that consumed him didn't really shock him. What did shock him was the total relief knowing there was no other man. "So what else is on your bucket list?" he asked again, trying to lighten the mood he had darkened with his stunt of jealousy. He realized he really didn't know Bonnie that well, which bothered him. He wanted to know everything outside of Orjyll.

Glancing up at the sky, she smiled, her features softening as a faraway look flashed across her face. "My bucket list is probably much different from the average Joe's." Her smile slipped slowly from her face. "To eat at a restaurant without having to watch my back. To laugh and keep that happy feeling before my reality sets in. To enjoy life and what it offers without fear of it ending prematurely."

Her emotions settled over him and he felt her sadness, but he also felt her need for normalcy. Once Orjyll was out of the way, and he damn sure would be wiped from the face of the earth, could Bishop give her what she so desperately sought? He was a Warrior. His life was full of danger. He had enemies of her kind and many of his.

"Silly, huh?" she said, not realizing what turmoil her words brought to him.

"No." He forced a smile. "Not silly at all."

"Do you have a bucket list?" Bonnie grinned up at him, excitement lighting her eyes. "I bet you do."

He shook his head. "No. Not big on lists." He glanced up at the sky. The sun was rising, making the snow glisten like glass. He wouldn't change the night he'd spent with Bonnie for anything, but he knew reality came with the sun. It was time they headed back, but he wanted more than anything to stay right here in this moment.

"Did I say something?" Bonnie frowned, still staring at him.

Now wasn't the time. He didn't want to ruin what they had shared. Maybe he was thinking too much about her bucket list. "No, you didn't say anything." He worked a real smile to his mouth and then pulled her up. "But I am going to have to get back."

"Dammit, I did say something." Bonnie sighed, then pushed her way up to her feet. "It never fails. My mouth always runs before my brain."

Bishop watched as she yanked his shirt off and tossed it to him. She was completely naked, her back turned toward him. She was beautiful. Rounded in all the right places. Not skinny, but womanly with curves that almost drove him to his knees. She bent over to get her clothes, and he almost did just that. He hadn't wanted to take her again, because he knew she had to be sore after their first time.

"I know better to open up because I always say the wrong thing." She continued her little rant, and actually, it was cute the way she was bitching herself out. "I'll never learn to just keep my mouth shut."

Reaching out, he grabbed her arm and turned her around. She looked adorable, standing there naked, holding her clothes and staring up at him. "You didn't say anything wrong, Bonnie," he said, then stopped her from looking away from him after she rolled her eyes. "You can say anything to me, and it won't be wrong."

"I am usually always right." Bonnie smirked with a cocked eyebrow. "Actually, I'm always right. No usually about it. But seriously, I don't really have a bucket list. Just things I think about that would be nice in my life every once and a while."

"And you will have that. I promise you." Bishop pulled her to him, then hissed as her naked body pressed against his. "Okay, you really need to get dressed. I'm having a real hard time controlling myself."

"Why are you having to control yourself?" Bonnie asked as her hand went south, but he caught it right in time.

"Because we need to take it slow. I wasn't too gentle toward the end, and I know you're sore." Bishop kissed her hand, then the top of her head. "Plus I'm sure Sloan is ready to kick my ass off the team. We need to get back."

Bonnie nodded, looking disappointed as she started to dress. "I'll transport you, but I'm not leaving."

"And I'm not leaving you here alone." Bishop frowned at her after pulling on his shirt.

"I won't be alone," Bonnie said absently, then turned to look up at him. "Kira should be here soon."

It didn't take Bishop long to figure out exactly what that meant. "No." He shook his head. "Not today."

"What do you mean, not today?" Bonnie ran her fingers through her hair. "The sooner, the better."

"I meant what I said, which is no and not today," Bishop said with a growl, pulling on his boots. Not ever, if he had anything to do with it.

"Bishop, you don't have any say on whether this happens or not." Bonnie dropped her hands from her hair to stare at him. "She is transferring my mother's powers to me, here, today."

Her words hit him hard. It wasn't in his makeup to just step back and say, *'Sure, put your life in danger for the rest of us while I stand here and watch.'* Fuck! "I can't let you do this."

"Then I will transport you now because I am going to do this." Bonnie slapped her hands on her hips and glared at him, her face red with anger. "This is not new information. This is what I said was going to happen, and it *is* going to happen."

"But I didn't agree to it," Bishop roared, losing his shit, but couldn't stop himself.

Bonnie didn't say anything at first. She simply stared at him and then slowly shook her head. Dammit, didn't she care that doing this could take her life? Well, fuck that. He cared enough for both of them, obviously.

"I don't need your permission." She cocked her head at him. "Though I would appreciate your support. This has to be done. I have to do this, Bishop."

"Why? Why you?" Bishop hated feeling helpless. Dammit.

"Because I'm the only one who can." Bonnie straightened her shoulders, the confidence in her voice and body language undeniable. "He has to be stopped."

Voices reached them, sending Bishop, who hadn't been paying attention to what was going on around them, into protective mode, pulling her behind him. He turned, ready to face whatever danger presented itself, but his eyes only found Kira, Ronan, Mira, Steve, and Ryker. "What the fuck is he doing here?"

"I asked him to be here," Bonnie said, then stepped out from behind him.

Okay, that fucked with him. She asked Ryker to be here, but never said a word to him about any of this until now. His eyes narrowed as he looked down at her. "You never said a word to me about this, but you asked Ryker to be here. What if I hadn't shown up last night?"

Her silence was such a blow, making him want to tear something to pieces. His hands clenched, his jaw tightening painfully.

"What about last night?" he growled down at her, not really knowing why he asked her that. No, that wasn't true. He did know why he asked her, and he wanted her answer.

Her head snapped back as if he had slapped her. "*What* about last night?" Bonnie shot back. Her eyes took on a haunted look. She sighed. "To me, last night was something I will never forget, Bishop. If today is my last day, that makes last night even more special to me. But last night does not give you any power over my decision to do this. To do anything for that matter."

"The fuck it doesn't." Bishop stopped himself short of shaking some sense into her. He let her go and ran his hands through his hair, so he didn't shake her out of frustration. "You could die, goddammit."

"Then I die," Bonnie whispered, then cleared her throat. "Long before I met you, my fate was set in motion. To be fair, Bishop, you weren't supposed to be a part of my fate. But you are."

He wanted nothing more than to grab her and… what? What in the fuck was he supposed to do? Run off with her? That solved nothing, and she would end up hating him.

"I can do this, Bishop." Bonnie put her hand on his arm as if that would reassure him. It didn't. "I have to do this."

"Why didn't you tell me last night?" Bishop asked, staring down at her, searching her eyes for the truth.

"Because I was afraid you'd leave," she replied matter-of-factly. "And I needed you."

Her words of need hit him hard, sending every emotion known to man throughout his body. Son of a bitch. Never in his life had he been so conflicted about what to do. He knew what he wanted to do, but also realized that would be a mistake.

"I understand if you need to leave. I'll make sure you get back." Bonnie wrapped her arms around his neck and held him tight, then whispered, "But it would mean the world to me for you to stay. If this is my last day, I want you here above anyone else."

Tipping her head up to his, he kissed her hard. "I'm going nowhere," he said against her lips, then pulled away slightly. "Don't die on me today, Bonnie Grail."

CHAPTER 20

*B*onnie never cried, but it seemed that's all she felt like doing around this man. Sad tears flowed as well as happy tears. So many mixed emotions spiraled through her. Her heart and soul had been torn from her so many times in her life. The things she had seen and had to do had hardened her to the point she felt as if she had only one emotion, and that was hatred. The numbness she felt for the situation was blossoming into tingles of feelings, and that reaction terrified her. Yet deep down, she wanted more of the numbness to fade. As she stared up into Bishop's handsome face, fear that this was it for her hit her hard. Last night and this moment would be the last.

Shaking her head and getting her thoughts back on track, there were no words. It was best she did what she came here to do, and whatever the Goddess saw fit to happen, would happen. And that, unfortunately, had always been the story of her life.

"I just want to say..." Steve's voice broke her attention away from Bishop, which she needed right now. "I'm not a fan of transporting."

"You're fine, Steve." Mira rolled her eyes as they walked closer.

"Actually, I'm not sure. I think my stomach and balls are somewhere else at the moment." Steve's voice did sound a little shaky.

"Transporting by magic isn't my favorite either," Bonnie agreed with a nod.

"We interrupting something?" Steve asked, looking around with a sly grin.

"If you'd been any earlier, then yes, you would have." Bonnie didn't have any problems being honest and she wasn't embarrassed. She glanced at Bishop to see his reaction and wasn't surprised to see him glaring at Steve.

"My man." Steve went in for a high five, but stopped at the growl coming from Bishop.

"Nice place," Kira said, looking around. "Yours?"

"Yeah," Bonnie said proudly, scanning the area. "Figured this would be as safe a spot as any. I don't want Orjyll to have any idea what's going on, and we're far enough away from anyone to have the power transfer be exposed." She didn't add that if this totally went down the shitter and killed her, this would be the place she'd want to go.

"What do you mean your place?" Ronan also looked

around with a frown. "There isn't even a house."

"Most witches have a special secret place that they go to in order to become one with nature. We're elemental witches," Kira replied, glancing at her mate. "I haven't been to mine in quite some time."

"Neither have I." Mira sighed.

"So, what exactly do you guys do in a secret place?" Steve frowned.

"Dance naked under the moon as we call upon the spells of our ancestors," Bonnie said with a straight face, then turned to grin at Ryker, who had remained quiet. "Isn't that right, Ryker?"

"Seriously?" Steve looked at Mira. "You dance naked out in the open?"

"Thanks, Bonnie." Mira frowned at her.

"I'm a warlock," Ryker said, then grinned. "The only dancing I do naked is if I have a woman with me."

"Now that's what I'm takin' about," Steve said, then got an elbow from Mira.

Bonnie chuckled, and looked toward Bishop, who wasn't smiling. He looked foreboding and angry. She guessed he wasn't in the mood for a bit of teasing.

"Are you sure you want to do this?" Kira picked up on Bishop's attitude obviously. "I promise to try harder. I can do this."

"I'm sure." Bonnie walked over to the blanket that she had spent the most glorious night on, and picked up her mother's journal that lay beside it. "I have read my mother's journal over and over again. This is my right. She even admits it but said she couldn't bestow that fate onto me. But it *is* my fate. We all know this. By rights, her power should be mine. With her powers, she knew I would go after Orjyll, sealing my fate once and for all."

"What do you mean, once and for all?" Bishop finally broke his silence.

"For a witch hunter, you sure don't know much about our kind," Ryker said with a cocked eyebrow. "Or was just killing us all you cared to learn?"

"I learned real well, especially how to take out warlocks." Bishop's answer was hissed in anger.

"You ever heard of the Rule of Three?" Ryker said, his eyebrow cocked and ignoring Bishop's statement. "By the look on your face, you have."

"That's beside the point." Bonnie threw Ryker a death stare, but Ryker totally ignored her.

"No, *that* is the damn point," Ryker shot back, then glanced at the blanket before looking back at her. "He obviously deserves to know."

"What's the Rule of Three?" Steve asked when everyone remained silent.

"It means that whatever she does to her father, because she is of his blood, will come back to her threefold." Bishop's voice shook in rage as he glared down at her. "And you want to pay that price, Bonnie?"

"It's my price to pay," she answered quickly, then

glanced away from him to look at everyone else, all of whom were watching her with worried eyes. This was exactly the reason for the aversion spell. She should never have dropped it. It was much easier when no one really cared or thought they cared.

"Bullshit," Bishop roared, his eyes black with anger. "It is *not* your price to pay. I can take that bastard down. I've killed powerful witches and warlocks, Bonnie. Why are you doing this?"

"Because it is my right." Bonnie sneered, getting angrier by the minute. "And I'm done with this conversation."

"Tough. I'm not." Bishop pulled her away from everyone. "What are you trying to prove by doing this?"

"Prove?" Bonnie sucked in her breath. "Did you just seriously ask me that? I'm not trying to prove anything. What I am doing is saving the ass of my coven, revenging my mother, and making sure my father's plan of taking over the world—making everything in his path utter chaos—is nothing but a distant memory. If I have to suffer for it, then so be it."

"And what about the people who care for you?" Bishop hissed down at her. "What about them? Should they just say, so be it? That is selfish, even for a witch."

The dig at her craft pissed her off, and it hurt just a little bit too. Witches were known to be selfish creatures, but if she was selfish as he obviously thought, she would have been jumping on her daddy's bandwagon and joining his taking over the world bullshit. Yeah, it hurt that Bishop thought this of her. Yet deep down, she had expected it, and that killed her.

Bonnie leaned up and whispered, for his ears only, "Just because I opened my legs for you, doesn't mean you can tell me what to do, Valentino." She grabbed his shirt, pulling him closer. "I am doing this with or without your support. The only selfish thing I have ever done in my life is to lift the aversion spell, which was obviously a mistake, and open myself up so just once in my life I felt wanted. So fuck you and your selfish witch bullshit."

The look on his face was priceless as she pushed away from him, but he grabbed her, tugging her back. "You go and do what you have to do, Bonnie. I will be right here, but it will be a race to see who takes out that bastard first. If I have to take that right away from you to save your life, then by damn, I will do it without regret. I would rather you hate me than be dead when I could have saved you. So fuck you right back."

Okay, so to say she was shocked by his words was an understatement. To say she didn't want everyone to disappear so she could open her fucking legs one more time for him would be one of the biggest lies she had ever told. And that was saying something 'cause she had told some doozies in her life.

Bonnie couldn't help the small smile slip across her lips. Damn, he was sexy when he was fired up and he was pissed off to a level she had never seen. It warmed her that he cared so much, but he needed to learn and learn quick that she wasn't a normal female in distress. She could and would take care of her own shit. "Then may the best—" She paused, looking for the right word. Her smile grew.

"—witch hunter," he added, his eyes narrowing even more.

"—witch," she countered quickly afterward, "win."

"Oh, I will," he promised, then grabbed her chin, tilting her face up. "I always win."

"Not against this witch." She touched his hand, then pulled it away from her face before turning toward Kira. "Let's do this."

She felt Bishop's eyes on her back as she walked away, but she needed to focus on the now. This wasn't something to play with and, in truth, he may win if she messed this up and freaking died. That wasn't even an option; it couldn't be an option. There was too much for her to do. Putting the bad thoughts to the side, she focused only on the positive.

"So is this going to be as intense as that just was?" Steve said, walking beside her, and glancing behind them at Bishop. "I thought Bishop was going to lose his shit for a minute."

"Just stay out of the way and you won't get hurt," Bonnie responded, then stopped. "Seriously, everyone needs to stay back. No matter what happens, do not come near either of us. If you can't do that, you need to leave."

"She's right." Kira looked around at everyone, her eyes stopping on Ronan. "Once we start, it cannot be stopped."

"I'll keep everyone back," Ryker promised, to which both Bishop and Ronan snorted.

"You can try, warlock." Bishop sneered, shooting him a deadly stare. Ronan didn't say anything, but he also gave Ryker a nasty glare.

Ryker ignored them. "I will do whatever it takes. Anyone breaking the connection will for certain be killing one, if not both of them."

Okay, that seemed to change the mood a bit. Bonnie swallowed hard before nodding at Mira, who waved her arm as another large fire sprouted from the ground. Mira walked back toward Steve as Ryker moved everyone a good distance away from Bonnie and Kira.

"I have to ask again," Kira said as a cloak appeared, draping around her, just as Bonnie's cloak appeared. They were identical in color with the dragonfly emblem proudly displayed on the back. "Are you sure about this?"

"Positive," Bonnie replied, and flipped her hood up. "If shit goes south, it's totally on me. I've forced your hand, but we both know this is what needs to happen."

Nodding, Kira smiled. "You've got this, witch."

"Hell yeah, I do," Bonnie vowed. Then lowering her head, she erased all doubts from her mind. Two memories came and went quickly. One was of her mother's smile, her hand reaching toward her, and then, just as quickly as it appeared, it was gone, only to be replaced by Bishop's handsome face as his hand reached out to her also. Both of them reaching for her wasn't lost on Bonnie, but she didn't have time to ponder it.

Soon, her mind went blank as both she and Kira spoke

in mumbled tones. There was no turning back now. It had begun. In the distance, thunder rumbled and lightning streaked across the sky. It was the beginning of the end.

CHAPTER 21

*B*ishop's body was wired as if thousands of electric bolts ran through it. He had to force himself to stand still as his eyes stayed on Bonnie. The sky had darkened as soon as Mira had called upon the fire that blazed multicolored flames. Black clouds swirled above them in every direction. Thunder surrounded them as lightning struck the field, not even fifty feet away. The wind picked up, giving Bishop only a glimpse of Bonnie's beautiful face as it moved her cape's hood in a peek-a-boo motion.

He could hear both women's mumbled words, but couldn't make them out. He stood, ready for anything, yet he felt helpless as he kept vigil, watching. He wanted to rile at the sky, at the unfairness of what could happen. If he lost her now, it would destroy him. The knowledge actually surprised him, but he knew for a fact that it would. Damn her and that aversion spell. So much time had been wasted by his true feelings being magically subdued. It still pissed him off. And now, within minutes, she could be lost to him.

As a rope of fire broke away from the blaze, both Kira and Bonnie held their arms out, hands fisted and touching each other knuckle to knuckle. The rope of fire floated above them as Kira's words became clearer.

"String entwined my powers bind." Kira's voice rang out above the wind that howled around them.

Bishop actually hissed when the rope of fire wrapped around each woman's wrist, snapping taut before running up their arms. He took a step, but Ryker threw out his arm, stopping him.

"No!" Ryker ordered, his head shaking slowly. "They do not feel it."

"Do you accept these powers until the end of time?" Kira continued, her voice chanting and lyrical.

Suddenly everything stopped. The wind, the swirling of the dark clouds, the rumbling of the thunder, and even the fire seemed to be frozen in time. When a streak of lightning stopped in midair as if waiting for the right moment to strike, amazement kept Bishop rooted. Never in his life had he seen anything like it. The air was electrified, and it seemed as if everything around them was waiting for Bonnie's answer.

Her head was bent, though he could still hear her whispered chant that was spoken so quickly it seemed out of place in the moment of everything being frozen. Even his own small movements were sluggish. Bishop wondered if maybe she had changed her mind. He was ready to get to her if he needed to, but he didn't know if he could even move quickly enough. He flexed his hand to be sure, his eyes shifting down to see his fingers move in slow motion. What the fuck?

Her voice grew louder, but he still couldn't make out the words. His eyes shifted to Mira. Wide-eyed, she stared as if anticipating something Bishop was clueless to. He couldn't move his neck as he once again shifted only his eyes to see Ryker's mouth begin to move, but he had no idea what in the hell the man was saying. Panic set in. Either something big was about to happen or something was terribly wrong. His eyes slowly returned to Bonnie, just as her voice went silent.

Nothing moved. Nothing at all. It was as if they were a painting. It was odd he even thought that, but that was all he could think this moment as... a fucking painting.

Bonnie's head snapped back, her cape falling off her head as her mouth opened wide. *"I accept!"* she screamed, her voice booming with an echo that went straight to his soul. Within seconds, all hell broke loose.

A burst of wind knocked everyone off their feet as if it had been held back by a force stronger than anything Bishop had ever felt. Only Bonnie and Kira remained standing. He quickly rolled to regain his footing, his eyes on Bonnie, who stood stiff, her body shaking slightly as thunder boomed around them. The wind blew them as if trying to push them away, but he refused to be moved. He heard Ronan cursing. His eyes quickly went to Kira to see her standing just as stiff, her teeth clenched and eyes squeezed tight.

Lightning began to strike near both women, but neither flinched. He felt the earth shake with each strike as he pushed his way closer to Bonnie.

"Don't!" Ryker hissed over the wind. "It's working. Just stay calm."

"Fuck that," Bishop growled as Bonnie's mouth opened in a silent scream. No noise escaped her throat, but her body jerked as if she was being shocked. The lightning picked up in strikes, getting closer and closer to the women.

"They're going to get struck." Ronan roared over the howls of the wind and thunder.

"I swear if either one of you goes near them, I will kill you myself," Ryker bellowed, grabbing Ronan and pulling him back. "Just stay the fuck back. Do not interfere... for their safety."

Nothing in his years of fighting witches, vampires, and other unworldly things had prepared Bishop for what he was witnessing now. The power radiating around him was impossible, yet it was happening. He would never have believed it if someone was telling him this tale. He would have called it bullshit. This was far from bullshit.

Sparks shot from the thin rope of fire around their wrists. Bonnie's body stiffened even more, and she bent back as if she was trying to pull away. It was more than he could stand watching her go through this. Three strikes of lightning hit at the same time. One behind Bonnie, one behind Kira, and one into the fire, sending showers of sparks everywhere. A thundering boom deafened him. His ears actually rang. The wind swirled around them, their capes blowing every which way, and then everything went dead, stopped immediately.

Bishops ears hurt, the ringing loud. His skin itched and his eyes burned, but they never left Bonnie, who remained in an awkward position with her back bent, mouth open, and her eyes wide looking into the sky. Suddenly, her mouth closed as she straightened her body back to normal.

Relief swiftly ran through him. It was over. She was alive and seemed unharmed. He glanced at Kira, who continued to stand and stare wide-eyed at Bonnie, whose mouth began to move again, but no sound was coming from her lips. He quickly looked back at Bonnie. Fuck! This wasn't the end.

"Powers unbind, the power is mine!" Bonnie said over and over again, her voice growing louder and louder with each chant.

Something made him look up—a noise maybe or just instinct. Out of a deep purplish-black cloud that swirled in all different directions, a lightning bolt descended toward the women. He opened his mouth in warning, but it was too late. The bolt hit their joined fists, running along the rope, sending Kira flying backward. It continued along the rope on Bonnie's arm, and suddenly, she was engulfed in electricity.

"No!" Bishop's bellow put the howling wind and thunder to shame. It took both Steve and Ryker to hold him down as he watched Bonnie's body literally being electrocuted in front of his eyes. He fought with everything he had to get to her, even dragged both men along with him. Ryker punched out, hitting him hard in the jaw, but nothing was going to stop him from getting to her.

Bonnie dropped to the ground on her hands and knees as the electricity seemed to slip from her body, disappearing into the ground. Mira ran to Bonnie as Kira crawled until Ronan reached to help her up.

"Bonnie!" Kira and Mira both called out.

Bishop roared as he threw both Steve and Ryker off him. He stumbled toward Bonnie, moving Ronan out of the way with a shove. He couldn't believe his eyes. She knelt on the ground, looking as if nothing had even happened to her. Bishop had watched as electricity had run through her body, yet she still breathed. It couldn't be, but it was. Shock and total relief made him feel a little weak.

"Let's not ever do that again," Bonnie finally said, her voice a little shaky. "Holy shit, that was intense."

Kira fell back on the grass, throwing her arm over her face. "Goddess, you can say that again."

"Are you good?" Bonnie asked Kira, who still lay with her face covered while Ronan stared down at her with a worried expression.

"No, not really," Kira said, then waved Ronan away. "I just need a minute. I've done a lot of stuff in my life with the craft, but nothing, and I mean *nothing*, compared to what we just did. I think I'll stick to basics from here on out. I cannot believe how powerful your mother was."

"Am I the only one who shit themselves?" Steve added

with a nervous laugh. "'Cause, son of a bitch, that was 'shit your pants' worthy right there."

"Are you okay?" Bishop ignored Steve as he continued to stare at Bonnie. He couldn't believe he was actually talking to her.

"Yes, I think so." Bonnie stood with Bishop's help. "It really worked. I can't believe it. I seriously had my doubts."

Those words hit Bishop the wrong way. "You had your doubts?" His voice was low and angry. "You. Had. Your. Doubts?" he repeated, punctuating each word.

"Uh-oh." Steve backed away, then reached for Mira. "He's about to blow."

"Well, yeah. Magic is always unpredictable." Bonnie shrugged, then smiled. "But it worked. I feel my mother's power. Actually, I'm consumed with it."

He could not believe she was so nonchalant about what she'd been through. Not much shocked him, but this shocked the shit out of him, and he didn't know if he liked it or not. No, he didn't like it at all, dammit.

"Do you have any idea what we all just witnessed happen to you?" Bishop said, trying to understand. Maybe she was crazy. No maybe about it. She was fucking crazy as hell—that was a fact.

"Ah, yeah. It happened *to me*, so I think I know better than anyone." Bonnie frowned, giving him a sideways glance. "What's wrong with you? It worked. I'm alive. It's all good."

Bishop just stared at her for a second before throwing his arms up in the air. His mouth opened, but honestly, he didn't know what in the fuck to say to that, so he just turned and walked away. He didn't know where in the hell he was going, but away from her for a minute was what he needed.

His strides were long and fast. He spotted a path through some trees and disappeared that way. Getting deep enough he knew he couldn't be seen, he stopped and tried to get a fucking grip on what he just witnessed. It wasn't easy.

The pent-up emotions were too much. He cursed, then punched out, hitting a tree directly in front of him. Not once, not even twice, but four times, and it felt damn good. Controlling his breathing, he closed his eyes for a moment and counted to ten, trying to regain control.

Magic was never something he was comfortable with. He had seen a lot of it, but this was something he had never seen. More than once, he'd thought he had lost her, and then when the lightning bolt ran over her body, he was more than sure he had definitely lost her while he stood watching. That would fuck with anyone, but to a Warrior, to a man like himself, it nearly destroyed him.

CHAPTER 22

*B*onnie watched Bishop walk away and frowned. Her excitement diminished with each step he took away from her. She really wasn't surprised by his reaction, so she didn't take it too much to heart. It actually showed he cared. He just didn't understand.

"Not everyone is fit for the world of witchcraft," Ryker said, breaking into her thoughts. "And not everyone understands. That was pretty dramatic. He didn't take it well. Don't be too hard on him."

Glancing Ryker's way, she frowned. "What? You're his champion now?"

"No, but I saw how much he cares for you, and well, I've been there," Ryker said, then pointed at her. "Don't ask."

Bonnie rolled her eyes. "Why do you think I'd care?"

"Because you're female." Ryker snorted, then glanced

up at the sky before lowering his gaze to her. "Good job. I didn't know if you could actually pull that off."

"Thanks." Bonnie took a step to make sure her legs were going to work. "Me either. Can you make sure they get back okay?"

"No problem," Ryker replied, but stopped her before she could walk away. "Don't push it, Bonnie. Rest before using your powers too much."

"Okay, Dad," Bonnie said in her usual sarcastic tone, but then put her hand on his arm. "Thanks, Ryker."

"Shit, I didn't do anything other than tackle that big son of a bitch before he could get to you." When she gave him a surprised look, he snorted. "I even tried to knock him out, but nothing was going to stop him from getting to you."

Bonnie nodded at that information, then said goodbye to Kira, Ronan, Mira, and a still shook-up Steve.

"You are one badass witch," Steve said, giving her a look of respect. "Never seen anyone get struck by lightning like that and live. Then again, come to think of it, I've never seen someone get struck by lightning. You fucking witches are crazy."

"That's what they say." Bonnie grinned at him, then headed toward where Bishop had disappeared.

Her legs felt like jelly and her body pulsed with energy, but she ignored it. Ryker was right. She needed to rest before practicing her newly acquired powers. Bonnie was excited to see what it all entailed. She was still trying to come to terms that she had her mother's powers added to her own. It felt right, and she knew this was exactly what she needed to defeat her father.

Heading further into the wooded area, she saw Bishop, his back to her. She stopped when he punched out, hitting a tree repeatedly.

"Kill my tree and you'll owe me a new one," Bonnie said with a frown.

"Bonnie, I'm really not in the mood," Bishop responded without turning around. "Your tree is fine."

Feeling a little weak and lightheaded, she slowly walked around him, so they were face-to-face. She eyed the tree to see some bark missing from where his fist had made contact. "Why are you punching the tree?" Bonnie asked, then cocked her eyebrow. "You mad, bro?"

Anger tightened his lips. No smile was to be seen. "How in the hell can you joke after what just happened?" His tone was low, tinged with a boiling rage.

Bonnie sighed, then held up her finger. Searching around, she saw a downed tree, headed that way, and sat down. "Sorry, I'd like to have this fight standing up, but I'm feeling a little shaky and need to sit down for a minute."

That seemed to get his attention as he rushed toward her to ease her down. "Dammit, you should have stayed where you were. I was coming back."

"Well, how in the hell was I supposed to know that when you just stomped off?" Bonnie growled, shifting her weight.

"I didn't stomp," Bishop growled back.

"You looked and sounded like a big old bear stomping away into the woods," she countered, waiting for his response. "Why are you so mad at me? What did I do other than survive? Or is that it? I survived, and now you feel like you have to make an honest woman out of me with a proposal of marriage after the night we shared? I promise not to force your hand, so to speak. And well, we both know there won't be no daddy with a shotgun."

"You think you're funny?" Bishop's eyes narrowed at her. Still no smile.

"Hilarious," she replied honestly. "Definitely funnier than Steve."

Bishop didn't respond. Instead, he looked away from her and stared out into the woods. Damn, what had she expected? No one got her. She was definitely different, but it was the way she coped. Humor. Maybe it made her more confident, even if people didn't find her funny. She really didn't know. What she did know was that humor kept her sane.

"Listen, I'm sorry. Not everyone gets me." She spoke her truth aloud. "Being a smartass has saved me from going insane. Seriously. Deal with a maniac that you know is of your blood. See all the fucked-up things he has done and is trying to do. Know he killed your mother and would kill you in a second flat. Be forced to do things you're not proud of. Fight every single minute of every single day to stay good when it would be easier to turn dark. Yeah, humor has kept me from the edge many times."

Finally, he looked down at her, but he remained silent as his eyes looked into hers. He was hard to read, that was for sure. He'd make a damn good poker player.

"I was scared today. I didn't know what was going to happen, but what I did know is that I'm amazing at my craft. No one can or ever will take that away from me. My mother's powers belong to me. No one else. The only reason I didn't get them at her death was that she didn't want to put me in the position that I have now chosen to be in. She knew her powers combined with another powerful witch could take Orjyll down. I *am* my mother's daughter, and I *am* powerful, and now, with her combined with me, this can all end. It is my decision, Bishop. No one else's. I have never had anyone in my corner. I've been alone all these years. You don't have to agree, you don't even have to understand, but please see how important this is to me. That's all I ask."

She went to stand, but it was a little harder than she thought it would be. She wobbled, but he reached out and steadied her.

"I'm sorry I worried you, but I'm not sorry that I did it. Maybe I should have explained the process, but to be honest, I didn't know exactly what was going to happen. I've heard about it, but never experienced the transfer of powers." Bonnie looked up at him. "We are so different, you and I. But having you there today made me stronger."

"How?" He finally spoke, even if it was only one word.

"Because, for the first time in my life, I had someone

there for me," Bonnie whispered, wanting him to know her true feelings. "Just me, and I don't take that lightly."

"Fuck!" he hissed, taking her in his arms. "You scared the shit out of me."

She smiled against his chest. "I think Steve had that same problem." She chuckled, holding him close. She then pulled away, all humor gone. "I know I acted like what happened today wasn't anything, was no big deal. It's just how I am. It's over. I survived. Kira didn't get injured. It was a win. Honestly, I wanted to back out so many times, but you being here gave me strength. I've never had that before. So thank you. And again, I'm sorry how I acted afterward."

"No you're not," Bishop said, cocking his eyebrow.

"Okay, I'm not." Bonnie shrugged in agreement. "It's just who I am. Flippant and whatevs. If I didn't have that, I would break. And breaking at any time for me is a death sentence."

"I'm sorry you've had to live like that," Bishop said, touching her cheek.

"I'm not." Bonnie grinned. "It's made me the badass witch I am today. Maybe deep down I wish I would have had a normal witchy upbringing, but I didn't. I've dealt with it just like I'm going to deal with what lays ahead. It's who I am. What I've had to be."

"Witchy upbringing?" Bishop laughed. His head angled back, and Bonnie swore at that very moment she would do anything to see him laugh like that more. Then he turned serious. "You are definitely a badass witch, but those days are over for you, Bonnie."

A hard knot formed in her stomach at his words. She had thought that before and needed to stay on course and make sure he realized her course wasn't going to change, even for him. "Those days will always be my future, Bishop. Until my father is dead, nothing will change. Not even me."

"I didn't say anything about you changing." Bishop frowned. "Soon, your life will be different."

Bonnie nodded but didn't agree. Having a different life was a thought she'd had a million times, only to be disappointed. Until it actually happened, she wouldn't hold her breath. "Listen, I'm starving and am feeling really tired. I guess I should get us back. I'm sure you have better things to do, and I've used up plenty of your time."

"You can have as much of my time that you want, Bonnie." Bishop kissed her softly.

"I think Sloan would argue that." Bonnie smiled against her lips. "But I'm seriously feeling a little weak, and I'm afraid if I don't transport us now, we'd be stuck here for a while."

"No complaints from me," Bishop replied, his tone serious as he moved a strand of hair out of her eye. "But next time we come here, can I please drive? Transporting is not really my thing."

Bonnie nodded, then yawned. "We'll figure something out," she replied, hoping she wasn't too weak to actually transport them to the right place. Transporting wasn't really her thing either.

"Hey!" Ryker's voice came out of nowhere. "I stuck around to make sure you were okay, Bonnie."

"She's fine," Bishop yelled back, sounding a little annoyed.

"Actually, maybe Ryker needs to help get us back." Bonnie yawned again. "I'm fine, but I'm really tired and am afraid I might transport us somewhere other than where we want to go. Sometimes that's not pleasant. Transporting isn't really my thing either. I failed miserably in witch school and ended up in the middle of the ocean once."

"Ryker, hold up," Bishop called out quickly as he picked her up in his arms. He headed out of the woods but looked down at her. "Are you serious?"

"No, there isn't witch school," she replied, putting her head on his chest. "But I did end up in the middle of the ocean."

"Ryker!" Bishop called out again, making her smile.

CHAPTER 23

*B*ishop had just hung up the phone when someone knocked on his door. Quietly, he headed that way. Bonnie had been asleep for almost forty-eight hours, and he was worried sick. Ryker said it was normal and that she should be coming out of it soon.

Opening the door, he saw Raven standing there, looking bored. "She up yet?"

"No," Bishop said, then stepped out of the way as Raven walked inside.

They headed toward the kitchen where Bishop was making breakfast. "She needs to wake her ass up so I can bitch her out."

"Why's that?" Bishop frowned, jerking away from the popping bacon grease.

"Because she didn't tell me what she was planning."

Raven sat down at the counter. "I'm supposed to be keeping an eye on her, and I swear she's harder to keep track of than any demon I've come up against."

Bishop grinned at that, then nodded toward the fridge. "Got some water and juice if you want some. Coffee is almost done."

"Thanks." Raven nodded but didn't move. "So, is she okay?"

"Ryker said this is normal after what she went through, but if the smell of bacon doesn't wake her up, I'm going to." Bishop had already decided he'd waited long enough to try to wake her. He had lain next to her, staring at her, watching to make sure she was still breathing, and fuck, it was driving him slowly insane.

While Sloan had put him on leave, he hadn't sounded happy about it. Not that Bishop gave a shit. He was not leaving his house until she was okay.

"I heard it was quite a show," Raven replied, then got up when Bishop cursed the popping bacon and pushed him out of the way, taking the tongs he was using. "Let me do it."

"Steve?" Bishop gladly handed over the job of cooking. He hated to cook but wanted something ready for when Bonnie woke up. Plus, he really did hope the smell of bacon would help wake her.

"Yeah." Raven grinned, shaking her head. "I'm sure it was embellished quite a bit knowing Steve, who said it was 'shit your pants' worthy."

Bishop rolled his eyes, leaning against the counter with

his arms crossed. "Actually, Steve probably didn't embellish much. It was definitely something I wouldn't have believed if I hadn't seen it with my own eyes."

Raven glanced at him over her shoulder. "Lightning actually ran over her body and she survived?"

He nodded with a cocked eyebrow. "It did."

"Damn." Raven turned back to the bacon. "Now I'm really pissed. That's something you aren't going to see every day."

"See what?" Bonnie's voice brought Bishop away from the counter and rushing her way.

"How are you?" Relief at seeing her up and awake shook him to the core.

Bonnie covered a yawn. "Actually, really good." She rubbed her stomach. "How long have I been asleep?"

"Too long." Bishop frowned, wrapping his arm around her shoulders and leading her toward the counter. "I was about to say fuck it and wake you up."

"The smell of bacon woke me up." She sighed, taking a deep sniff. "Goddess, that smells good. I'm starving."

Bishop smiled with a chuckle. "Bacon does it every time. No one can sleep through bacon."

"Hey," Bonnie said, just now noticing Raven at the stove. "You switch jobs?"

Raven glanced at her, then pointed the tongs at her. "Me and you have some talking to do, but not until after you eat."

"What did I do now?" Bonnie sighed, then held up her hand before Raven could say anything. "Hold that thought. Coffee. I smell coffee."

Bishop poured her a cup after helping her on the stool. He grabbed the cream and sugar. Bonnie made her coffee to her liking, blew on it, and then took a sip. He couldn't stop looking at her. She had a beautiful sleepy look to her, and it was sexy as hell. If the circumstances were different and Raven wasn't there, he would be picking her up and taking her back to his bed.

"Okay, now you can answer," Bonnie was saying to Raven, who put the plate of bacon on the counter.

"How do you want your eggs?" Raven asked, putting her hands on her hips. When Bonnie didn't answer, Raven cocked her eyebrow at her. "I'm going to make sure you're fed before chewing your ass out. How?"

"Scrambled," Bonnie replied, then glanced at Bishop when Raven turned away to make her eggs.

Raven grunted, but turned around to fix the eggs.

"And I thought I wasn't a morning person," Bonnie said, then snorted with a frown as she looked around. "It is morning, isn't it?"

"Yes, it's morning." Bishop smiled down at her and had to fight against taking her into his arms. She seemed too innocent and small sitting there, peering up at him. His protective instincts kicked into high gear. He reached out and touched her cheek. He was surprised when she leaned into his hand. Raven setting down a plate full of scrambled eggs with a loud plop had him pulling his hand back with a growl. He glared at Raven.

"What?" Raven glared back at him before turning to get two pieces of toast from the toaster and placing them on Bonnie's plate. "She needs to eat."

Bonnie buttered her toast, looking between Raven and Bishop. She grabbed a few pieces of bacon, taking a bite with a sigh. As she chewed, Bonnie continued to peer at the two who were both looking at her. "Aren't you going to eat?" she asked them both, and both shook their heads. "Okay then. Go do something because I'm not taking another bite while you both stare at me like I'm a caged animal."

Raven laughed, then walked around the counter toward the living room and sat on the couch. "I don't do dishes," she said to Bishop as she passed.

Bishop frowned at Raven, then walked around to start cleaning up. "I didn't ask you to cook. You just took over," he mumbled, then gave Bonnie a sideways glance when she chuckled. "And you. I was not staring at you like you were a caged animal."

"It was a figure of speech," Bonnie said over the rim of her coffee cup.

"I know what it was," Bishop replied, as he made quick work of the dishes. Turning once he was done, he noticed her plate was already empty, and he smiled. "You want more?"

She shook her head. "I'm good, but thank you."

"Good." Raven walked over, putting her phone in her

back pocket. "Now, how in the hell can I keep an eye on you or have your damn back if you don't tell me what you're up to?"

"Um, well…," Bonnie said, then rolled her eyes. "I've never been good with telling people what I'm up to."

"Yeah, think I got that." Raven huffed. "I had to find out everything from Steve. You know you're going to be a damn legend with that guy going around singing your praises."

"I'm far from a legend." Bonnie replied thoughtfully, then stood up from the stool. "Though, that does have a nice ring to it."

"Don't worry," Raven said to Bishop. "I won't let her head get too big."

"Good luck," Bonnie teased, then glanced up at Bishop. "Can I use your shower?"

"Of course," Bishop said, then took her hand to lead her toward his room.

"Don't leave," she said to Raven. "I want to talk to you both, but not until I have a shower and clean clothes."

"Do you need me to have someone bring you clothes?" Bishop said, his brain only thinking of her naked in his shower and nothing else. How desperate was that? She'd just gone through an ordeal, slept for nearly forty-eight hours, and all he could think about was her wet and naked.

"I'm a witch," Bonnie reminded him, then squeezed his hand. "I think I can handle clothes."

"I'll be here unless you decide to slip out a window or something," Raven called out after them. "I'm not the one who disappears."

"Again, I'm a witch," Bonnie responded with a sigh. "No window needed."

"I said *or* something."

Bishop cut Raven off as he shut the door to his room. "She's persistent."

"She is." Bonnie nodded, then stopped. "But I trust her."

They stood and stared at each other. Even relieved that she was awake, he was still worried about her. "Are you sure you're okay?"

"I'm fine." Bonnie patted his chest. "I really am. Have you been here the whole time?"

"Of course," Bishop replied. "I wouldn't leave you alone."

Bonnie glanced away from him, biting her lip before she quickly grabbed him up in a hug. "Thank you," she whispered, giving him a squeeze.

Picking her up, he held her against him. "You don't have to thank me, Bonnie."

"But I do." Her voice shook slightly. "When I woke, I was confused, not really knowing where I was. I started to panic until I heard the muffle of your voice, and then I knew I was safe."

"You are very safe," Bishop assured her, kissing her softly. "Now, you best go and get that shower before I take you in there and bathe you myself." If she only knew how close he was to doing just that, but he wanted to make sure she was okay before that happened, and it definitely *was* going to happen. Bishop set her on her feet and turned her toward the bathroom.

Glancing at him over her shoulder, she gave him a tempting smile before disappearing behind the closed door. Bishop grunted and quickly turned and rushed out of the bedroom before he said fuck it, and went in there to do what he warned her he would do.

CHAPTER 24

*A*fter quickly finishing her shower, Bonnie dried off, her mind racing. The towel rubbed a sensitive spot on her shoulder, and she frowned, knowing exactly what it was. Catching her reflection in the mirror across the bathroom, she walked up to it and stared at herself. She looked no different, even with her mother's powers. She rolled her eyes at that thought, knowing darn good and well her appearance wouldn't change because of that, but inside, she was different. She felt a confident acceptance that she had been searching for her whole life. Having a part of her mother was the key to everything.

The burning on her shoulder couldn't be ignored, though. Twisting, she angled to see the heart-shaped mark blazing red. It had flared when she had first seen Bishop. She had chalked it off to maybe irritating the mark, but as time went on, she knew that wasn't the case. Each interaction with Bishop had sent her mark into overdrive. Now it throbbed with a beat of its own. He was her soul mate. No question about it.

Slowly, she twisted back and looked into her own eyes. She not only saw herself, but part of her mother as well.

"I will do you proud," Bonnie said to her reflection, though she spoke the words to her mother. "I know this is not what you wanted for me, but it's the decision I made. Soon you can be at peace."

For just a brief moment, she smelled lilac, and then it was gone. It was a whiff from her past and home. Warmth fluttered through her, as if being caught up in a loving hug, the sensation enfolding her as a sad smile spread across her face.

"I feel you, Mama." A tear slipped from her eye. "And if that was you sending the dreams, thank you. I don't really understand them all, but I will figure it out."

The feeling left her quickly. Knowing that was her mother's way of telling her she was present and at her side had Bonnie using her magic to dress. Without a second glance at herself, she hurried out of the bathroom and out of Bishop's bedroom. It was time, and she had never been as ready as she was at this moment. Not only did she have her mother's powers, but she also sensed she now had her blessing. Nothing would stop her now.

Glancing around, she saw Raven and Bishop at the counter talking. They stopped to look at her.

"I had a dream," Bonnie said, then frowned. "Actually, I had a lot of dreams, which is odd because I don't dream."

"Wait a minute." Raven frowned, shaking her head as if trying to keep up. "What?"

"I had dreams, and I think my mom was trying to tell me something," Bonnie said, then looked at Bishop. "I need to see Viktor."

"Why do you need to see Viktor?" Bishop asked while Raven nodded in agreement to his question.

"I don't know yet." Bonnie frowned in confusion, but headed toward the door, then stopped and looked back at them. "Well, are you coming, or am I going to have to do this on my own?"

Raven and Bishop glanced at each other, then stood and headed her way.

"Good." Bonnie nodded and headed out the door. "Try to keep up."

"Don't be a smartass," Raven warned her, heading to her bike.

"No promises," Bonnie said, stopping when Bishop stopped by a car. "Where's your bike?"

"Car is safer," Bishop said, opening the door for her, but she refused to move.

"Bike or transport." She gave him that ultimatum, really hoping he picked the bike. Actually, she had a feeling he'd pick the bike since he had an aversion to transporting. "Your choice."

Bishop cursed, slamming the door closed before stomping toward his bike. "Stop being bossy."

"That's like telling me not to be funny. Ain't happening." Bonnie snorted, climbing on the back of his bike. "And stop stomping around like a big old bear."

"Bonnie," Bishop warned, glancing over his shoulder at her.

"Yes," she answered innocently.

"Don't be a smartass, and I don't stomp like a damn bear." Bishop started the bike and revved it a few times.

"Yes, you do," she replied with a small grin before wrapping her arms around his waist. Feeling his strength against her was exhilarating and made her feel alive. She could really get used to this.

Bonnie enjoyed the free feeling the bike gave her. She didn't want to slow or stop. Even urged Bishop to go faster, but he just shook his head. She frowned, but then glanced at the streetlights and made sure that they changed to green, so they didn't have to slow. Bonnie knew she was going to have to work on her magic and soon, but first, she needed to follow up on her dreams before they escaped her. It was a clue on how to find Orjyll; she just knew it. Because of no red lights, they pulled into the compound in record time.

She jumped off the bike with Bishop's help, then followed him and Raven into the compound. Viktor was just coming out of Sloan's office.

"Damn, it's good to see you." Viktor pulled her into a hug. "Heard all about it."

"I'm sure Steve told a tall tale." Bonnie downplayed

what happened, but Viktor gave her a look that said he knew Steve hadn't. "I need to talk to you."

"Sure." Viktor frowned down at her, then looked at Bishop.

"Bishop!" Sloan's voice came from his office.

"Shit," Bishop hissed, then grabbed Bonnie's hand.

Bonnie frowned. "He doesn't sound too happy."

Jared walked by just at that moment. "Obviously you don't know Sloan that well. That's his happy voice."

Not really wanting to go in there, Bishop wouldn't let go of Bonnie's hand and tugged her along with him.

"Good to see you, Bonnie." Jared gave her a nod of respect. "Can't wait to hear about it... without Steve's theatrics."

Goddess, what had Steve told them? She didn't have much time to think about it before she was inside Sloan's office, standing beside Bishop.

"You coming back anytime soon?" Sloan glared at Bishop, and Bonnie felt a tinge of guilt since she was the reason Bishop hadn't been doing his Warrior duties. He then looked at Bonnie, his features softening slightly. "Bonnie, I'm glad you're okay. Quite a story we've heard."

Before Bonnie could open her mouth, Steve walked in, standing right in front of Bonnie with wide eyes. He reached out and poked her in the shoulder, pulling his hand back quickly, surprising her.

"What in the fuck are you doing?" Bishop growled, pulling Bonnie back away from Steve.

"Sorry," Steve said, then went to do it again before Bishop knocked his hand away.

"Touch her again and lose the hand," Bishop warned, his eyes narrowing.

Bonnie rolled her eyes, realizing what Steve was doing. "I'm not full of electricity, Steve." She saw the disappointment in his face and felt for the guy.

"Damn." Steve frowned, then grinned. "Girl, I just want to say that was… awesome. I mean, it freaked me the hell out and I was worried about you, but holy shit—"

"Steve," Sloan warned, then looked back at Bishop. "So, when can I expect you back? Jax and Blaze did a raid last night and found more newly turned vampires in cages."

"Fuck." Bishop shook his head.

"Now." Bonnie let go of his hand, pulling away. "You can expect him back now."

"Good." Sloan gave a nod, then began shuffling through papers. He held one out toward Bishop. "I need you and Viktor to check this place out. We have confirmation from a reliable source they're running a blood ring through their business."

"Wait a minute." Bishop frowned, not reaching out to take the papers, letting Viktor do it. "I didn't—"

Bonnie pulled him back and glared up at him. "I don't need a babysitter," she whispered, giving his arm a squeeze. "I'm fine. You need to go about your life, Bishop."

She watched different emotions flitter through his eyes before he bent down and whispered into her ear. "You are my life, Bonnie."

It felt like she had been surrounded by electricity all over again, just by his words alone spoken in such a deep timber. Her heart beat like a fast drum, pounding harder and harder. Hell, even her knees went weak. What was this man doing to her? And seriously, how did she respond to that?

"Thank you" was her response, and immediately, she wished she could pull the words back. *Thank you?* What in the hell was that? Feeling her face flame hot, she cleared her throat nervously.

Bishop actually chuckled, even while looking irritated. "You're welcome."

"I've got Raven," Bonnie added, not really knowing what else to say. "She'll make sure I don't do anything stupid."

Bonnie glanced behind her to see Raven staring at them with a smirk. Rolling her eyes, Bonnie turned back to Bishop. He was also looking at Raven with a cocked eyebrow.

"I'll make sure she doesn't do anything more stupid than she already has." Raven reiterated what Bonnie said, but not in a flattering way. Bonnie guessed she was still irritated with her for ghosting her more than once.

"See." Bonnie sighed after tossing Raven a dirty look. "I'm in good hands."

When Bishop still seemed to hesitate, Bonnie put her hands on her hips. "Dammit, don't make me disappear, because I will. I will not disrupt your life any more than I already have." Bonnie glanced around, hoping that everyone in Sloan's office was preoccupied and not listening to their conversation. She was relieved to see Viktor looking over the paper he took from Sloan, and Jared as well as Steve standing around Sloan's desk talking. That left Raven, who thankfully was gone. "Don't do this, Bishop. I'm fine," she said after looking back at him.

For a long moment, Bishop remained silent as he stared down at her. Then his eyes slightly narrowed as he leaned toward her. "You disappear, I will find you."

As those words left his lips, she couldn't stop thinking how full his lips actually were. Goddess, she was turning into one of those women who couldn't keep a straight thought when a handsome man was being all alpha on her. And she kind of liked it. Ugh, this definitely was getting complicated.

CHAPTER 25

She was right, which pissed Bishop off. Dammit, he was torn with what to do. Glancing over her head at Viktor, who gave him a cocked eyebrow, he cursed. "Raven!" Bishop called out toward the empty doorway.

Raven appeared quickly with a smirk. "You bellowed?"

He heard Viktor chuckle, but ignored him as well as Raven's smart-ass remark. "Don't leave her side unless someone replaces you."

"No one can replace me, but don't worry. I've got her," Raven answered with a straight face. "Should I follow her into the bathroom while she takes a piss, Master?"

"Not in the mood, Raven." Bishop all but growled his warning. He glanced at Bonnie to see a grin quickly disappear as she tried to look innocent. Damn, these women were going to drive him insane.

Again, he had to admit Bonnie was right. Would he admit it out loud? That was a big fuck no. But the more he was out in the field, the chances of finding that son of a bitch Orjyll before her was in his favor.

"I swear to be on my best behavior," Bonnie said, and he knew she was trying to sound obedient, but was failing in a big way. He didn't believe her for a minute.

"What did you need to talk to Viktor about?" Bishop figured it best to drop it instead of calling her out and starting a war before he left her.

"Yeah, what's up?" Viktor asked, handing Bishop the paper from Sloan.

"I had dreams, but they were confusing. I know they were from my mom," Bonnie began with a frown. "How much did you know about what my mother could do with her powers?"

A haunted look flashed through his brother's eyes but was quickly gone. Bishop knew Viktor still had guilt where Emilia was concerned, but Lacey, his mate, had helped him fight those demons.

"Emilia was amazing with what she could do," Viktor responded matter-of-factly. "What do you want to know?"

"Could she track magic?" Bonnie asked, her brow furrowed as if afraid of the answer.

Viktor thought for a minute, his eyes going to Bishop. "Remember when she found that coven that you and I walked past hundreds of times?"

"Damn, yeah, I forgot about that." Bishop grinned, grabbing onto the memory. "I lost a hundred dollar bet with her on that. She never said how she did it, though."

Bonnie clapped her hands together. "Great!" she said excitedly.

"Come to think about it, we had a case of a warlock who was using his craft by working his way into married women's beds. He was an ugly son of a bitch. He made sure the husband came home to find them. It was always women with money." Viktor shook his head. "Damn, that was a mess. A friend of your mother's was one of them."

"I remember that." Bishop laughed. "He was ugly as sin, going around using magic on unsuspecting females. Your mom called us in on that one."

Bonnie grinned, but two creases quickly appeared between her brows. "You guys didn't kill him for that, did you?"

"Nah," Viktor replied with a huge smile. "She wanted us to because she was so mad, but we just hung him naked with special rope Emilia gave us and let the husbands take care of him after she put a binding spell on the asshole. Wasn't his name Gomer something or another?"

"Yeah." Bishop nodded. "Damn, I forgot all about that." It was good to remember some of the fun times he and his brother had in the past. It wasn't always horrific.

"Did my mom ever find out you didn't kill him?" Bonnie asked eagerly, and Bishop realized he had more to offer Bonnie than he thought. He remembered a lot about Emilia. He made a mental note to tell her more about her mother when the time was right.

Bishop shared a look with Viktor. "Yeah, she wasn't happy about it. Gave us hell as a matter of fact."

"But to answer your question, she did find him," Viktor replied, looking thoughtful. "I'm not sure how, but she had a unique way of finding anyone with magical powers."

Bonnie nodded but didn't say anything. Bishop watched her closely and could almost see her mind working. "Why did you ask?"

"Just trying to get a handle on what she could do. What I need to work on to make finding dipshit easier on all of us," Bonnie replied honestly. Her brows then dipped. "But I promise not to go looking for him today, so go on and do what you have to do."

"Yeah, let's get out of here. I want to get finished early so I can take my girl out to dinner," Viktor said, as he headed for the door.

"Keep your phone on while you're out with your... girl." Sloan called out after him. "Everyone, and I mean, *everyone* is on call."

"Dammit," Viktor cursed as he quickly exited the room.

"That goes for you too," Sloan warned Bishop before going back to talking to a grinning Jared and Steve.

"Guess he told you, huh?" Bonnie smiled and cocked an eyebrow.

"Don't think I didn't catch that 'promise not to go

looking for him *today*' comment." Bishop didn't even look Sloan's way, but continued to look down at her.

"Damn, he's smarter than I thought," Raven said, gaining a glare from both of them. "I caught it. Didn't think he would, though. Men are a—"

"Raven," Bishop warned with a deep grumble.

"Pain in my ass," Raven mumbled, then pushed off the wall. "Come on already, man. She's fine. Stop being all weird and shit. I've got her till you get back. I'm not letting her do anything I wouldn't do."

Bishop's eyes narrowed on her. "That's not a comforting thought."

"You have no idea," Raven mumbled again with a snort, then slammed her mouth shut.

"I have a lot of work to do before I even think of looking for dipshit," Bonnie reassured him, but it fell flat. "No worries," she added, giving him that innocent look she had perfected.

He wanted to believe her, he really did, yet he'd come to realize she did things to her own beat. While he actually respected her for that, it also scared the shit out of him. He needed to find that bastard and soon, because if he didn't, she would.

"Are you fucking coming or not?" Viktor stuck his head through the doorway, glaring at Bishop.

"He's coming," Bonnie and Sloan answered in unison.

Bonnie grinned, then grabbed his hand and walked him

out. "Now, don't be stomping out of here like a big old bear," Bonnie scolded, making him roll his eyes.

"Why do you keep saying I stomp like a bear?" Bishop grumbled, squeezing her hand gently.

"'Cause you do." Bonnie walked him straight to the door.

"Yeah, you kind of do," Raven said behind them.

"Can you give us a minute?" Bishop glared at her over his shoulder.

"Hey, you said not to let her out of my sight." Raven held up her hands. "Make up your mind, bear boy."

"Be nice." Bonnie pinched his ribs, but he hardly felt it.

"She's really getting on my nerves." Bishop pulled Bonnie out the door, away from eyes.

"She's funny." Bonnie shrugged. "And she *was* doing what you told her to do."

"Not when *I'm* with you." Bishop wondered what in the hell he was doing. He had only really spent any amount of time with women for one thing—sexual satisfaction. Was he crazy giving up his bachelor lifestyle to be driven insane? Staring down into Bonnie's large, beautiful eyes, he knew the answer to the question. He *was* crazy, and he *was* fucked.

"Be careful," she said, then started to go back inside. Immediately, he stopped her, then hauled her up in a kiss.

"No, you be careful and stay out of trouble," Bishop ordered, then kissed her again, hard and intense.

"Stop that shit!" came over the intercom. "If I can't be with my woman, then by fuck you can't be with yours." Sid's voice echoed around them.

"Jesus!" Bishop shook his head and flipped the camera off. Viktor stood laughing by his bike as Bishop headed his way. "I need a new fucking job."

Climbing on his bike, he glanced up to see Bonnie with a half-grin on her face. With a wave, she turned and went back into the compound, but not before she peeked a look over her shoulder at him.

"She's up to something," Viktor said over the roaring of his bike. "I'd know that look anywhere."

Yep, he was going to go in-fucking-sane. "Shit!" He pulled out his phone, sent a text, then put it in his back pocket. With a woman like Bonnie, he'd always need a back-up plan.

CHAPTER 26

*B*onnie headed back into the compound, her thoughts a little jumbled. She was confused about her relationship with Bishop. Sure, she'd let him be her first. He was also protective… though, he *was* a Warrior, and wasn't that what they did—protect? Yeah, she was a little confused.

"So, what kind of trouble are we getting into?" Raven asked, breaking her out of her thoughts.

After glancing around to make sure they were alone, she walked closer to Raven. "I really need to go somewhere so I can work on my magic. And I might need some volunteers." Bonnie frowned, then shook her head. "No, scratch the volunteers. I think I need to practice first."

"Are you sure?" Raven looked disappointed. "I know some real assholes I can call."

A laugh burst out of Bonnie before she sobered and sighed. "Well, keep them in mind 'cause I'm going to need some, and soon." She peered toward Sloan's office, making sure she had the all clear. Looking back at Raven, she said, "You ever transport?"

"I refuse to ride on a broomstick." Raven's eyes narrowed. "I like you, but don't like you that much. My bike is right outside."

"Yeah, well, my field is too far for the bike." Bonnie frowned. "And that's so cliché. Witches do not ride on broomsticks, though that would be awesome. I hate transporting."

"You need a field? I got a field." Raven snorted, walking toward the door. "Come on."

Once outside, standing by Raven's bike, Bonnie had second thoughts. "This might not be a good idea. I'm sure my jackass of a father has people everywhere, and there's no doubt they will be able to feel the magic I'm going to be releasing."

"Good." Raven shrugged her shoulder. "Saves us time from having to find the piece of shit. Let him wonder what in the hell is going on. I figure he probably thinks you're helping Kira, and that's exactly what we want him to think."

Raven had a point, though Bonnie really hoped Orjyll didn't know she now had her mother's powers. When dealing with the asshole, it was best to come at him with a surprise. It threw him, which was how he made mistakes. She'd seen that firsthand. Bonnie wasn't naïve enough to think this was the case, though. He had too many people working with him. They would be foolish to underestimate him. That was something else she had seen. While he didn't have his full power, Orjyll was still very dangerous. Even though Bonnie was so ready for this battle to be over—one way or another—she wanted to make damn sure she was ready to take on whatever he had to throw at her.

"True," Bonnie agreed after a beat, getting on the bike. She then spoke her thoughts aloud. "I just need to make sure I'm ready."

Raven glanced at her from over her shoulder. "Bonnie, you're ready. You've been ready since the day that fucker killed your mother. You know it, I know it, and fuck anyone else who has doubts. Plus, you got some badass motherfuckers who've got your back. Don't forget that."

Bonnie stared at Raven for a few seconds before her smile grew. "Damn, I think I got a girl crush." Never having had backup before, Bonnie had a hard time knowing how to accept it, so of course, she went to what was reliable in her life... jokes. Then again, she kinda did have a girl crush going, but dammit, she wished it wasn't so hard for her to accept this new idea of someone actually on her side. A "ride or die" person. Her mind went to Bishop. It felt good, really good, but it also scared the shit out of her. She'd been wrong about things in her past concerning people, so her trust level was low, almost nonexistent, but she was learning to appreciate not being alone.

"Then you've got good taste, bitch." Raven grinned and started her bike. "Now, hold on to your ass 'cause I'm taking you on one hell of a ride."

"Shit." Bonnie grabbed on to Raven as they flew out of the parking lot. Bonnie didn't feel fear once, even when Raven ran a red light, and they almost got smashed by a truck. She realized real quick she better have her magic ready because Raven was not lying about taking her on a hell of a ride. She just needed a little reassurance it wasn't going to be a ride to hell.

Hitting a dirt road, they rode at a much slower pace. The road narrowed to a trail before disappearing into some trees. They continued up and down paths until they rode out into a clearing. Raven shut off her bike.

"Will this do?" Raven got off, looking around. "I do some target practice here and never got any complaints. No one around to complain."

"It's perfect." Bonnie gazed around the area, her eyes flicking up to the sky. It looked like snow. The air was chilly with a slight breeze brushing by, leaving goose bumps in their wake. Quickly, she changed her clothes using her magic. Dressed in jeans, boots, and hoodie with the words *Hocus Pocus, I Need Tequila To Focus*, she was much warmer.

"Nice shirt." Raven leaned against her bike and smirked.

"Thank you. It's one of my favorites." Bonnie nodded, glancing back at Raven. "You're kinda making me self-conscious."

"Tough," Raven replied without missing a beat.

Rolling her eyes, Bonnie turned back around and was a little at a loss. She always used spells for most of her magic, but from what she understood from her mother's writings and hearsay, her mother could make things happen without the spells. Well, she was her mother's daughter, so she needed to remove her head from her ass and get busy. Time was wasting, and Orjyll was becoming eviler by the minute, the fuckwad.

With a sigh, she realized she really needed to be more ladylike. Her thoughts and language were horrid, but then again, when had that ever bothered her? It got her point across and if somebody didn't like it, then they could fu—

"Not impressed," Raven called out behind her, cutting off her thoughts. "I'm bored."

Eyes narrowing over her shoulder, she grinned when the bike rolled quickly from behind Raven, sending her stumbling backward. No spell. Just a thought. Holy shit, she was going to like this. Cocking her eyebrow, Bonnie grinned. "Still bored?"

∾

*B*ishop jumped through the window, his boots pounding the ground as he chased the son of a bitch. Damn, he was fast and zigzagged like a crazy man. His rage propelled him forward. Blood ran into his eyes from the large gash on his forehead, but he swiped it away without missing a beat. The fucker had surprised him with a crowbar as Bishop came out of the basement.

The asshole kept looking over his shoulder, checking to see if Bishop was still behind him. Suddenly, the crowbar that bastard had hit him with came sailing toward him. Bishop went to his knees, sliding under it, then back on his feet in a fluid motion. He swore if he caught this fucker, he was going to torture his ass for a while before he took him back for questioning.

"Give up, asshole." Bishop leaped over a downed tree. "You stop now, I'll let you live."

"Getting tired, old man?" the guy yelled as he jumped a creek, Bishop following close behind.

Seeing a thick broken limb, Bishop swooped it up in a run, glad it was thick and heavy. Without missing a beat, he whipped it at the man's legs, sending him to the ground. Bishop was on him within seconds of him going down. They rolled, throwing punches, but Bishop was too much for him. The guy was fast, but he couldn't fight like Bishop, not even close.

"How does it feel to get your ass beat by an old man?" Bishop said, then jerked him to his feet. "Huh?"

"Listen, I didn't do that back there." The man looked behind Bishop from where they came from. "All I was to do was keep guard. I didn't even go down in that basement."

"Then how do you know to deny anything that was in the basement?" Bishop growled, putting silver handcuffs on him. "Guess you think I'm old *and* stupid?"

The not-so-tough guy now tried to plead his case, "Dude, I just needed some money."

"Plenty of legit jobs out there, even for a vampire," Bishop said, walking him through the creek. "Orjyll isn't legit."

"But the pay is good." He'd admitted to working for Orjyll, which was what Bishop wanted to know. "And it's cash. All I had to do is guard. That's it."

"And you fucked that up," Bishop said, scanning the area to make sure no one was lying in wait for them. He knew Viktor had called in reinforcements when he'd gone after this asshole. "What's your name?" He was young and probably turned before his twenty-first birthday.

"Joe," he finally said after a few minutes of probably wondering if he should even be talking to Bishop or not.

"Well, Joe, you're going to be confronted by some scary-ass Warriors in a few minutes," Bishop said, figuring if he could get him to talk before the others scared the shit out of him, that would be best. "Your attitude and answering questions without being a smartass is going to determine whether you live or die."

"Didn't think the VC could do that to people. They have rules." Joe tried to look over his shoulder at Bishop, but Bishop gave him a shove to keep him going.

"Oh, we do have rules. *Our* rules." Bishop snorted, then glanced at the darkening sky as snow began to fall. "So, you want to go ahead and fill me in on what happened in that basement?"

"I don't know, man," Joe said, shaking his head. "I never went down there. I swear it. Whatever is down there has nothing to do with me."

Bishop was done. He was pissed and he was done. Other Warriors were pulling in, but Bishop walked past them, his large hand on the back of Joe's neck as he led him past everyone. Pushing Joe through the door, he guided him toward the basement steps. He thought about pushing him down the steps but didn't. Nice guy? Fuck no. He wanted answers, and if the fucker broke his neck, they wouldn't get any.

The smell of death hit him as soon as they entered the yard, but as they started down the staircase, it was so rank he almost gagged. Bishop had smelled death before, many times, but this was different somehow.

They rounded the corner where Viktor and Sloan stood among cages that were stacked on top of each other. Bishop's eyes scanned the carnage. Sickness and complete rage made him squeeze the back of Joe's neck to the point he cried out.

"Oh God," Joe cried out and gagged, then tried to look away, but Bishop refused to let him.

"God is nowhere in this basement," Bishop growled, then jerked his head back around. "Look, you son of a bitch. I don't even want you to blink." Bishop watched the man's reaction, and either the guy was a highly skilled actor or was telling the truth and really hadn't known what was in the basement.

Bishop continued to grip his neck so Joe couldn't look away again, but his eyes also scanned the area. Not one cage was empty. Each had a vampire inside—all dead by a silver bullet gunshot wound to the forehead. Women, men, and kids… well, teenagers, but kids to Bishop. The youngest looked to be about sixteen. They were all starved. Their gaunt features and sunken eyes told that story.

"I want to know who did this," Bishop hissed as he pushed Joe toward one of the cages that held a younger vampire.

Suddenly, Joe stiffened, his handcuffed hands trying to get into his pocket as he started twisting.

"What are you doing?" Bishop growled, then looked into his blank eyes. Joe was no longer there. Joe began to thrash as if in a panic to get into his own pocket. Bishop heard his wrist crack. He was breaking his own bones just to try to free himself. "Fuck!"

Viktor rushed over with Sloan, and they subdued the man enough for Bishop to reach into his pocket. He pulled out a small square plastic liquid-filled packet. It looked like a Tide POD. Viktor quickly checked his other pockets.

"That's the shit others who've been caught have taken." Sloan bent to look at the pod Bishop tossed on the ground. "But he's a vampire. I only remember humans doing this. Can that shit take one of us down?"

Bishop glanced at Viktor, who was looking at him. "Looks like Orjyll has a new game." Viktor cocked his eyebrow.

"Get Bonnie here, now," Sloan ordered Sid, who'd entered the room with a curse of rage as he took in the scene.

"On it," Sid said, then disappeared back up the steps.

Not wanting to involve her in this, Bishop knew he had to think of more than himself. He stood looking down at Joe, who still thrashed around trying to get to that pod. Viktor was right. Things were changing, and they'd better make damn sure they were on the winning team.

CHAPTER 27

*B*onnie was wearing herself out, but she was in awe of what she was able to actually do. And yet, she respected her mother's power, keeping control at all times. Okay, a few times things got a little crazy… like when the tree she'd uprooted had headed straight toward them. Yeah, Raven wasn't too happy about that. That woman could cuss.

Tired and hungry, she decided it was time to quit. She felt confident to this point that she could control herself and not take out the good guys, but she needed a little more practice. The thing about magic was once you lost control, you lost yourself in the magic, and it could overtake you in a matter of seconds. Power was heady, meaning once you tasted it, you wanted more and more and even more. Bonnie had seen many good witches and warlocks become so obsessed with power that they lost themselves to the dark side. She refused to be one of those people. Never would she disrespect her mother or herself in that way.

She wanted to try one more thing before they left, though. Closing her eyes, she focused on the elements. Fire she could do. Rain was iffy; she got a sprinkle with a little thunder and a poof of lightning, but next she wanted to try wind. She had done all the elements before, but with a spell. So far, anything she had tried was with just a thought. Feeling a breeze pick up, she opened her eyes to see the trees across the field sway in a gentle motion. Nothing crazy. Again, she closed her eyes and focused harder.

The only sound was the creaking of bare frozen tree limbs and… "Old Town Road" by Lil Nas X.

"What in the hell?" Her eyes popped open. She turned to see Raven with her gun out, rushing toward her.

"Shit!" a male voice sounded, but there was no one there.

"Steve?" Bonnie frowned, searching the area. Raven stopped before her with her gun drawn.

"I'm going to start shooting at air," Raven warned, her tone hard.

Steve appeared with his hands outstretched. "Whoa." Steve held his phone in one hand, the song still playing. A moment later, it went quiet. "Dammit, put the gun away. Sorry, thought this fucking thing was on silent."

"What are you doing here being all invisible and shit?" Bonnie moved Raven's pointed gun away from Steve.

"Good way to die." Raven put her gun away.

"Yeah, well, Bishop wanted me to follow you," Steve blurted, then frowned. "Damn, I just dropped him in it, didn't I? Ah, fuck it. He figured you guys were up to something and wanted me to follow you to make sure you were okay."

"So he doesn't think I can handle the job and sent *you*?" Raven sounded offended and looked pissed, extremely pissed.

"Looks that way, but you didn't hear that from me. I'll lie my ass off," Steve said, then looked over their heads, his eyes growing wide. "Is that a tornado?"

"What?!" Bonnie spun, her eyes as wide as Steve's. "Uh-oh."

Sure enough, there was a small funnel heading their way, blowing anything and everything out of its path.

"What in the hell do you mean, uh-oh?" Raven backed up, taking Bonnie with her. "Did you do that?"

"Maybe." Bonnie stumbled, but Steve and Raven caught her. Okay, dammit, she needed to focus.

"You think you can *maybe* stop it?" Raven yelled over the roaring.

Closing her eyes, Bonnie tried to focus, but Steve and Raven were distracting her with their "Fucks" and "Oh shits." Okay, she could do this. She could feel the strength of the wind pushing her back. Raven and Steve both held on to her while trying to keep their footing. If she didn't stop this thing, which seemed to be growing in strength, innocent people could be hurt, even worse, be killed all because she screwed up and lost focus. This was definitely a learning experience on what not to do when facing asswipe and his army of witches and vampires. *Don't be distracted.*

"Bonnie!" Raven shouted, and Bonnie peeked to see the funnel growing and looking very angry. Yeah, the twisting thing looked pissed off and heading straight toward them. Bonnie buckled down. She could do this. Feeling something burn in her chest and deep inside her soul, she pictured the funnel shrinking, becoming smaller and smaller. She continued to do this until finally, the wind stopped pushing against her.

Opening her eyes, she was relieved to see the funnel disperse and disappear into the sky. Her legs buckled, but Steve caught her.

They all stared out at the now empty field without saying a word.

"What in the hell are you looking at?" another male voice called out from behind them.

They all jumped, turning around, and screaming—Steve screaming the loudest.

"Fuck!" Steve shouted, his hand on his chest. "Fuck! Man, you scared the shit out of me. Did you see that?"

"See what?" Charger frowned, then looked behind where they stood to where Steve was pointing.

Bonnie's heart was beating so hard it made her dizzy. Damn, that was close. Too close. "You didn't see that?"

Charger's eyes narrowed. "What in the fuck are you guys smoking back here?"

"Did you do that?" Steve looked at her wide-eyed, totally ignoring Charger.

Rolling her eyes, Bonnie glanced once again behind her, then looked at Steve and then Raven. "Let's keep this between us, 'kay?"

"Shit." Steve snorted. "You think I'm going to be able to keep that secret? And I thought watching you being swallowed up by lightning was intense. That was nothing compared to this because my ass was on the line this time." Steve stabbed his finger at the empty field.

"What are you doing here?" Raven asked, her voice sounding normal, as if they didn't almost get swallowed by a tornado.

"I'm here because obviously, no one here can answer a fucking phone," Charger said, glaring at Steve. "And you've got a tracker on your bike still."

"Why do you have a tracker on your bike?" Bonnie asked Raven with a frown.

"It's protocol for a Guardian." Raven glanced away from Charger. "I just haven't removed it yet."

"We need to go," Steve said, pulling his phone away from his ear. "Sloan wants you."

"Me?" Bonnie pointed to herself. "What did I do now?"

"Don't know," Steve said as he headed toward the path through the woods. "I was too busy getting my ass chewed for not answering Bishop's call. I mean, excuse the shit out of me. I was almost blown to smithereens by a tornado. But does anyone care about that? Nope, they sure as fuck don't."

Bonnie noticed Charger looking at both her and Raven. She just shook her head. "Don't ask."

"Didn't plan to," Charger said, but once again, he glanced over their heads before turning away. "Bike is out by the road. Meet me out there."

"Why do men always have to bark orders like we have to listen to them?" Bonnie followed Raven to her bike. "And why do they have to look sexy as hell doing it?"

Raven glanced at her phone as she got on the bike, then put it in her back pocket. "We don't have to listen. Steve just texted me the address." Raven started her bike. "And he's okay."

Bonnie snorted. "Charger is fucking hot and you know it. You're such a liar."

"Shut up." Raven revved her bike, then took off in the opposite direction Charger and Steve went.

"Hey, where we going? They went that way," Bonnie said, then gasped when Raven sped up toward the opposite side of the field.

"Just because they bark orders doesn't mean I have to follow them," Raven called out, taking a quick turn heading up a big hill. "Hold on. This may get a little sketchy."

Sketchy wasn't a word Bonnie would use during her bike ride from hell. This was definitely a more challenging trail than what they were on before, but she had to give Raven credit. The woman could handle a bike. It had to be twice as hard with her on the back, but Raven even laughed a few times during a few very dangerous maneuvers. She was crazy. Maybe even crazier than Bonnie was, and that was saying something.

They broke out of the woods and onto a road. Hearing a bike roaring up to them, she looked back to see Charger pulling up beside them. He didn't look happy. He slowed just long enough to give Raven a disapproving glare before speeding past them.

"I think he's pissed," Bonnie yelled over the roar of the bike.

"He's always pissed," Raven shouted back, then sped up, passing Charger with reckless abandon. This time it was Raven who gave him a nasty glare as they passed.

If Bonnie wasn't mistaken, a look of respect flashed in his eyes, but it was gone when he looked at her. For the rest of the ride, they rode close together, catching up to Steve. They pulled up to a large house with a lot of activity.

Once parked, they all got off their bikes, and she scanned the area for Bishop. Disappointed at not seeing him, she headed toward the house but stopped when she heard Raven's and Charger's raised voices.

"You do not put civilians in danger just to show your ass, Raven." Charger was growling the words loudly. "You're lucky you are not under me anymore because I'd be writing you up."

"She was not in danger," Raven replied, her voice even and calm. "Why am I even responding to you? You never listen to a damn word I say anyway."

"I was safe," Bonnie said, knowing she had to stick up for her girl. "Raven wouldn't do anything to put me in danger."

"Watch yourself, Raven." Charger leaned toward her. "I'm watching you."

Bonnie cocked her eyebrow at that, then glanced at Raven whose calmness from a few seconds ago went bye-bye.

"Why is that?" Raven leaned in even closer. "Why now? Huh? You sure as hell didn't care when I was a Guardian. Why now that I'm a Warrior?"

Steve, who stood beside her, whistled under his breath. "Damn, girl has a bite."

"Shush." Bonnie wanted to hear what Charger was going to say to that, but was disappointed because he didn't say anything at all. He actually turned toward her. "Come on. They want you inside."

He gently took her elbow and directed her toward the house. That was when she saw Bishop covered in blood, and everything else going on around her disappeared.

CHAPTER 28

*B*ishop and Viktor dragged Joe up the steps. It was one of the hardest damn things he'd ever done. The man was fighting them every step of the way. He was under some kind of spell, which clued them in that he was probably newly turned and was once a half-breed. His eyes were blank, but his body fought them as he tried to get to the pod that had been in his pocket, which now was in Slade's possession.

Viktor barely dodged a blow to his nuts and growled, "I'm going to knock this fucker out."

Honestly, Bishop was wondering why they didn't go ahead and do that, but Bonnie should be there any minute, and they needed answers. He had a feeling this guy was going to spill everything, so knocking him out would only delay that process.

Not wanting Bonnie anywhere near the basement, he made the decision to bring him upstairs. Once in the kitchen, Viktor and Bishop slammed him on the kitchen table, scattering everything that had been on it everywhere. Adam and Sid came in.

"Bonnie's here," Adam said, then helped Viktor hold down Joe as Sid took Bishop's place.

"Hurry the hell up." Sid struggled against Joe's legs.

Bishop left the kitchen and hurried outside. She was watching Charger and Raven having an exchange before she turned, her gaze landing on him. Bonnie's eyes widened and he realized even though he was probably healed, his blood was still all over him.

"How bad are you hurt?" She ran toward him and he couldn't help but like the worry for him in her eyes . She scanned his body and frowned. "Not your blood?"

"You sound disappointed." He cocked his eyebrow at her. "Yes, it's my blood, but I'm already healed. Got hit in the head with a crowbar." Bishop rubbed the area.

"Someone hit you with a crowbar in the forehead, and you're waltzing around with a possible concussion?" Bonnie put her hands on her hips. "Does Slade know?"

"Ah, not sure." Bishop shook his head. "I'm fine, just bloody. And I don't waltz."

Bonnie rolled her eyes, then nodded. She looked behind him at the house, then back to Bishop. "I'm glad you're okay. So what's going on? What does Sloan need me for?"

"Bishop!" Steve called from the front door of the house. "Sid said if you don't get back in there, he's going to kill the guy. He sounded pretty serious. That dude is going insane."

"What's he talking about?" Bonnie asked as Charger walked up with Raven.

"Bonnie." Slade headed toward them before Bishop could answer her. He held out the pod in the palm of his hand. "Do you know what this is?"

Bishop saw definite recognition in her eyes as well as emotion. "Yeah." Bonnie's voice was hard. "It's what Orjyll gave to everyone. He would put them under a spell, so if caught, they would take it. Orjyll had a twisted way of having people be loyal to him. He trusted no one. Expected anyone if caught to expose him.

"What would it do to a vampire?" Slade asked, his tone serious and concerned.

Bonnie reached out to take the pod, but Bishop grasped her wrist, stopping her. "It's fine. It has to be ingested. When Orjyll first thought of this sick punishment for being caught, he had two different kinds." Bonnie took the pod, holding it up. "Then realizing he could just add a little bit of silver to the poison, he could kill two in one, so to speak. When you hold it up, you can see flecks of silver."

"Flecks?" Charger also looked at the pod she held up.

"Yeah, only the best for the bastard. No liquid silver for him." Bonnie gave the pod back to Slade. "There's such a small amount that a vampire can carry it on them without it causing any type of issue. But once ingested, that's a different story."

"And these dumbasses agreed to this?" Raven said, taking the pod from Sloan and holding it up so she could see.

"No." Bonnie snorted. "No one in their right mind would agree to that kind of loyalty to a psychopath. It's the spell. Why do you think he's trying to produce more and more half-breeds?" She didn't wait for an answer. "So he can control them with magic. If they are too strong, he gets rid of them. Even half-breeds."

Thinking of what lay inside the house behind him in the basement made Bishop curse to himself at the unfairness those innocents suffered just because this sick fuck wanted to control them.

"Speaking of which, seeing that pod means one of Orjyll's guys survived." Bonnie looked back to Bishop. "Is he going crazy right now? Is that what Steve was talking about?"

Damn, Bishop was regretting calling her in. He could see her battle-ready, though he really didn't want her involved. But that wasn't fair because she was involved more than he was comfortable with. He needed to step back, make sure she was safe, and let her do her thing. That's what a real man would do. While he was an alpha, he was also fair. She was strong, no doubt about that. Stronger than any woman he had ever known.

"Yes," Bishop said, then stopped her before she could pass him to go inside the house. They stared at each other for a long moment, but then Bishop turned and escorted her to the kitchen.

"What's the smell?" she whispered as she walked in, her gaze taking in everything.

They could hear the commotion coming from the kitchen—Warriors cursing and thrashing going on. Sloan, who stood just outside the kitchen door, turned to look at them.

"Can you do anything for him?" he asked Bonnie without explanation. "Sid is about ready to kill him, and we really need this guy alive."

"I'll try," Bonnie said, but Bishop stepped in front of her and entered the room first.

"Hold him," Bishop ordered before letting Bonnie completely in the kitchen. He felt her looking around him, but he made sure Joe was secure.

"What in the fuck do you think we've been doing for the past ten fucking minutes?" Sid growled, then cursed some more.

Bonnie stepped around Bishop, and it took everything he possessed not to grab her and take her away from all of this. He kept having to remind himself that this was what her life had consisted of way before he'd met her. As much as he hated it, she was needed here, and he had to support that. Support her.

Staying as close to her as he could, Bishop focused on Joe. His arm slipped from Adam's grip as he thrashed violently and would have hit Bonnie if Bishop hadn't pulled her back.

"Dammit." Adam grabbed his arm again. "Sorry. This dude is determined."

Sloan came in to lend a hand. Once they got control again, Bishop let her go. She walked up to Joe and laid her hand on his forehead. She closed her eyes and began to chant low, her words unrecognizable to anyone in the room. She had a hard time keeping her hand on his forehead, but she managed to do it, her eyes closed the whole time. Finally, Joe started to quiet, the thrashing dwindling to only jerks of his body.

Bishop watched Joe's eyes begin to clear and come into focus. They widened at seeing all of them around him and realized he was being held down. He began to fight again, but for different reasons. He was freaked out.

"Where am I?" he yelled as he jerked, trying to break their hold. "Get off me."

Stepping into Joe's vision, Bishop carefully moved Bonnie out of the way. "Remember me? Crowbar to the forehead?"

Joe stopped trying to fight as he stared at Bishop. "Ah shit," he cried out, then looked around at everyone again. "What happened? Why am I on the table?"

"Because you were going crazy," Sid grumbled. "I'm letting you go, but if you even try anything, I will kill you. Got it?"

He nodded and glanced at Bishop. "I ain't trying anything. I just want to get up."

Everyone looked at Sloan, who bobbed his head. Joe sat up slowly and rubbed his face. "Did I black out?"

"Were you a half-breed before being a full-blood?" Bonnie asked, her eyes observing the guy carefully.

When he nodded, she sighed, then looked at Bishop. "Did you pull a gun on him?"

"No," Bishop said, shaking his head. "Why?"

"Because the spell begins when the person knows there's no escape." Bonnie still watched Joe carefully.

"We handcuffed him," Viktor clarified; he also stood ready if the guy went berserk again.

"Spell?" Joe frowned, his voice shaky. "No one put a spell on me. I'm a vampire."

"If you were previously a half-breed, then yes, you can have a spell put on you." Bonnie frowned. "Did you meet Orjyll, or are you just one of his lackeys?"

"Never met that guy, but he's the one who was paying me. Heard his name a few times and figured he was the main dude." Joe looked confused as hell. "Listen, all I know is I answered an ad online for work. Got a text to meet up with some guy at Melly's Brew Crew in downtown. Don't know his name, never asked and he never gave it. He gave me the address here and told me the times I needed to be here to keep an eye on the place. Said there would be a bonus if there were no problems, and if there were problems, to take care of it. He gave me a phone number and cash."

This time everyone but Joe looked toward Adam. "Truth." Adam nodded. "All of it."

"Sorry, man." He glanced at Bishop. "I just needed the money and was doing what I was told. I shouldn't have hit you with the crowbar. I can't even believe I did that."

"No, you shouldn't have," Bishop agreed, shooting him a narrowed look.

"Spell," Bonnie said absently, pulling out her phone. Bishop watched her search for something, then held the phone out toward Joe. "Is this the guy?"

"Yeah, that's him," Joe replied with a frown. "Who is it?"

"Wyrick," Bonnie said, but not to Joe. She looked straight at Sloan. Sloan had unfinished business with Wyrick after being shot by him.

"I swear I never went in the basement. If I had, I would have walked away. That is not something I would ever do." Joe shivered as he glanced toward the basement. "I just thought I was working a little security detail for the guy. I didn't even have a key. I came in after seeing the door was open, and then you came up from the basement."

Bonnie looked at Bishop. "What's in the basement?"

Joe started to answer, but Bishop pointed at him. "Shut it," he ordered, then peered down at Bonnie. She didn't need to see what was down there, and *he* definitely didn't want her to see what was down there. Hell, he wished he hadn't. "You don't want to go down there," he said to Bonnie, but by the look on her face, he knew that's exactly where she was going to go.

CHAPTER 29

One thing Bishop needed to learn about Bonnie was when she was told she shouldn't do something, she was sure going to do it. She couldn't help it. Maybe she had a problem with any type of authority. Perhaps she was too much of a free spirit, but now she needed to see what was in the basement. By the looks on everyone's face, she knew it wasn't good, and she probably would regret her stubbornness. Obviously, it had everything to do with her bastard of a father, so not going down there was not an option.

Surprised Bishop didn't stop her, she walked to the door then down the steps. Turning the corner, she saw the cages immediately. What took her a minute was to process what was inside them. Steve, Damon, and Duncan were busy as they carefully removed bodies out of the cages.

The odor throughout the house didn't really register with her upstairs, but now the pungent odor of death hit her. Stepping further into the basement, she felt Bishop behind her. She knew he was there and actually appreciated his presence because she was afraid she was going to go into shock.

Men, women, and teenagers filled the cages. Their naked bodies gaunt from starvation. She stepped even closer to see the gunshot wound in one woman's forehead, her lifeless eyes staring at Bonnie. Overwhelming guilt slammed into her. If she looked close enough, Bonnie knew she would see blame in the woman's eyes.

"I could have stopped this," Bonnie whispered as her eyes went to a young guy in a smaller cage curled up in a ball, his lifeless eyes staring toward her.

"That's enough." Bishop grabbed her shoulders and turned her away from the horror, but she still saw it. She knew she would see it for the rest of her life.

She let him lead her upstairs back into the kitchen and toward the front door, but she stopped and looked first at Joe and then Adam. "Did he have anything to do with any of that downstairs?" Bonnie asked, her voice low and even. She didn't even give Adam time to answer before she yelled, "Did he?"

"No, he didn't," Adam said, then shook his head. "I would tell you if he had."

Bonnie nodded, then looked toward Sloan. "Do you need me for anything else?"

"No," Sloan replied, giving her a knowing look that made Bonnie want to scream.

They all knew she could have stopped this carnage from

happening a long time ago, yet she hadn't. She could have taken Orjyll out, but didn't.

"Get me out of here," Bonnie said, looking away from the stares directed at her.

"You got her?" Raven said as they passed. "I'm going to stay here and help out."

"Yeah," Bishop answered as he quickly led her outside and to his bike.

Bonnie felt like she was on autopilot, her mind replaying the horror in the basement of that normal-looking house. Hate and rage filled her more than ever before. She didn't even realize when they started to move, but somehow, she had wrapped her arms around Bishop, her head leaning against his back as the scenery passed by in a blur.

"I could have prevented it," she whispered, then closed her eyes in disgust. Disgust at the man whose blood ran through her veins, at herself, and her self-loathing began to consume her.

Before she knew it, they were at Bishop's place, getting off the bike and walking into the house. She moved one foot in front of the other until she slowed and stopped completely. Suddenly it all became too much. Her body shook as if she couldn't keep her emotions under control, and the anger, absolute rage, fear, and disgust were going to explode. Panic overwhelmed her suddenly. Squeezing her eyes shut and fisting her hands, she opened her mouth and screamed, unleashing her fury.

She felt Bishop wrap her up into his large, strong arms. Not restraining her at all, but instead, giving her a sturdiness in which to let go of everything. Years and years of mental anguish poured out of her. Still in a somewhat sane frame of mind, she heard glass shatter and knew she needed to control her magic. She couldn't lose herself enough to let her power go on a rampage. No, that would be saved for later. Not today, but soon. Very soon.

As quickly as her scream came, it stopped. In his arms, her shaking quieted. She had never lost control like this, ever, and wondered why now. Deep inside she knew. Never had she had support before—someone on her side. It had always been her and her alone. For the first time in her life, she could let go, and it would be okay. Now the tears came, hard and fast. Sobs of pain racked her body. No rage, only pain. It was as if her emotions were taking over and deciding when to release and how. It was odd, but it was time. Past time.

Bishop didn't say a word as he held her. His large hands rubbed her back, allowing whatever she needed. Finally the tears slowed, the sobs subsided, and her emotions, while still there, were not as raw.

"What did I break?" A sniff followed her whispered words.

"A few windows," Bishop said, his mouth pressed to the top of her head. "No worries. I know a witch who can fix them with a wave of her hand."

Bonnie did just that, without even looking. She pulled away from his chest and rubbed her eyes. "Sorry about that," she said, before realizing she wasn't really sorry. "Actually, I'm not. Thank you for allowing me to… lose my shit."

Bishop gently smoothed a strand of hair behind her ear. "Bonnie, we all need to lose our shit. And I'm glad you retracted that apology because I wasn't going to accept it. Everyone needs someone to vent to. Viktor has always been that person for me. I usually punch him in the face, but we all vent differently. I'm honored to be that person for you."

"So I could punch you in the face and it be like a free-bie?" Bonnie said with a grin, but it quickly crumbled into a sob as her thoughts went back to the basement. How could she even smile or joke? "Goddess, if I would have taken him out when I had a chance, those people would—"

"Don't even think of blaming yourself for that." Bishop's voice hardened slightly.

"How can I not?" She looked up at him, her eyes full of tears and anger. "Do you know how many times I could have but didn't? I was so close to the bastard, and I didn't even try." She looked away from him, but he stopped her.

"Look at me, Bonnie." Bishop's eyes searched hers. "You were on your own. Now you aren't alone. You have many behind you, and we will get the bastard. Together. We are going to do this together. You're a smart woman. If you really believed at any time you could have killed Orjyll, you would have. I believe that with no doubts."

Biting her lip, she nodded, then shook her head. "Those

people." A tear slid down her cheek. "They died because they didn't suit his purpose, didn't they?"

Bishop said what she already knew, "Yes."

"How can someone be so evil?" Bonnie asked, not really expecting an answer. Instead, she felt she needed to toss out the thoughts that terrified her the most. "His blood runs through my veins."

"You are nothing like him. Do you hear me? Nothing!" Bishop took her face in his hands, forcing her to look at him. "You also have your mother's blood in your veins, and that is much more powerful. Never forget that. Emilia was a beautiful soul, and so are you."

Bonnie nodded, praying he was right. It was a fear of hers. She actually had a mean streak, and definitely wasn't what you would consider sweet, but so far, the evilness she had seen over the years with her father had never come out of her. But once she came face-to-face with Orjyll, that evilness that was a part of her was going to have to come out, and it terrified her.

"Promise me something," Bonnie said quickly, her eyes widening.

"What?" Bishop asked, not promising anything.

"Don't let me hurt any of us." Bonnie thought about the tornado from earlier. "This has to happen soon. I did practice, but my mother's powers, well, let's just say I can understand Kira's anxiety while she possessed them. It could take years to learn to control. We don't have years."

"I promise." He leaned down to kiss her but stopped

before he made contact. "I want to kiss you, but I'm sure I still have blood all over my face."

Bonnie leaned up and kissed him instead. "You don't, and if you did, it's your blood." His promise meant more to her than he could even know. She trusted him to pull her back if she lost control. He was a witch hunter and would probably know before she even realized it.

He tugged her into his arms and held her close. "Now you promise me something."

"Anything." She surprised herself at her own answer and how quick she was to promise him something when she didn't even know what it was. "Within reason," she added.

He chuckled, then looked down at her, turning serious. "You don't do this alone. If I'm not around and something happens, you wait for me. We do this together."

Wow, this was a hard one. Could she promise him this? Did she even want to? Doing a quick soul search, she admitted she needed him by her side. Actually, she wanted him by her side. This was a first for her, and it felt good. "I promise."

He gave her a narrowed look. "That was a long hesitation."

"I didn't want to lie to you, so I had to think about that one for a minute." She followed with a smile.

"You look tired." He searched her face. "I'm going to go shower, get this blood off me. Then if you're hungry, I'll fix us something to eat. You okay?"

"Yeah." She nodded, her lips curving upward as he kissed her on the forehead before he turned around.

"I'll be right back."

Standing there, she felt suddenly lost. What in the actual hell? Shaking her head, she made her way to the couch and sat down. Glancing down, she saw herself wringing her hands together, then pulled them apart and stood up. She paced around for a second and figured out what the problem was. She didn't want to be alone. Not now. Tomorrow it may be different, and she'd want her space like she usually did. But right now, she needed him. At least to be close to him. She didn't want to remember what she had seen in that basement, and it seemed he was the only thing in her life that could make her forget.

Rushing toward where he'd disappeared, Bonnie stopped at the bedroom door. When she heard the shower, she slowly walked toward the bathroom, shedding her clothes as she went. She didn't even second-guess herself. Was it an abrupt decision? Definitely. Did she care? Definitely not.

Stopping before the shower, she saw him through the glass. Bishop stared straight at her. His eyes roamed up and down her body as he opened the door. He held out his hand, and she took the last few steps needed. As she moved to underneath the warm water and into his arms, she knew this was exactly where she belonged.

CHAPTER 30

*B*ishop let the hot water wash the blood away. Eyes closed, he took this minute to calm himself. Seeing Bonnie in so much pain totally did him in. It was hard to watch, but all he could do was be there for her. If he could take her pain and rage away, he would with no questions asked.

Wanting nothing more than to swoop her up in his arms and carry her inside the shower with him, Bishop knew that would be selfish. As much as he wanted it, it wasn't the time. So instead of doing what he wanted, he left her to get her thoughts together. Maybe that was the right move. Maybe it wasn't. It was hard to tell with Bonnie. She was so independent, which he didn't understand, but respected.

With a sigh, he went to grab some shampoo when he heard the door open. Slowly, he turned only his head to see her standing in the doorway through the glass panel of the shower, her beautiful body bare. She looked lost but determined. She wanted him, needed him as much as he needed her. The knowledge hit him hard, filling him with a longing to be the best man he could for her.

Opening the door, he reached out his hand, giving her the opportunity to change her mind. Thank fuck she didn't. There wasn't even a hesitation as she walked forward, taking his hand and stepping inside the cubicle with him. He couldn't even express how that made him feel. She came to him, and he fucking soared. Holy shit, he was losing his mind.

The water glistened off her body as it beaded against her skin. She was beautiful in all ways. He reached out to touch her face, but she stopped him as she reached for the soap. Lathering her hands, she put the soap back, then massaged the suds into his chest, shoulders, and arms. Her soft hands roamed up his neck, to his face as she caressed his features, her eyes following her hands. Her fingers played with the area he had been hit, her gaze quickly going to his as if making sure she wasn't causing him any pain. The pain thrumming through him was further south than his forehead. He throbbed painfully with need, but he continued to let her have her way. Shit, he was more than happy to let her have her way.

She glanced down between them, and he could tell a grin formed across her lips. Her hands followed her gaze as she cupped him, then began to explore in earnest. Bishop gritted his teeth, his head falling back as his eyes closed. One hand went against the glass, and the other stayed fisted to his side. It took every ounce of self-control not to turn her around, bend her over, and slide into her body.

"Make me forget, Bishop." Her whispered words opened his eyes as his head snapped down to stare at her. "Only you can make me forget, even if for a short time."

He didn't need to be asked twice. Clasping the back of her head, he brought their mouths together in a kiss so hot his toes fucking curled. His free hand ran all over her body, loving the slick feel of water on her skin. Her breasts pressed against his chest, sliding all around the slickness of the soap and water. It was almost more than he could take without losing his shit. Her fingers tightened against his cock as she continued to play with him. He lifted her leg to rest on his hip as his fingers found her core. Bishop pumped one finger, then two inside her, and she was more than ready for him, but he wanted this to last. He didn't know if he could last, but he was going to try, dammit. Pulling their mouths apart, he picked her up high enough that her tits were face level. He began with one, sucking her puckered nipple and biting before moving to the other. He couldn't get enough of her. Bonnie's cries and moans had his cock so hard he hurt.

"Spread your legs and straddle me," he ordered, and she did. He slowly let her slide down his chest. The feel of her pussy riding down his bare skin had him growling. "Let me know if I hurt you. This may get a little…"

"Out of control," she finished when he couldn't seem to find the right words. "Good."

Her words had him sinking her onto his cock. Her body swallowed him so tightly he had to fucking control himself so as not to end this before it even started. His jaw tightened, his eyes narrowing as he kept himself deep inside her, not letting her move. Not yet.

"You look so angry." She touched his mouth with her thumb, running it along his bottom lip. "You should really smile more."

"Not angry," he replied, his teeth clenched. "Just trying to get control so I don't hurt you." Or embarrass himself, he added, but not out loud.

"You won't hurt me." She tried to move, but his hands wouldn't allow it. So she wiggled, making him moan and growl at the same time. "Come on, Bishop. Let loose."

He cocked his eyebrow at her, then gave her a wicked grin. "Let loose?" He carefully plastered her back against the glass and hoped to fuck it would hold.

"Please" was her one-word response.

Bishop pulled out quickly, but slowly pushed his way back inside her just to make sure she was ready for him and that she wasn't in pain. The look of pleasure radiating from her eyes told him she was absolutely fine. With only one purpose in mind, he began to "let loose." As he pounded into her, she slid up and down the glass panel. Her breathing came in loud bursts. She gripped his neck so she could pull herself up and ride him. He stood with his legs braced apart, letting her have her way and damn, did she. He watched her breasts bouncing, his gaze going back to her face to see her wide-eyed and watching him.

Knowing she was close and he was way past close—though he could hold off all night just so she could have more pleasure—he took control again. Sliding her off him, he set her on her feet, then turned her around.

"Put your hands on the glass." His voice was low and husky with his demand. When she did, he stepped back to see the beautiful sight of her displayed for his eyes. Damn, how many times had he pictured this in his mind, in this shower... fuck, any shower? Many fucking times. She glanced back at him from over her shoulder, and he cursed at the "come fuck me" look in her eyes. Giving himself a few strokes, he moved behind her and eased himself inside her tight heat. Grabbing her hips, he didn't start out gentle. Not this time. She was ready for him.

"You are fucking beautiful," he said as he continued to pump into her. One hand remained on her hip as the other ran along the smoothness of her spine, then dipped around to feel the fullness of her breast. He pinched her nipple, making her moan. He wasn't much of a talker during sex, never had been, but the picture of her accepting him in this manner sent the words right out of his mouth. Yeah, he was definitely not a talker but a doer, and he was fine with that as were the women he'd had in his lifetime.

Right now, only one woman mattered to him, and if she wanted him to recite a fucking poem, he'd be pussy enough to do it just to be inside her. Jesus, he was most definitely under her spell, pun totally intended, and he'd never felt more content.

Bonnie didn't respond other than the moans, sighs, and cries of pleasure. Again he was fine with that. When she whimpered and began to push back against him to meet his thrusts, he knew she was at the edge. As was he. His large rough hand slid from her breast and along the smooth side of her stomach, where he found the part of her core that would send her over that edge. With a second of hesitation—because he didn't want this to end —he realized that this was actually the beginning. Whenever he could have her in his bed, shower, kitchen, yard, wherever in the fuck he could, he would have her.

Working his fingers, he thrust in and out, his eyes roaming the glass to make sure it was holding, and smiled as she screamed out in pleasure. This scream— compared to her earlier scream—was the only scream he ever wanted to hear from her. With a few last thrusts, he also lost himself, even felt lightheaded for a moment, and had to grab for something to steady himself. Fuck, that had never happened before. Getting his shit together quickly, he pulled out, then slowly helped her straighten up as he turned her and tugged her to him.

They stood that way for a while, each lost in thoughts of their own. Her breathing regulated, though her body still shook, just like his. Eventually, she pulled away from him to stare up into his eyes. Without a doubt, he knew he loved her. He absolutely loved this woman, and even when she had used the damn aversion spell, his mind and body knew it.

"I love you, Bonnie Grail," he said, his eyes connecting to hers. "And if you don't love me, you will."

~

Swallowing hard, Bonnie had longed to hear those words from someone... anyone. How sad was that? Day in and day out, she only lived with hatred that she projected or received. Sure, she had friendships here and there, but she'd never trusted anyone with her heart or soul. And if she loved that person, they would be given free rein to both. She tried to think of something smartass to say, but it stuck in her throat. That was new. Goddess, why wouldn't words come? Swallowing once again, praying he didn't hear the gulp, she frowned. "How do you know?"

Okay, that shocked him, or at least his widened eyes stated that fact. "That I love you?" He frowned with a shake of his head. "What kind of question is that?"

"A good one from where I'm standing," she replied, then cocked her head. "Bishop, we've been thrown together by circumstances out of our control. You know next to nothing about me. What I like to eat, my favorite color, if I snore, what my favorite movie is, or who I would ask my guy to give me a pass on if I met them."

Bishop listened intently to her without saying a word until that last part. "Pass on what?"

"You know, if we were together..." She did a quick glance at him and then down at herself. "...not just naked together, but together *together* and I saw Jason

Momoa, you—or my significant other—would give me a pass to sleep with him."

"The fuck I would!" Bishop roared, making her jump as the glass panels shook. "Who is this Momoa bastard. I will kill him now."

"Seriously? *Game of Thrones*? *Aquaman*?" Bonnie eyed him, then realized he had no clue who she was talking about. "Okay, that's beside the point."

"No, *this* is the fucking point. You are mine. No passes will be given, ever. For anything." Bishop clipped her chin up to look into her eyes.

Her heart beat frantically at the look he was giving her. Damn, it would be so easy to just jump into his arms and declare her true feelings, but her ending hadn't been written yet, and until it was, she couldn't do that to him. Could she?

"Your favorite color is black. You do snore. Any movie is your favorite if it makes you laugh, and fuck this Jason Mosa fucker." Bishop cocked his eyebrow at her as if daring her to tell him he was wrong. She couldn't because he was right.

"Momoa," she corrected, then shook her head. "So you're telling me if we were together *together*—"

"We are together *together*," he growled, glaring down at her.

"—and I gave you a pass, you wouldn't take it?" Bonnie rolled her eyes. "Come on. I mean, really? Any woman on this planet… you wouldn't screw if I gave you the go-ahead? J.Lo? A Kardashian?"

"No, I would not." Bishop crossed his arms as he stated his answer firmly. Then he looked a little puzzled. "What is a Kardashian?"

Bonnie couldn't help it; she laughed so hard, and it felt so damn good. The look on his face was priceless. She couldn't believe they still stood in the shower after a round of amazing sex, and then he announced he loved her, but all she could do was question him. What was wrong with her? He was close to perfect. Why was she doing this to him? To herself? *Just tell him your true feelings, bitch. You love him too. Just fucking say it.* All this was going through her mind as her laughter died down.

Her eyes met his golden gaze, and she knew that she could never leave him wondering about her true feelings for him. All the bullshit she just spouted had nothing to do with anything other than her fear. Reaching up, she cupped his cheek.

"I do love you, Bishop." Her gaze dipped to his lips, then back to his eyes. "I've known it for a long time."

He pulled her into his arms and kissed her deeply. When he pulled away, he said, "You sure like to make things hard, don't you?" He picked her up and carried her out of the shower toward his room.

"Keeps it interesting." She smiled and nipped at his neck. "And Bishop."

He stopped and looked down at her. "Yes?"

"Fuck Jason Momoa." She touched his full lips with a sexy grin. "He has nothing on you."

Bishop tossed her on the bed, making her shout out in

surprise. "You're right, but now I feel I have to prove that to you."

"You already have, but please prove anything and everything you need to, Warrior," Bonnie teased, then laughed when he playfully attacked her.

Right now she was going to live her truth. She loved him —wanted him to see who she really was. Bonnie believed he did love her, but very soon, what they were about to go up against would be the real proof of how strong that love really was on his side. She hated to be so guarded, but nothing was forever. She'd learned that the hard way. Bishop was a good man. She would not see him go down for things she had done in her past. *That* was how much she loved him.

CHAPTER 31

*B*ishop was enjoying his time with Bonnie, but he knew when his phone buzzed, their time of enjoyment was about to end, for now. After hours of talking, with lovemaking in between, he had learned so much about her, but she was holding things back from him. That was okay. He looked forward to spending the rest of his life learning about her. She was fascinating, funny, and had a good heart.

Smiling at her as he passed her at the kitchen sink where she was cleaning up their dinner, he grabbed his phone. He opened his text from Viktor.

Get dressed and be ready. Shit is going down. Be there soon.

"Bad news?" Bonnie asked as she closed the dishwasher and started it.

Bishop watched her, hating to break their moment of normalcy. "Every text from Viktor is bad news," he teased, then frowned. "But I don't know for sure. He's on his way over here." He left out the "shit is going down" part for now.

"Maybe they found out more information," Bonnie said, and he could hear the hopeful tone in her voice. She wanted this over, and so did he, but he also wanted to keep her safe. Keeping things from her wasn't in the deal, though, and he had to remember that. He agreed to be a team with her, and he needed to stick with that.

"Maybe," he said, then wanted to change the subject. "Can I ask you something?"

"Sure," she said slowly, a little nervously.

"You spent almost half an hour cleaning the kitchen." He cocked his eyebrow at her. "You're a witch. Why not use your magic?"

Bonnie shrugged. "Sometimes I like to feel normal, ya know? Doing chores like that sometimes helps keep me grounded. I can do things without using my craft."

"I didn't say you couldn't." He grinned, really liking sparring with her. She was quick with a comeback and never really got angry, just even. The sparkle in her eyes said she was definitely up to something now.

"Though I can do some pretty cool stuff." Her eyes dropped as an evil mischievous grin appeared on her lips.

He felt the zipper on his jeans start to go down as his button popped. "So you like to play with fire, do you?" He headed toward her, making her laugh. She tried to escape him around the counter, but he jumped it and landed directly in front of her. She backpedaled, but he stalked her, enjoying the chase.

"I do." She gave him a saucy grin. Then she tried to take off, but he was way too fast.

He grabbed her from behind, lifting her off her feet as he headed toward the couch, but the knocking on the door stopped him. "Shit!"

They both stilled as they looked toward the door. Reality was knocking, and it was time to let it in. He set her down, then turned her. Cupping her chin, he kissed her, then turned to go to the door.

"Bishop." She reached out, grasping his arm. He angled to look at her. "Thank you for helping me forget, even if it was for a short time."

Rushing into his arms, they both ignored the pounding on the door. Both knew that once the door opened, things were going to change. Neither wanted that change but knew they had no choice.

"I love you," they said in unison.

Forcing himself to let her go, he headed for the door.

"Ah, hey," Bonnie called, and when he turned around, she motioned toward his crotch with a chuckle. "You might want to fix that."

He looked down to see his zipper down and button unsnapped. Pulling his zipper up, but leaving his pants unsnapped, he gave her an "I'll get you for that" look. He opened the door to find not only Viktor, but Raven,

Ryker, Charger, Damon, and Steve at the door. "Come in." Bishop stepped back as they all walked inside.

"We got more information from Joe," Viktor said, nodding to Bonnie. "We found the ad he responded to. It seems that ad is an ongoing thing. It's for security at different locations. Said they will train. No experience necessary. I hope I'm wrong, but it looks like there are a lot more houses out there like the one we just found."

"I answered it, and we got a reply," Steve said, glancing at his phone. "We have a meeting set up at Melly's Brew Crew in an hour. Said he'd be wearing a red tie."

Bishop had a really bad feeling. "And who is the *we* in this scenario?"

"Blaze is going to shift. He should be here any minute," Viktor said, then looked at Bishop. "Everyone else is also meeting here."

"That's not going to work." Bonnie cut in, looking around at each of them. "Melly's is a witch hangout. They will pick him out in minutes. Any witch or warlock who can't identify a shifter when in shifted form needs to hand in their magic card. We aren't a trusting lot... if that hasn't been made clear. And I'm sure if it's not Wyrick, whoever it is will be a witch. I could be wrong, but I doubt it."

"He's good," Damon said, as if that was the end of it, but by the look on Bonnie's face, Bishop knew it wasn't.

"Didn't say he isn't," Bonnie replied, her brows dipping. "But you're going to waste an opportunity because you aren't listening to me again."

"I agree with Bonnie." Ryker broke into the conversation. "Chances are they're going to know that Blaze has shifted, especially if they're suspicious of who they bring on in the first place."

"And when haven't we listened to you?" Damon said, ignoring Ryker. Before Bonnie could open her mouth, he shook his head, apparently rethinking his question. "Yeah, okay, don't answer that."

"So who do you suggest?" Ryker grinned as if knowing her answer.

"Me, of course," Bonnie replied as if everyone should have known that.

"No." Bishop shook his head, not liking the idea at all.

"Ah, yes," Bonnie shot back. "I can change my looks, and before you say, *won't they know you're using magic,* it's a witch hangout. There will be all kinds of magic going on. We need information, someone on the inside. If any single one of us walks in as ourselves, then game over, especially if it's Wyrick. We don't know who is going to show, so my plan to get information is the best."

Bishop didn't like this at all. So many things could go bad, and he didn't want her in the middle of it. Okay, he knew he said they were a team, but dammit, that was before shit was ready to fly. Another knock on the door had him cursing as he went to answer it. Blaze and the rest of the Warriors filed in, including Sloan.

"So everybody on board with what's about to go down?" Sloan said, his presence filling the room.

"Yes," Bishop said at the same time Bonnie said, "No." *Fuck!* She gave him a narrowed glare before looking back at Sloan.

"You send Blaze in there in shifted form, he will be called out," Bonnie said without missing a beat.

"Wrong." Blaze shook his head, looking a little offended. "No one will know."

Bishop watched Bonnie and Ryker share a look. He knew when Bonnie got her head stuck on something, she was not going to let go. It didn't matter that she had a room full of Warriors glaring at her, with two of them looking pretty pissed she was changing the plans. Sloan and Blaze both narrowed their eyes toward her.

"Okay, shift into..." Bonnie looked, around tapping her finger against her lip. "Sid."

"Fuck, man," Sid grumbled. "I hate when shifters change into me. Freaks me the fuck out."

"Freaks us the fuck out too," Jared muttered, then grinned. "Two Sids. The horror."

"Fuck you." Sid glanced toward Blaze, who now was the spitting image of him. He did an exaggerated shiver. "Damn, that's fucking creepy."

Bonnie turned her back, then motioned for Ryker to do the same. "Okay, now mix yourself up so we can't possibly know."

Glancing at Sloan to see how he was reacting to this, Bishop was surprised he seemed very interested in what

Bonnie was doing. He then looked her way when she turned around.

"Wait." Jared held up his hand, stepping into the middle of the room. "I'm sorry, but I cannot let this pass. I've got a hundred that says neither Bonnie nor Ryker can tell who is who. Any takers? Come on, Tessa needs a she shed."

Sloan growled, shaking his head in irritation while bets were made. Even as serious as this shit was, the Warriors knew how to take the edge off. And every single person was on edge. He noticed Bonnie was looking at him. Everyone seemed to be betting against her and Ryker.

"You in, Bish?" Jared asked him.

"Yeah, put me in for... Bonnie," Bishop said, not wanting to bet at all because dammit, she was going to put herself in a dangerous situation, and he really didn't know if he could let her do it. He didn't want to go back on his word to her, but his protective instincts were on overdrive.

"Thank you." Bonnie gave him a beautiful smile over her shoulder. "The odds are definitely in your favor."

Snorts from the Warriors sounded throughout the room as both Sid and... Sid—aka Blaze—rolled their eyes at the same time, which was fucking weird. He hadn't paid attention, so he really didn't know which one was the real Sid.

"Okay, turn around and lose," Jared said with a huge grin, rubbing his hands together.

Bishop watched as both Ryker and Bonnie turned

around. Each of them looked at both Sids. Bonnie didn't even hesitate before glancing at Ryker.

"Should you do the honors, or shall I?" she asked with a confident grin.

"Witches first." Ryker stepped back, wearing a matching grin.

Bonnie looked back at both Sids and pointed. "The Masked Warrior is Blaze on the left."

"I fucking love that show," Steve said, breaking into the silence of the room.

"So do I!" Bonnie said, her eyes widening at Steve. "I knew the Rottweiler was Chris Daughtry. I called that."

"This season is gonna be off the char—"

"If you say one more word, I am going to kill you." Sloan cut Steve off with a jab of his finger, then looked toward both Sids. "Is she right?"

The Sid on the left shifted back into Blaze. His eyes narrowed in confusion. "How?"

Before Bonnie could answer, Bishop saw two Damons step up. Another thing about the Warriors was they took nothing to chance. They wanted to make damn sure she was right. Jax had shifted into Damon.

"Holy shit, didn't see that coming," Steve said, then backed away as both of them growled at Steve. "Two decapitators. I'm out."

"The original Damon is on the right." Bonnie didn't even hesitate after glancing at the two. "Guys, we can do this all night, but I'm going to be right every single time. As I said, witches and warlocks are a suspicious lot. Now, if I passed Blaze on the street as Sid, then no, I probably wouldn't know he's a shifter because I'm not paying attention. Whoever is meeting at Melly's is going to be ready for anything, and that includes a Warrior in shifter form. You keep underestimating Orjyll, and I keep telling you that's a big mistake."

Bishop did agree with Bonnie on that part. They had underestimated the bastard. Orjyll had lived too long. It was time. This needed to be over. Unfortunately—he glanced at Bonnie—the woman he loved more than anything was the key to ending it.

CHAPTER 32

$\mathcal{B}$onnie stood outside of Bishop's as she got ready to go. It was all moving so fast. For months nothing, and now it was go time. But she knew that was the way it worked when dealing with things out of the ordinary like this.

They wanted her to wear an earpiece and a mic. Even though she wasn't comfortable with that, she reluctantly agreed. They decided to send Raven in with her, two girls out for the night kind of thing so as not to draw suspicion until they saw who was showing up in a red tie. Raven wasn't too well known around the area, so Bonnie agreed. Too damn bad she wasn't a witch. Bonnie had fought against Ryker going in because he wouldn't like her plan, and she couldn't afford for this to get fucked up. This was it.

A car came sliding into the driveway, speeding toward them and stopped suddenly, almost hitting Slade and Adam.

"Are you fucking crazy?" Adam yelled, stomping toward Jill, who got out of the car. "You almost hit me with my own fucking car. Wait a minute! Dammit, Jill, stop hotwiring my car."

"Leave the key and I won't have to," Jill said, not at all concerned with Adam's anger. "Hey, babe. I wasn't going to hit you." Jill patted a frowning Slade as she passed him.

"No!" Ronan pushed past Bonnie, heading straight toward the car when Kira got out of the passenger side.

"Um, where's Mira and Drew?" Bonnie didn't like that they were unprotected. Jill and Kira were supposed to be with them.

"They're fine," Kira answered, ignoring Ronan. "I'm not letting you do this alone."

Steve came out of the house, stopping immediately at seeing Kira and Jill. "What in the hell are you doing here? Where's Mira and Drew?" Steve repeated Bonnie's question.

"Everybody just chill." Jill rolled her eyes. "Do you honestly think I'd leave them unprotected? Steve has been texting Mira everything, and Kira threw a fit. I couldn't let her come alone like she planned, so I called Dillon. He's with them, so freaking chill the hell out already. And by the way, when are you going to bring Dillon and Philip back on?" She glared at Sloan.

"Jesus!" Sloan swiped his hand down his face. "Jill, shut the hell up."

"For now, but seriously, we need them," Jill said, having to have the last word.

"If things go wrong, he will have two of us, leaving only Mira and Drew," Bonnie said to Kira, ignoring the drama going on; she couldn't focus on that right now. She was actually glad to see Kira. It fit her plan well for Kira to go with her to the meeting, but never would she have asked for Kira to do this. It had to be her decision.

"Things aren't going to go wrong." Kira tilted her chin up as she glared at Ronan. "Now, what's the plan?"

Ronan cursed long and hard, but then looked at Duncan. "Mic her."

Bonnie nodded, then turned toward Bishop while Ronan filled Kira in. "Wish me luck," Bonnie said, then leaned close to him and whispered, "I won't embarrass you in front of the other Warriors and give you a hug."

Pulling her into his arms, he kissed her hard, then lifted his lips from her. "You could never embarrass me." He growled down at her, "Watch your ass, witch. And remember, I'm keeping our deal, and I expect you to do the same. *Do not* put yourself in danger. I will be close and watching your every move."

"Watching my every move?" Bonnie frowned, feeling guilty and hoping that he was not going to make her promise anything. She was already going to break their deal and knew it. Man, she hated herself right now.

"Raven is wearing a camera so we can watch. I'll be in a van across the street watching everything," Bishop said, then stopped her from looking back at Raven. "Be careful, Bonnie."

Bonnie snorted, her throat tight with emotion. She wanted to tell him so much but knew she couldn't. "Careful is my middle name." She kissed him once more before pulling away. "See ya later, Warrior."

Her legs felt wobbly as she walked toward the car. Her eyes stared straight ahead, not wanting to look at anyone in fear of them calling her out. She felt Bishop close behind her and sighed as she felt him against her back when he reached around and opened the car door for her. Without looking his way, she got in the driver seat as Raven got in the back, and Kira slid into the front passenger seat. Her eyes went to Ryker, who gave her a nod; she just looked away.

"Bonnie." Bishop leaned down in the door. She looked up at him, doing her best to hide behind the façade she had perfected after so many years of having to play people. He was the one person, the only person she had to play, and it was going to tear her heart out. "I love you."

"And I love you," she whispered, and accepted his kiss. Then he was gone, shutting the door. The breath she was holding escaped, sounding loud in the quiet car. Static appeared in her ear a moment later.

"So, what's the plan?" Kira said, turning toward her. "The real plan."

"Yeah, was wondering the same thing," Raven said from the back seat. "Wanna fill us in now, or we just winging it?"

Bonnie knew Kira had interfered with the mics, and obviously so did Raven. "The plan is… it ends today." Bonnie first looked at Kira, then in the rearview mirror at Raven. So as not to get anyone suspicious, she started the car and pulled out. Vans and cars followed her, but then fell back. "Kira, you know how to trail a transport path?"

Kira snorted. "Give me a challenge," she replied, then her head snapped toward Bonnie. "What in the hell are you planning?"

"Don't," Raven said, turning to look behind them. "Don't tell us. Adam could be reading any one of us, and the less he knows, the better."

"Shit on a broomstick." Kira sighed, leaning her head back. "Okay, I'm stopping the interference before they freak out."

"Raven, do you copy?" Duncan's voice boomed in Kira's ear.

"I copy," Raven said calmly. "We heard you, just a little static on our end. Am I clear on yours?"

"Yeah," Duncan said, and Bonnie wished she could pull the damn thing out of her fucking ear. It was driving her insane, and it was hard for her to focus. "Kira, Bonnie, do you copy?"

"Yes," they said at the same time.

Sloan's voice came over the line. "I want silence."

"Sorry, boss." Steve's voice followed. "But I just want to say something."

"Shit," a few voices echoed, Sloan's the loudest.

"I just want to say thank you, ladies." Steve's voice held a tinge of emotion. "Each one of us Warriors would give our left nut—"

A few snorts, groans of "Jesus," and sighs came over the line, but Steve ignored them as he continued, "—to have you safe somewhere. But we all know what would happen if any one of us went in there. All hell would break loose, and we would miss this chance. Just be careful and, Bonnie," Steve said, then the line went silent.

"Yes, Steve," Bonnie said as she glanced in the rearview mirror to see Raven roll her eyes, but a smile curved her lips.

"You are one badass chick. Anyone who can produce a tornado that nearly blew my ass away is all right in my book." The respect in Steve's tone was sincere.

"Thanks, Steve." Bonnie smiled, then added, "This is going to work. It's for Drew, so she doesn't have to grow up the way we did."

The line went silent for just a second before Bishop's voice came over the line. "Tornado?" He sounded confused.

Before Steve could go on an explanation spree, which would indicate she may not be ready for any of this, she quickly said, "Silence," trying to mimic Sloan's voice.

A few chuckles came over, but then nothing. "Okay, time to disguise."

Glancing over at Kira, she saw that she had completely changed her looks. She grabbed the steering wheel. "Go ahead. I got it."

Bonnie did the same before taking control of the wheel again. Her stomach cramped with nerves as she saw Melly's up the road on the right. The parking lot looked full.

"Okay, that's freaking creepy," Raven said, then put her face in between them, looking back and forth at each of them. "Wish I could fucking do that."

"Raven, watch for demon activity." Charger's voice came over their earpiece. "Use the code if you spot one. Kane and I will be close."

"Duh" was all Raven said, gaining a growl from Charger and a few chuckles from the Warriors.

Bonnie parked, then turned to look at Raven. "They'll know you?"

"Possibly," Raven said, then cursed. "This isn't really a hot spot for them, but you never know."

Bonnie frowned, wondering if her mother's powers combined with her own would allow her to pull off a glam spell on a full blooded vampire. Worth a shot. Glancing around, Bonnie quickly snapped her fingers, and Raven didn't look like Raven anymore. "Holy shit, that actually worked." Bonnie's eyes widened before looking back at the road. "Okay, if something happens to me, this look will vanish, and you will be you again, so watch your ass."

"So you could have done that to Blaze?" Bishop's voice sounded suspicious and a little bit angry.

"Surprisingly, I think I could have," Bonnie said, then frowned. "Then again, maybe not." She did not want Bishop to make her pull the car over so Blaze could be the one going to meet Mr. Red Tie. That was not in her plans.

Raven glanced in the rearview mirror and frowned. "You gave me gray hair?"

"It looks good on you." Kira grinned. "Seriously, it actually looks amazing."

Looking at herself again, Raven turned this way and that. "It does look pretty cool."

"Can we stop with the fucking beauty shit for a second and focus," Sloan hissed, not sounding happy at all. "I swear to God, when this fucker is dead, I'm quitting. If I had a beating heart, I'd have already died from a heart attack. Get your asses in there and get this done before I really get pissed off."

All three of them rolled their eyes, and Bonnie remembered the necklace around Raven's neck, which was actually a camera, was pointed directly at her. She just gave it a wave, then got out of the car, with Raven and Kira following.

Paying their entry fee at the door, she walked in, gaining some attention, but not much. They headed toward the bar, ordered a drink, then waited—for what Bonnie wasn't sure yet. She knew she would soon find out.

"Raven, move around a little bit and scan the place so

we can see the layout," Bishop said, his voice sending Bonnie's heart racing.

Raven did just that as a man walked up to her, blocking their view. "Damn," the man said with a low whistle, trying to be smooth and failing miserably. "Never had me a vampire before. What's your name?"

Moans at the man's come-on came over the line, except for one that was a low growl. Bonnie really needed to get this fucking earpiece out of her ear. Soon. Even with this idiot distracting them, she scanned the room, looking for someone with a red tie as she sipped her drink.

"Notta." Raven sighed, her tone bored with a tinge of irritation.

"That's a beautiful yet unusual name," he said, then gave her a sleazy smile. "What's your last name?"

"Chance," Raven replied, making Bonnie choke on her drink. She glanced at the guy whose smile was fading.

"Chance?" he said, his tone not so pleasant.

"Yeah, Notta Chance." Raven glared at him. "Now get lost, asshole."

"Boom," Sid said, then laughed. "Damn, Raven, that was fucking harsh. Funny as fuck, but harsh."

"Bitch," the smooth guy said, but walked away quickly.

"You don't even know, fucker," Raven mumbled at his retreating back, then nudged Bonnie. "Eleven o'clock."

"Wyrick," Kira whispered through clenched teeth.

Bonnie glanced that way, and sure enough, it was Wyrick wearing a red tie. Good, he wasn't on to them... yet. He thought he was meeting anyone other than them. Bonnie took nothing for granted. She waited for him to sit down, then their eyes met. She turned to set her drink on the bar, then took the earpiece out.

"What are you doing?" Raven hissed as she turned around, waving down the bartender. "Put that back in."

"Remember what I said." Bonnie gave Kira a sideways glance putting her hand over her mic. "Trace the transport path."

She heard Bishop yelling through the earpiece; her name was bellowed. Using her magic, she made it disappear before turning around toward Wyrick. Making her way to the table, she opened herself up to the Bonnie no one had met, other than the sick fuckers she had spent most of her life with—her bastard of a father included. Wyrick, she didn't know well, but he was up her father's ass, so he deserved to meet the bitch she was about the become.

"Red tie," she said as she walked up to the table, then sat down. Bonnie was glad he actually seemed taken aback. It was always good when you knew something the other person didn't, and it proved he didn't know shit. He actually looked around a little frantic. "Is there a problem?"

"No, actually, I'm a little shocked that you're a woman." Wyrick quickly tried to collect himself. She could tell his type didn't like surprises. Boy, was he in for a real shocker. "I was expecting a man."

"Careful," Bonnie warned him with a cocked eyebrow. "Some may think you are discriminating."

She watched carefully as he regained his composure. He studied her closely, then seemed to relax. Yeah, he was gaining his confidence back, and she didn't fucking like it. In fact, she despised this man. He had an "I'm better than you" air about him that just rubbed her the wrong way, and he'd shot Sloan, who was growing on her. Yeah, Wyrick was a piece of shit who was going to go down, but right now, she needed him.

"So what made you decide to apply to the ad?" He leaned back in his seat, then gave the waitress a dismissive wave, not even looking at her. Yeah, she'd like to strangle him with that ugly-ass red tie. What a pompous ass.

"Why does anyone answer a job ad for? A job, dumbass," Bonnie said, then smiled when his eyes widened. Yeah, it was time. Fuck it. She was done with the game. Glancing toward Raven, she looked straight at her necklace and mouthed, "I'm sorry" before turning back to Wyrick. "Now, let me ask you a few questions, Wyrick."

CHAPTER 33

"What in the fuck is she doing?" Sloan said behind Bishop, who was sitting watching the monitor half out of his chair and ready to take off at any signs of trouble.

Bonnie had taken out her earpiece, but her mic was still attached. He watched horrified when she looked toward Raven, as if looking straight at him, and mouthed the words, "I'm sorry."

"Stop!" Bishop shouted over the line, shutting everyone up and trying to focus on what the hell was going on.

"Who are you?" Wyrick's voice was fainter than Bonnie's, but still very audible.

"In about five seconds, this place is going to be full of VC Warriors," Bonnie said as Bishop watched her change back into herself. "So I suggest you get us out of here real quick and collect that bounty. What do you say? I'm sure Daddy is anxious to see me."

Bishop was out of his chair and busting through the back of the van, the doors flying off their hinges. He didn't look as he crossed the street, and a car slammed into him. He jumped just in time—not to take too much impact on his legs—and rolled over the hood and landed on his feet. He heard others running behind him. Reaching the door, he knocked the bouncer out of his way, fighting through the crowd, his eyes frantically searching.

As if in slow motion, he saw Bonnie reach across the table, Wyrick grabbing her hand. His shout of "Stop" had both Wyrick and Bonnie looking his way. Their eyes met, and he saw regret before she looked away. Just before they vanished, Raven leaped through the air and grabbed onto Bonnie as all three of them disappeared.

"No!" Bishop bellowed, sending everyone scattering out of his way. He knocked over chairs, tables, and a few people getting to the table Bonnie had been at. She was gone. Fuck! Bishop pushed over the table, and even picked up a chair and threw it against the furthest wall. The place had emptied out quickly. The only ones in there were the Warriors and the owner, who was throwing a fit about her place getting wrecked.

Glancing down, he saw a folded-up piece of paper. Bending, he picked it up and opened it.

Witch Hunter,

I know that you are furious with me right now, but please don't be. This was the way it had to be. I haven't forgotten our promise to each other, and I still consider us a team, and what a team we make. The witch and the witch hunter. Though sometimes one has to take one for the team. This time that was me. Next time it can be you. Kira can hopefully trace the transportation path, but if not, I hope to come back to you after this is done. I don't plan on letting saggy ass win to rule the world. How embarrassing that would be. Trust in me, Bishop, that's all I ask. For once, I may be able to make someone proud, and if that someone is you, all the better. Please understand, that's all I ask.

I love you,

Your Witch

Bishop stared at the note, rereading it a few times and feeling so many emotions. He even grinned at one point. Holy fuck! Folding it back up, he put it in his pocket, then turned toward Kira. "Can you trace her?"

"I'm trying," Kira said with both hands over her ears. "Just give me a minute. It's confusing. I lose it at a certain point."

"Shit," Bishop hissed under his breath. His body was wired; he could not let her do this alone. That was not going to fucking happen, but he had to find her first. His eyes spotted Ryker, who stood where Wyrick had been sitting, his eyes closed. "Ryker?"

Ryker shook his head, holding his hand up. "Shut up," he growled, and everyone did.

Over their earpieces, they heard a weird sound, as if something was scratching at someone's mic. Different tones, some low- and high-pitched radiated over the line, making the Warriors cringe due to their superb hearing. Without a doubt, Bishop knew it was Bonnie's mic. A loud pop had everyone pulling out their earpiece, other than Bishop. He held his hand up to his other ear, blocking out the cursing as he listened, but nothing other than silence greeted him.

Dread and a feeling of hopelessness overwhelmed him, sending his rage to the limit of no return. He would not lose her. Rushing toward Kira, he clasped her shoulders, making her look up at him.

"Please, Kira," Bishop pleaded, but seeing the look in her face told him that it was useless. She couldn't trace her.

"I'm so sorry," Kira whispered as tears filled her eyes. "I've tried, but I keep losing the path at the same point. I'll keep trying."

Bishop nodded, dropping his hands. Ronan clapped him on the shoulder as he took Kira in his arms, walking her away. Glancing over his shoulder, he saw Ryker in the same position, his eyes closed. Walking that way, Bishop stopped in front of him.

"Can you trace them?" He knew his voice sounded hopeful. Fuck, that's all he had at the moment was hope that someone could tell him where in the fuck she was. He was holding on by a thin thread.

"Yes," Ryker mumbled, but didn't open his eyes. "Almost there."

It took everything he had not to shake the shit out of Ryker to hurry him up. If anyone hurt Bonnie, there was going to be hell to pay. He had killed many witches in his time and never once with a smile. But this time... this time he would smile his way through the killings if anyone fucked with what was his.

Bishop stood as still as he could, the wait driving him insane. Once this was over and she was safe, he was going to... what? Bust her ass? Possibly. Rage at her? Doubtful. Hold her and never let her go? Definitely.

"Got it," Ryker said as he opened his eyes. "I can only transport a few more, other than Bishop. The rest are going to have to wait until I get the exact location. I can only follow the path. It doesn't give me an address I'm afraid."

"I can transport a few." Kira stepped up with Ronan right beside her. "Including Ronan."

"Damn straight," Ronan growled, his eyes narrowing, obviously not happy with her going, period. "You are going nowhere without me."

"I don't know who is going to take me, but I'm going. Raven can only handle a few demons, and I'm sure there's a few there." Charger stepped up.

"You know I'm going." Viktor also stepped up, then looked at Bishop. "You ready for a blast from the past, brother? Looks like we're going witch hunting again."

"The question is... are they ready?" Bishop said as his eyes turned black as night. He looked at Ryker, then grasped his hand in a manly grip. Viktor put his over theirs. Then under his breath, Bishop added, "I'm coming, Bonnie. Hold on."

~

*B*onnie stumbled, her stomach still churning from the transport. Goddess, how she hated it. Glancing at Raven, stunned that she'd tagged along by grabbing her just before Wyrick transported them, she saw her gag.

"Son of a bitch." Raven shook her head, then glared at Wyrick before grabbing him by the shirt and headbutting him. "That sucked."

"You bitch." Wyrick threw his arms out as silver chains appeared, heading straight toward Raven, but Bonnie was quick, throwing her hand out and sending them on a different path before disappearing altogether.

"Play nice, children," Bonnie said, then let her eyes take in where they were. They stood in a yard outside a huge building that looked almost exactly like the Warrior compound. There was a wall around it with a gate, almost identical. Very odd. There were enough differences for her to see that, in fact, it wasn't the compound. "I see Orjyll still isn't very original."

"Noticed that, did you?" Wyrick said after giving Raven a nasty glare. "Orjyll liked the layout of the VC Warrior compound."

Bonnie rolled her eyes and knew Wyrick didn't appreciate it. Good. The more she could irritate him, the more his focus was off Raven. "So, are we going to stand out here all night or you going to collect that bounty? Maybe start your own little compound, follow in your hero's footsteps. That is if you live long enough. Sloan Murphy is really looking forward to seeing you again."

"You're a real smartass, aren't you?" Wyrick sneered as he led them toward the front of the building.

"So I've been told," Bonnie said, then got Raven's attention by eyeing her necklace. Raven slowly grabbed it and moved it around so whoever was watching could get a good layout of the place. When they stopped at a door, Wyrick knocked loudly. "Ah, Daddy didn't give you a key?"

Wyrick turned so fast Bonnie wasn't ready for the backhand across her face. "I've had enough of your mouth." Wyrick blocked Raven's punch, pushing her back, his glare full of hatred. "I'm going to have fun watching them kill you."

"What, you too much of a pussy to do the job?" Raven snapped at him, but Bonnie reached out, holding her back.

Bonnie spit out blood, keeping herself as calm as she could. She needed to get inside, have Orjyll in front of her before she let loose the power that was just bubbling at the surface. Bonnie knew for a fact Wyrick had no idea she now possessed her mother's power, and she really hoped Orjyll thought the same. "You will regret laying a hand on me."

"I seriously doubt that," Wyrick spat as the door opened. He stepped aside as Raven went in first, then Bonnie, followed by Wyrick.

Walking around them, Wyrick led them into a large room. Bonnie's eyes took in the extravagant, bold colors of silk and velvet that adorned the long windows. It looked like.... Hell, she couldn't even think of what it looked like. A mess for sure, but definitely Orjyll's style. Gaudy as hell.

"Make sure they stay here," Wyrick told two men who were shooting pool. They put their pool sticks down, then stood, arms crossed as they stared at the women while Wyrick disappeared into another room shutting the door.

"Okay, no offense, but your dad is a fucking loon," Raven said as she looked around. "And has a thing for the Warriors it seems. Holy shit, if I didn't know better, I'd think we were at the compound, minus the velvet and silk."

"Wait till you meet saggy ass." Bonnie smirked. "This is nothing."

"Quiet!" one of the men ordered.

"Fuck you," Bonnie and Raven said at the same time.

Suddenly, the room filled with both men and women surrounding them. "Oh, Daddy dearest must be ready to make an appearance," Bonnie said, with so much disdain the two men glanced at each other.

"Hey, change me back," Raven said, holding up a strand of her hair. "It's really hard to be a badass bitch with gray hair."

"Eh, not true. I've known some real badass gray-haired women." Bonnie glanced at her but did as she was asked and changed Raven back to her original self.

Looking around at everyone as if bored, she began tapping her foot. Everyone was staring at them. Guess it was time to get her shit started. She was hoping for backup, but it looked as if Kira wasn't able to trace the path. Dammit. She knew Raven could telepathically let them know where they were, but only if they knew exactly where that was.

"So, guess most of you know, I'm Bonnie." She turned around, eyeing every single one of them. "Grail. With the bounty."

No one said a word; they just stared at her. Yeah, this was how it went. They were loyal to dickhead. Not one of them would disobey him. She knew the routine well.

"Not a very talkative group," Raven said at her back. "They all witches and warlocks? I don't feel demons."

"Demons come and go. They don't always play by his rules." Bonnie grinned, giving one of the warlocks a wink. "Unlike these pussies."

"Got a mouth on you, don't you?" the warlock said with narrowed eyes, trying to intimidate.

"Shit, you should hear me." Raven played along with Bonnie's "no care" attitude. Okay, actually, she wasn't playing along; that *was* Raven's attitude.

Bonnie looked over her shoulder at the door, then back at the warlock. "What's wrong?" she goaded. "Not important enough to be inside the big boy room?"

"Don't, Simon," a witch beside him said when he took a step toward Bonnie. "She's just trying to get to us. Wait. We'll have our turn soon enough."

"Looking forward to that." Bonnie gave her a smile and

a nod. "Okay, I'm tired of waiting for asshole to make his grand entrance."

Bonnie headed for the door she knew Orjyll was behind, and just as expected, everyone moved at once. Raven cursed, getting into a stance ready for anything.

"I'm going to give you all a warning." Bonnie looked around at them. "I am going into that room, and if you try to stop me, that will be the biggest mistake of your sucky cult-like life."

With Raven, she headed toward the door, and sure enough, everyone rushed them. With lightning speed, Bonnie stuck out her arm and spun in a circle. Every single person flew off their feet, other than herself and Raven. She was surprised they didn't try to use magic. Interesting.

"I warned you," Bonnie said just as the door opened.

"Daughter!" Orjyll's voice sent shivers of hatred through her body. "Now, is that any way to act when I've invited you into my home."

Preparing herself mentally to face her father, she turned and frowned. He stood there in a multicolored... hell, she didn't know what to call it... cape maybe? It looked like velvet curtains with the rod still on it. He has lost his mind and fashion sense for sure.

All she could think to say was "What in the hell are you wearing?"

Just then, the warlock who had been running his mouth earlier rushed her from the side. She thrust her hand out, stopping him in midrun, then used her power to send him sailing out the silk-covered window. She didn't even look his way, but instead, continued to stare at Orjyll, and she liked what she saw in the depth of his eyes. Confusion mixed with a little bit of fear. He never did like anyone more powerful than him.

"Someone's been working on their magic," Bonnie said as a large smile spread across her face. She couldn't wait to tell him whose powers she now had. Yeah, it was a night for reveals. "Have you?"

CHAPTER 34

$\mathcal{B}$ ishop, along with Ryker, Viktor, Charger, Ronan, and Kira found themselves inside a room full of people just as a man rushed toward Bonnie. Before he could get his bearings, the asshole was flying through the air and out the window.

"Ryker!" Orjyll said, then clapped. "And Kira. Oh my, this is definitely my day. Now, if Mira and Drew come, we can be one big family."

"Is he delusional?" Raven said, but Bonnie didn't answer as she was staring at a very angry Bishop.

Yeah, that's right. He said with his eyes, "I'm fucking pissed." But then he saw her face; it was red, bruised, and it looked like her lip was split in the corner. "Did someone hit you?" His voice was menacing as he stared at her.

"Wyrick," Bonnie answered without hesitation. "I'm sure Sloan will give you a shot or two before he kills him."

Bishop's eyes went straight to Wyrick. "You're a dead man." He pointed at him, just to make sure Wyrick knew he was threatening him.

Hearing stomping coming up behind him, Bishop turned to see the guy who had flown through the window running back inside. He was furious, and the fury was directed toward Bonnie. He never made it even close. Bishop punched out, hitting the guy in the temple, sending him straight to the ground. Cranking his neck back and forth, he looked back at Bonnie.

"Thanks, babe." She smiled at him with a nod. "Hey, no hard feelings, right?"

"No problem. And we will discuss this later," Bishop said, then motioned toward Orjyll. "Continue."

"I see you've made some friends," Orjyll said, not sounding so confident. "Why don't you introduce me."

"Two witch hunters, VC Warriors, and Dark Guardians is about all you need to know, but honestly, I'm the one you really need to worry about," Bonnie said, making Bishop grin.

Even as pissed off as he was, he was proud of her. Yeah, she went back on her word, but they would settle that soon enough. He was just relieved he found her, and she was okay. Now he had her back, and he'd kill any moth-erfucker who tried to harm her.

Suddenly, there was all kinds of commotion as the rest of the Warriors arrived. The room was full to capacity.

"Looks like we have an old-fashioned stand-off," Sid said as he looked around, then his gaze went to Orjyll. "What in the fuck are you wearing, old man?"

"Did you ever see that Carol Burnett show when she played…. Fuck, what was her name?" Jared snapped his fingers as if trying to remember.

Bishop's eyes scanned the room, and he saw a lot of confusion. Shit, he understood. There were times his fellow Warriors confused the fuck out of him too. In the worst of times, they cut up, but he'd quickly learned that was their game plan—to confuse and conquer while having a laugh or two. "Scarlet O'Hara, *Gone with the Wind*."

"Yeah, that was hi-lar-ious," Jared said, then frowned when one guy headed toward him. "Buddy, you're fucking up."

"Jenson. Stay," Orjyll ordered, and the guy stopped immediately.

"Wow." Jared cocked his eyebrow, looking from Orjyll to the guy. "Jenson. Sit."

A few chuckles rumbled from the Warriors, Bishop's one of them. He knew Viktor was thinking the same thing as him. Why weren't these people trying to use magic? He took a quick glance at the guy on the floor, who was either dead or just knocked out. He didn't really give a shit either way.

"Enough!" Orjyll shouted, his face a mask of anger. "How dare you come here and insult me."

"We dare because of you wearing shit like that." Sid eyed him in disgust. "That, whatever it is, insults me."

Sloan stepped forward, past Bishop to stand next to Bonnie. "We didn't come here to insult you." Sloan's voice was calm, almost too calm. "We came here to kill you."

Bishop watched Wyrick closely. He could see the fear in his eyes as he did everything he could not to look directly at Sloan.

"Starting with you." Sloan pointed right at Wyrick.

"My house. My rules." Orjyll sneered at them all. He flung his curtain cape back and waved his arms.

"Be ready," Viktor hissed, but Bishop was keeping his eye on Bonnie. Her body began to shake slightly. Suddenly, chains began to drop from the ceiling.

Bonnie chanted something in a loud voice, and the chains dropped harmlessly to the ground. "You really need to come up with some new tricks, dickhead. Predictable since you've already done this one," Bonnie said, then took a step forward. Bishop also stepped forward as did everyone else. "Where is Vanessa's boy?"

A woman next to Orjyll stepped up in front of him. "Dead or alive?"

"Roberta seems to want the bounty." Orjyll's smile was pure evil.

"Alive, since I'm breathing," Bonnie answered her. A snort followed. "Seriously, Daddy-o, you need to find smarter bitches."

"I wasn't talking to you." The woman's hand shot out, sending a lightning bolt toward Bonnie, who easily deflected it.

"Damn, that reminded me of Wonder Woman," Jared said, impressed.

"Dude, you are watching way too much television," Sid replied, just as the woman tried to hit Bonnie again.

Before anyone knew what was happening, the bolt was deflected, and the woman was wrapped in a rope, her hands by her sides. "How was that, Ronan?" Bonnie asked Ronan, who tipped his hat at her.

"Couldn't have done better myself," Ronan said, but his voice was low and slow in his cowboy twang.

"You want that bounty, bitch, you're going to have to try harder than that." Bonnie said flippantly, but with a underlying dare.

"Okay, I'm getting fucking bored." Damon's voice rumbled through the room.

The Warriors all seconded Damon's statement, but Bishop knew it wasn't this easy. Something was getting ready to happen and it was going to be a shit show. He had been in many situations like this before to know with witches, everything was unpredictable.

~

They were getting to him. Bonnie knew that better than she knew her own name. It was exactly what she wanted and needed. Wyrick had undone her magical rope on the woman, who was staring daggers at her. She needed to get Wyrick out of the picture, and fast. He was absolutely the most power-ful. Something odd was also going on, but she couldn't put her finger on it yet.

"Do you really think you are going to win?" Orjyll took a step toward Bonnie, his hatred for her finally showing. "You are nothing. Always have been nothing. Tell me, daughter—"

"Don't call me that," Bonnie hissed, her eyes narrowing.

"But you are my daughter. Nothing can ever change that," Orjyll said, his words penetrating only slightly the wall she built around her heart where he was concerned. "But tell me, do your new friends know exactly who they are protecting? What you've done for me?"

Bonnie stood straight, her shoulders back and chin held high. "I did what I had to do to survive," Bonnie said evenly. "And the only regret I have during that time is not killing you then."

"You wound me." Orjyll put his hand to his heart, a fake expression overcoming his face. It only lasted a minute before he laughed. "Sorry, I just can't. Do you really think I care anything for you? I feel nothing. You are a piece of dirt under my shoe. You are just like your mother. Thinking you are better, when in fact, you are just like me. More so because my blood runs through your veins. You cannot ever defeat me because I will always be a part of you."

Bonnie bit the inside of her cheek as she let him spew his hate for her. It fueled her for what was to come. "Are you finished?" she asked, making sure her voice was void of emotion.

"No, actually, I'm not," Orjyll said before looking from her to the rest of the Warriors standing behind her. "Just know that what I've started will never end. Even if you somehow defeat me today, which is impossible, nothing will change. Someone is ready to step into my shoes and fulfill my destiny. But make no mistake, the end for you is coming. The army I have created is vast."

"Jesus, is he done yet?" This time it was Steve who broke the silence. "Where in the hell is this army you keep talking about?"

"Oh, they are coming. Being trained just for you." Orjyll hissed as he pointed at them all, his eyes wide with excitement. "You have no idea what is in store for the mighty Warriors."

Bonnie's eyes caught movement behind Orjyll. She leaned slightly to see an old woman with her eyes rolled back in her sockets, showing only white, her mouth moving in a chant. Shit, all of Orjyll's ranting was a distraction. She glanced at Ryker, then Kira.

"Binding." Bonnie hissed the warning to them. She tested her own magic and felt it strong and true. She glanced at Ryker, who shook his head at her. Dammit. She then looked to Kira, who stared at her in a panic. Before she could do anything, Kira stiffened, her body coming up off the ground as her toes dragged the floor going toward Orjyll. "No!" Bonnie stepped in front of Kira as she began to fall, but Ronan caught her.

"Ah, Bonnie. Don't ruin the fun." Orjyll laughed as he

tried to look around her at Kira. "I'm going to get your mother's powers one way or another."

"Get her out of here," Bonnie ordered, then turned toward Ryker, who gave her an "I'm going nowhere" look.

"Stop them," Orjyll demanded, and suddenly Ronan stopped as if running into an invisible barrier. "Come now, Warriors. You cannot possibly win against our magic now that your witches are powerless. Their magic is bound. Once again, you are on the losing side. Not only will I kill you, daughter, but I will kill Kira and take your mother's powers. Then only two Grails will be alive. And it's obvious from this display that will be easy."

Bonnie's eyes narrowed as they looked first at Bishop, then the rest of the men. Turning slowly, she glanced at Sloan. "Wyrick is yours."

Sloan gave her a nod, then a slow smirk formed across his lips. She then looked toward Orjyll.

"I'm going to give you one more chance to answer my question," Bonnie said, her voice loud and clear. "Where is the boy?"

"I have no use for that boy," Orjyll said in disgust. "Pike was the one using the kid to control Vanessa. But since they killed him, I doubt you'll ever find that brat."

"Good to know." Bonnie needed confirmation that she knew what he said was true when Adam gave her a nod. She lifted her arm and snapped her fingers. The barrier surrounding Ronan and Kira was gone as Ronan walked out of the room.

The old woman, aka hag, looked shocked as she shook her head. "That can't be."

"Oh, but it can, hag." Bonnie didn't usually like to talk disrespectfully to the elderly, but this old bitch needed to go. She was full of darkness. It oozed out of her. Then she smiled at the woman when the hag tried to use her magic. "Problem?"

"What are you?" The old woman stepped back, fear evident on her face.

"It's *who* are you," Bonnie corrected her, then looked at Orjyll when she answered, "And I am my mother's daughter."

"No." Orjyll looked over her head where Kira disappeared, then back to her in shock.

"Oh, yes. And can I just say this feels so damn good right now? Is it bad for me to... you know, rub it in?" Bonnie felt the breeze begin to pick up. It was time to show this bastard exactly what he messed with. "You have done nothing but brought evil into this world, and it's time it stopped. I now have my mother's powers transferred to me. I lived, and now you will die."

"Silly girl." Orjyll shook his head and dropped the cape from his shoulders. "Do you take me for a fool?"

"Yes," Bonnie answered honestly. Suddenly, there was an audible click. She turned her head to see guns held by an invisible force to each Warrior's head. A sudden case of tunnel vision hit her as her mind went blank with despair. No, this couldn't be happening. Slowly, she looked around to see every single witch and warlock facing Orjyll with their eyes rolled back showing only white as their mouths moved in a chant.

"And once again, you were wrong." Orjyll clucked his tongue at her. Goddess, she hated that sound. Hated him. "Take my hand and transfer Emilia's powers to me, and they will live. Don't, and they will die. The choice is yours."

"Those powers will do you no good. Mira, Kira, and Drew will still live." Bonnie's voice held strong. She would not let him see her fear.

"No." He shook his head. "Not true. They are not controlling the guns. I am. I am feeding off their magic. Why do you think I have so many with magical powers around me?"

"Stealing their magic," Bonnie corrected him. She now knew why none of them were using their magic. Her bastard of a father was using and stealing their powers for his own. Tricky, but not unheard of. Wyrick definitely had a hand in making this happen. He was lying low and she knew why. He was terrified of Sloan. Good, she needed Wyrick's focus elsewhere.

"Stealing. Feeding. Makes no difference to me." Orjyll reached out his hand toward her. "Time is running out. Save them or watch them die. Oh, and did I mention they all are loaded with silver bullets?"

Bonnie reached out her hand but stopped before they made contact. She knew if she used her powers to get rid of the guns, she wouldn't be fast enough to get them all.

Someone would die, and she couldn't handle that. Testing just how powerful she was at this moment was not worth the risk.

"Drop the guns, and then you can have not only my mother's powers, but mine as well. I will do whatever you want." Yeah, Bonnie was lying out her ass. If he was stupid enough to do that, she'd kill him on the spot.

"Bonnie!" Bishop's voice made her cringe. "Don't. He's going to kill us either way."

She turned to look at him, their eyes meeting. The gun pressed against his temple. "I have no choice."

Orjyll came closer to her, then leaned down. "You lose. You all lose, again. He's right. Either way, they will die." He looked up at them all with a smile of victory before glancing back at her. "But you, I think I will keep you alive so you can live with what you did to your... friends."

Knowing this was it, she slowly glanced back at Bishop. Dammit, she had to do something and fast. Suddenly, a foreign feeling overcame her. A voice inside her head, faint at first, grew louder.

"You can do this, Bonnie. Trust in the magic. Trust in my power. Let yourself go." Her mother's voice kept repeating inside her head. Her eyes became very sensitive as did her body. Tingles of energy pulses crossed her skin to her bones. *"Trust in the magic. Trust in my power. Let yourself go."*

Bonnie began repeating the words. She felt her eyes rolling in the back of her head. She didn't fight it. She did as her mother's words said: trust in the magic, trust in her power, and she let herself go. With her body going rigid, she was completely aware of everything that was happening. She could see clearly, more clearly than she had ever seen before.

Turning to see the guns pointing at her people, her friends, her love, Bonnie leaned her head back and screamed an inhuman roar. Her arm swept in an arc as the guns all dropped to the ground. Lifting her head, she saw Orjyll with his hands over his ears, staring at her in horror. With just a thought, he was picked up and held above her.

Hearing footsteps coming toward her, Bonnie threw up an invisible wall between them and herself, as well as Orjyll. It was only them; everyone else was separated. "No, you lose!"

CHAPTER 35

*B*ishop tried to get through the barrier, but dammit, he couldn't. He ran around, but there was no way in. Bonnie continued to hold Orjyll in the air. He called out to her, but she seemed lost, as if she didn't hear him.

Chaos was going on around him, but he didn't care. All he cared about was getting to Bonnie. "Fuck!" He pounded on the invisible barrier, calling her name over and over again, but nothing worked.

He could see Orjyll's mouth moving, but couldn't hear. His eyes went to Bonnie's emotionless face. Fuck, she looked so lost. Thinking back, he cursed, then put his hands together. He swore if this didn't work, he was going to lose his shit. He began to chant the words from so long ago that Emilia had taught him. The words came easier and faster. Opening his eyes, he felt his hands slip through the barrier like butter. Holy shit, it worked.

Once his hands were through, his body quickly followed.

"You are nothing," Orjyll was screaming at her. "You can kill me, but you will still be nothing. You are rotten to the core, Bonnie Grail. You will never win. Not over me."

Bishop saw red as he reached up, grabbing Orjyll by the throat and pulling him down to him. "You will die knowing that she will live. She is everything you are not. Bonnie is nothing like you, you son of a bitch."

Tossing him against the barrier, Bishop looked toward Bonnie. Her eyes were back to normal, but they still had that blank stare. He turned her toward him but kept Orjyll in his sight.

"I can't do it." She looked up at him. "As much as I hate him, I can't do it. If I do, that means it's true. I'm just like him, and I'm not. I'm nothing like him."

"No, you're not," Bishop said, then glared at Orjyll. "Drop the barrier, and we will deal with him. You do not have to be the one."

Bonnie nodded, and the barrier dropped. "I'm sorry."

"Never be sorry for being good, Bonnie," Bishop said, then handed her off to Viktor. Just as he turned, he saw Orjyll smile at him.

"Big mistake," Orjyll said just as Wyrick threw a gun his way. "You're right, Bonnie. You are nothing like me. A winner."

Bishop called out a warning, but it was too late. The gun

fired. He watched in horror as Bonnie flung herself toward him, her hand outstretched. Everything slowed, just like the day in the field when her mother's power was transferred to her from Kira. The bullet stopped inches from his chest and hovered. Only his eyes met Bonnie's as the bullet fell to the ground.

It was as if the room exploded in motion as the wind whipped through, knocking some people down and pushing others back. He watched as Bonnie stared at the bullet meant for him for a second before she looked up at the woman, then to Orjyll. Rope appeared, tying each of them. With movement from Bonnie's hand, the woman was shoved across the room by an invisible force while Orjyll struggled against his bonds. A large wooden beam appeared, and Bonnie walked toward it with Bishop following closely.

"You sent me a video of my mother once," Bonnie said, her voice edged with rage. "Because of you, I will never be able to wipe my mother burning to death from memory."

Orjyll fought against the rope while he was being moved by Bonnie's magic—her mother's magic—to the wooden beam. "She deserved it. She betrayed me," he hissed at her. Hatred and rage filled every word.

"And I think it's fitting that you die the same way." Bonnie ignored him. "Didn't think I had it in me, but you've proved me wrong by almost killing another person I care about. Guess I do have it in me, Dad, you piece of shit."

Bishop watched as Bonnie held her hand out, a swirl of

flames circling her palm. She looked toward Viktor. "Would you like to be a part of this?"

Viktor held out his palm. Kira joined them, her hand held out. Orjyll was now against the beam, his eyes wide with fear as he also watched the flames dancing in their hands. Kira tossed the first bit of fire to the wood that appeared.

"That is for me and my sister, you bastard." Kira hissed, her eyes narrowing with hatred.

Viktor did the same, then spat on the floor just before the flames licked its way toward Orjyll. He didn't say a word, just backed up.

Bishop looked down at Bonnie, he saw that she stared at the fire in her hand. She glanced up at him when he held his hand out toward her.

"What about you, bitch?" Orjyll screamed at her. Fear, pain, and rage radiated from his voice. "Go on! Do it. Do it! I fucking dare you. You don't have the guts."

Bishop held out his hand, and her eyes raised to his. "I got you."

With very little hesitation, Bonnie let the fire leap from her hand to his before dropping her own to her side. She stared up at Orjyll. "Whether I toss the fire to seal your fate or not, you are defeated, but not by my hand alone. You are nothing to me."

Bishop tossed the fire from his hand into the already burning wood, his eyes going up to Orjyll's rage as he glared down at them. "Fuck you!"

"This isn't over!" Orjyll shouted, his voice screeching. "I swear this will never be over. I've started something you cannot stop. I will be back to finish it."

"Burn slowly, then rot in hell," Bonnie said, then turned away from him for the last time.

They walked outside just as Blaze was going in. Bonnie stopped, then turned to look at her father, who was screaming in agony as the flames licked at his body.

"Come on. You don't need to see that." Bishop urged her away, but she kept her ground.

Bonnie continued to stare. "Actually, I think I do. Maybe it will replace the image of my mother burning to death."

Grabbing her in a hug, he wished like hell he could take it all away from her. He would if he could, but unfortunately, that couldn't happen. All he could do was be there for her to lean on. Hopefully, that would be enough. Her words were blunt but truthful. Bishop was relieved when she looked away from Orjyll.

"Sloan, I swear I didn't mean to shoot you." Wyrick's voice had the three of them looking that way.

Kira walked up to Bonnie. "I can't believe it." She hugged Bonnie tightly. "Thank you."

"It's over. And we did it together," Bonnie said, then started to turn back again as if to make sure Orjyll was still back there, but Bishop stopped her.

"Neither of you need to see it. Blaze is taking care of him," Bishop said, moving them along. "And I don't want to miss this. I've never seen Sloan in action, and I really don't want to miss it."

For the most part, that was true, but he also knew Bonnie was struggling with what just happened. He was damn proud of her. She was one hell of a woman, and she was his.

"We've been friends for a long time. Orjyll put a spell on me." Wyrick wiped the blood from his nose.

"Lie," Adam said as he leaned against a tree, arms crossed and watching with a smirk on his face.

Sloan spun, kicking Wyrick across the face, knocking him across the yard. Wyrick got up slowly, his eyes finding Bonnie. "Unbind me, please. Give me a fair shot."

"Nope." Bonnie shook her head. "There was nothing fair on your part when you shot Sloan."

No words came from Sloan's mouth as he continued to beat the shit out of Wyrick. It was a silent ass-whooping, a one-sided ass-whooping. Bishop almost felt sorry for the guy. Nah, that was a fucking lie. He was loving every minute of it. As if Sloan grew bored of beating the shit out of Wyrick, he unleashed a series of unmerciful punches that dropped Wyrick to the ground... again. Picking him up by the hair, Sloan glared at Wyrick

"I told you I'd get you," Sloan growled, then in one swift move, he had him in a headlock, and with a fierce twist, broke his neck. He dropped him without a glance. "Traitor," Sloan spat before walking off.

"Holy fucking shit," Steve said breathily, as if he had

been holding his breath for weeks. "I will never ever piss that man off again."

Ryker walked up after passing Wyrick's body, giving it a glance. "Good job," he said to Bonnie, then reached out and shook Bishop's hand. "Most of those people in there were under a spell from the old lady. We got her too. She's not going anywhere but to the witches council for punishment. Sloan gave the okay. Don't worry. She will be locked away for life. They don't mess around."

"What about the female with Orjyll?" Bishop frowned, his eyes scanning the area.

"She took a pod," Ryker replied, then shrugged. "Guess she'd rather die than be taken. No one saw her do it, but Slade confirmed it."

Bishop nodded as Ryker walked away. He then looked down at Bonnie, who was staring up at him.

"Take me home," Bonnie said, then leaned against him. "I just want to be away from all of this."

Bishop led her away from the building before realizing he didn't have a vehicle. Shit. "Ah, I think you might need to take me home." Bishop groaned, hating the fact that he was going to transport one more time and dammit, it would be his last.

~

*H*anging up the phone, she smiled at Bishop, who was staring at her. "That was Mira."

"I figured." He smiled at her, then opened his arms as she crawled up on his lap.

They hadn't been home for even half an hour before the calls started coming in. The only person she hadn't heard from was Raven. "Did you see Raven before we left?"

"Yeah, she was talking to Charger." Bishop rubbed her arm.

"Really? Interesting?" Bonnie whispered, laying her head on his shoulder.

"Why is that interesting?" Bishop glanced at her with a cocked eyebrow. "You aren't playing matchmaker, are you?"

"No," Bonnie said, then shrugged. "Maybe. I don't know." Feeling agitated, she climbed off his lap. Dammit, her mind wouldn't stop. She felt out of place or something. She didn't really know what was wrong with her.

"Bonnie, what is it?" Bishop sat up, watching her closely.

"I don't know." Bonnie stopped pacing around, then wiggled her body in a weird way. "I just have this weird feeling. Like, what am I supposed to do now? Shouldn't I feel free? I mean, the wicked warlock is dead. Saggy ass is no more. The curse is lifted. I'm not hunted anymore. At least, I don't think I am. But what am I supposed to do now? That was all I knew."

"I guess those feelings are normal," Bishop said, then frowned when she gave him a sideways look. "What?"

"You guess?" Bonnie threw up her hands and rolled her eyes. "I was hoping for… *Bonnie, yes, those feelings are absolutely normal. You're going to be fine. You're not going insane. You will have a life now that you aren't being hunted by your evil father.*"

Bishop actually grinned as he stood up, but instead of grabbing her and holding her, he crossed his arms. "You are *absolutely* normal, you *will* be fine, you're *not* insane, and you *will* have a life with me. How's that?"

Biting her lip, she nodded. "Better."

"Good. Now how about your little stunt of breaking our deal?" Lines appeared between Bishop's brows. A grin quickly followed when she glared back at him.

"How about we hold off on that until tomorrow?" she countered.

"Fine." This time he did grab her and hold her tight. "Your mom would have been so proud of you."

"I heard her, you know," Bonnie whispered into his chest. "When I saw those guns pointed at everyone, especially you, and I got so confused and afraid, I heard her talking to me."

"I don't doubt it. She was a very special lady. Just like you." Bishop kissed the top of her head.

"I do think he was right, though." Bonnie shivered, thinking of Orjyll's words. "This isn't over. Someone will take his place."

"We've been dealing with this for a long time. What matters is you and the rest of the Dragonfly Coven are safe. We will face whatever is to come when it gets here," Bishop answered, his voice serious and deep.

"It just seems too easy." Bonnie said, not able to get that thought out of her head. "And another thing. What if one of the witches did the same thing I did with Ryker? He could still be alive. They could have transported him and…Goddess, what about Vanessa's son?" She felt panicked as if nothing had really been resolved.

"Bonnie, he's dead. You're safe." Bishop cupped her cheek. "And the boy is top priority. He will be found. I promise you."

She pulled back, nodding and staring up at him. She prayed to the Goddess he was right, and he probably was, but something deep inside her warned that it had been too easy. Deciding to push that feeling back for now, she smiled. "So, where do we go from here, witch hunter?"

"Wherever we want, witch." Bishop grinned down at her. "But only on one condition."

"What's that?" Bonnie frowned, not liking the sound of that.

Bishop reached behind him, then knelt in front of her. "Wherever we go, you go as my wife, my mate." He opened his hand that held a tiny box. "Will you marry me, Bonnie Grail?"

Staring wide-eyed at the box, Bonnie slapped her hand over her mouth in shock. Tears filled her eyes as she went speechless.

"I wanted to do this after a nice dinner, maybe dancing.

This is probably the wrong ti—" Bishop didn't sound too sure of himself when she didn't answer right away.

"Yes!" she said loudly and quickly. "Yes! Yes! Yes!"

She watched him slip the perfect, most beautiful ring on her finger before she jumped into his arms, knocking him backward onto the floor. After kissing him hard, she pulled away with a big smile, but then it began to fade. "Thank you for making me always forget the bad."

Bishop pushed a strand of hair behind her ear, his eyes never leaving hers. "Soon there will be nothing bad for you to forget, and only good for you to remember."

A teardrop fell on his cheek before she moved and laid her head on his chest. Her love for this man over-whelmed her. She trusted him with everything she possessed. She knew the worst was yet to come, but for tonight, the bad was over. Only good remained, and he lay beneath her. She closed her eyes, enjoying the feeling while it lasted.

"Bonnie," Bishop whispered against her ear.

"Hmm?"

"What's this about a tornado?"

Bonnie's eyes popped open, and a smile spread across her face. Maybe, just maybe, things were going to be okay.

Printed in Great Britain
by Amazon

55303616R00190